# From Antiquity to Independence

# From Antiquity to Independence

Compiled and Edited by

*Shankar Kashyap*

The Impish Lass Publishing House
Mumbai

**From Antiquity to Independence**
1st Paperback Edition
Impish Lass Publishing House
Published: 2020



From Antiquity to Independence is a work of fiction. The names, incidents and characters portrayed in it are the product of the author's imagination and their personal experiences and opinions. Any resemblance with actual persons, living or dead is entirely coincidental.



Cover page design by Jyotikant Mishra

# About the Editor

*Shankar Kashyap is an Orthopaedic Surgeon from the UK specialising in Hip and Knee replacements with intense interest in ancient history, particularly ancient Indian history. He has published over 25 scientific papers in peer reviewed scientific journals over the years before delving into writing books. His first book, A Kangaroo Court was published in 2011 with great critical reviews. Researching for over 25 years into archaeological and literary history of India resulted in the Harappa series. Harappa Trilogy, published during 2012-2015, was well received both by the critics and the readers. He has since published a crime thriller. The Retribution based on a real event that occurred in 2000 in the UK. He has also published two poetry books – Lady in Red (a collection of love poems) and Musings of a Romantic (a compendium of poetry). He has published many short stories and poems in journals and books as well as in a number of anthologies. He is a recipient of many national and international awards for his books. He is also an accomplished painter with his paintings exhibited both in India as well as in the UK.*

*He writes regularly in his blogs at https://shankarkashyap.wordpress.com/ and https://harappaseries.wordpress.com/*

# Introduction

India as a country is as disparate as can be from time immemorial. As to who the people of India are is a question that has been raging for thousands of years. The DNA analysis of skeletons of our ancestors from the Harappan civilisation has thrown more questions than answers, partly due to vested interests hijacking the results to suit their propaganda.

Human existence in the Indian subcontinent of one type or another goes back to at least 70,000 years with the Homo Sapiens coming out of Africa. Other species of the Genus Homo have been living in India long before the Homo sapiens came. There is evidence for the Denisovans in the foothills of the Himalayas and there is evidence of humans in the ash of the Toba eruption (Jwalapuram in Andhra Pradesh) 72,000 years ago.

Middle of third millennium BC was the golden era of Indus Valley Civilization or Harappan Civilization. It stretched from the river Indus and Hindu Kush mountains in the west to the Ganges-Yamuna doab in the east, Himalayas in the north and the Arabian Ocean in the south. The area was over a million square miles and the biggest empire of the time, bigger than Sumerian or Egyptian civilisations put together.

After the Last Glacial Maximum about 13,000 years ago, the Himalayan glaciers receded just far enough north to leave a vast fertile alluvial plain between the Hindukush mountains in the north west and the Aravalli hills in the east. This area was flooded every year like a clock work by the river Indus. This vast land was fed by waters of seven great rivers – Sindhu (Indus), Parushni (Ravi), Vitasta (Jhelum), Vipasa (Beas), Sutudri (Sutlej), Asikni (Chenab) and Saraswathi (Gaggar-Hakra).

The Indus Valley civilisation was at the peak of development in the middle of the third millennium BCE with several large urban centres such as Mohenjo-Daro, Harappa, Kalibangan, Dholavira and Rupar. The excavations show uniform developments across the area, suggesting area wide communications, exchange of ideas and resources across the vast land. The Harappan seals have been discovered as far away as Mesopotamia and Egypt in the west and in places at the southern tip of Indian sub-continent, suggesting travel and communications over vast distances. This vast civilisation appears to have disappeared around 1900 BCE. There are several theories for their demise.

The question of Aryan Invasion Theory (AIT) has been raging ever since Max Muller's famous statement – "Indra stands accused" of destruction of the Harappans. India has come a long way since then and the so called Aryan Invasion Theory has received a well and truly lifetimes worth of battering. India as a subcontinent has developed from a place of occupied by pre-Homo Sapiens before the Young Toba Eruption 70 odd thousand years ago to one of the most advanced civilisations during the third millennium BCE only to be invaded by numerous hordes of foreigners – Greeks, Persians, Scythians, Mughals to name a few. They have not only taken riches from the land we call India, but also left a legacy of rich culture, music, poetry and architecture behind. The cave drawings of Bhimbetka caves are a testament to the enduring legacy of over 30,000 years of human habitation – a veritable Facebook track of time on rock.

There is evidence of Harappan civilisation extending from Balkh in the west to the eastern banks of Yamuna in the east and the Himalayan ranges in the north to the Vindhyas in the south. India as a conglomerate nation came into being with the Magadhans, consolidated by Chandragupta Maurya and further firmly entrenched by the great Ashoka in the third century BCE. Prior to that the subcontinent was a mixture of several kingdoms and tribes.

This book is about a country with several thousand years of history told, not by experts or historians or academics, but men and women like you and me. The stories reflect the passion, hate, aspirations, visions and disappointments as well as a hope for the future. The country is going through a period of turmoil and rapid development just like Europe did during the Industrial revolution couple of centuries ago. This disparate collection of articles is nothing, but a reflection of what India truly is – a disparate collection of individuals – 1.2 billion of them.

*Shankar Kashyap*
*Newcastle upon Tyne*
*United Kingdom*
*January 2020*

# Index

**Section VIII**
**Mughal Empire – 1526 CE – 1857 CE**



**Section IX**
**The Marathas – 1627 CE – 1818 CE**



**Section X**
**The British Raj – 1857 CE – 1947 CE**



**Section XI**
**Mythology**

# Section 1
## Harapppan or Vedic era.
### *(7500 BCE to 1600 BCE)*

Harappan civilisation dates back to 7000 BCE, with origins in the west at Baluchistan (Mehrgarh) and in the east in Haryana (Bhiranna). It reached its peak during the middle of third millennium BCE with highly advanced urban civilisation with public roads, water supply, drainage, weights and measures. The civilisation appears to have disappeared around the middle of second millennium BCE. The causes for this are still being debated and no firm conclusions have been drawn. There are many experts and Indologists who firmly believe that the Harappan civilisation and Vedic civilisation are one and the same. Despite numerous attempts at dating the ancient Vedic scriptures, there has been no consensus as to who composed them or when they were composed. They have been dated to 6$^{th}$ millennium BCE to as recent as 600 BCE. This book does not give me enough space or time to go into the details of pros and cons for various arguments. Suffice to say that there is a school of thought, which firmly believe that the Harappans composed the Vedas.

There are at least two major battles described in the Rigveda – one fought on the banks of river Parushni (Ravi in Punjab) between the descendants of Puru and the Avestan from the west. The seventh book of the Rigveda describes another battle on the banks of the River Parushni and at the same time another battle on the banks of river Yamuna. The root cause of both these battles goes back to the story of emperor Yayati, which we are all familiar with. When Emperor Yayati asks his five sons to help him reverse the curse by sage Shukra – Yadu, Turvasha, Dhruhyu, Anu and Puru, all of them refuse except the youngest son Puru. When the time comes for abdication, Yayati hands over the central part of the empire – Ilavarta to Puru and the surrounding countryside to the other four sons. This obviously generates an enmity which is carried on for several generations. Dasharajna is a war between Sudas, the sixteenth descendant of King Bharata and a confederacy of ten kings led by Abhyavartin Cyamana on the other. This has been portrayed as a battle between right and wrong. The battle is of significance as the outcome of the battle decided the characters and events of the two other epics – Ramayana and Mahabharat. If the results of the battle were different, the stories of the two epics would have been completely different. In my opinion, Dasharajna should be considered the third epic of India.

Briefly, King Sudas is the son of Pijavana and the grandson of King Divodasa. King Divodasa expanded his kingdom centred on the mighty river Sarasvati. He wages a bitter war against the Dasyu king Sambara and destroys 99 towns in the kingdom of Ujjala with the help of God Indra. Sudas inherits this kingdom and he further expands his kingdom in the east, west and north under the guidance of the sages Vishwamitra and Vasishta. The countries in the south were not considered important enough to be conquered or fought for. The expansion of the kingdom leads to jealousy by the surrounding tribal kings. They join hands, are led by King Cyamana from Ariana (Abhyavarta or present day Iran), and attack Sudas on the banks of river Parushni. King Shimyu of Bhedas leads a minor group of tribal kings of Yaksu, Ajas and Sigrus and attack Sudas on the eastern border on the banks of river Yamuna. Ancient rivalry between Haihayas and the Bhrigus come into force during this battle. Vitahavya, a descendant of the famed Haihaya Emperor Sahasrabahu sides with Sudas whereas the Bhrigus join the confederacy of ten kings

We have two excellent articles in this section dealing with the Vedic period and the Harappans. The first one even though somewhat technical, it is worth reading with enormous amount of well-researched information. It is penned by eminent authors – Mr S Krishna Kumar and Pt S Gowri Shankar. They have explained the Vedas and their relevance to present day in detail and makes it easier for mere mortals like us to understand the complex subject. Second and third articles super-impose contemporary images on an ancient theme making it very interesting read indeed. Dominic Arivarasu definitely kindles your interest with the current controversy about the recent scientific declaration of DNA/RNA studies of Rakhigarhi skeletons.

# Significance of Vedas in the Modern Day and 21st Century

*Pt S Gowri Shankar and*
*Mr S Krishna Kumar*

### *Who is Pt S Gowri Shankar?*

*Pt. S. Gowri Shankar from Mumbai, started his academic pursuit at the young age of nine. On the instruction of Kanchi Kamakoti Peetam Mahaswamigal, he was inducted into the Vedic Gurukulam at the well-known Vedic Patashala in Salem (TN) and was under intense Vedic studies and training in the Guru-Shishya Parampara for over eight years. After intense study of the scriptures and Sanskrit language, his abiding interest in spirituality propelled him to attain degree in Vedic Science and Bharatha Shastra from reputed Madras Sanskrit College of Madras University. With an in depth knowledge of scriptures and decades of spiritual legacy behind him, Panditji, as he is known as, has been tirelessly propagating knowledge on Vedas, Indian culture in India and abroad.*

*Panditji has travelled across the globe giving discourses and conducting workshops. He has given lectures to cosmopolitan audience within the USA, Canada, the UK, Singapore, Nepal, Malaysia, South Africa, Mauritius, Kazakhstan. Fluent in Vedic Language (Granth), Tamil, Sanskrit, Hindi and English, Pt. S. Gowri Shankar has an easy style of teaching supported by structured power point presentations.*

***Who is Mr S Krishna Kumar?***

*S. Krishna Kumar from Dombivli, is 62 years young, a retired Vice-President –Finance of a reputed IT company and an Ex-Faculty Professor for management students, is not only a media writer, freelancer and an author but also a social activist, dramatist and actor.*

*He also participates in the popular talk shows of TV channels and indulges in public speaking. He has participated in over 35 shows of CNN-IBN, NDTV, NDTV Profit, Times Now and so on. He has been widely interviewed by all sections of the media for his multifaceted roles and activities.*

*Being a good orator, he is regularly invited by schools and colleges to be the judge and moderator for their college events and debates. He is a music buff too.*

*S. Krishna Kumar is the executive editor of The Impish Lass Publishing House & one of the award winning editors. He has edited & compiled seven anthologies for the ILPH, so far (Are We Mere Spectators, Meticulous Men of Mettle, Jamboree Jubilation, Speak Your Mind (which was sent to Hon'ble PM and a letter too received from the PMO), Yes Boss, Hat Tip & The Travellers' Diary.*

# Significance of Vedas in the Modern Day and 21st Century

If one must take up a debate or wish to write about the essence and importance of Vedas, it will take a long time. The Vedas are descriptive and exhaustive and cover a wide variety of subjects including rituals, knowledge, worship, medicine, education, Vaastu, astronomy, astrology and many others.

Vedas lead us to Upanishads, Puranas etc. which are also quite descriptive and enlightening.

This article is focusing only on the "relevance & significance of Vedas in the modern day & 21st Century."

We have tried our best to collate those important parts and sections of these subjects as described and enshrined in the Vedas. And, we have highlighted them with clear references from the Vedas and their several elements, supplementary subjects and cases, in a way that even a layman can understand the importance and contents.

***The Vedas;***

These are the most ancient religious texts which define truth for Hindus. They got their present form between 1200-200 BCE. Hindus believe that the texts were received by scholars direct from God and passed on to the next generations by word of mouth.

The Vedas, sacred hymns of praise, were among the earliest sacred texts of Hinduism. The name Veda means "knowledge" in Sanskrit, an ancient Indian language used for many sacred texts. Hindus consider the Vedas to contain eternal knowledge not written by humans but revealed to them by 'Brahman.' Upanishads and Vedas are two terms that are often confused as one and the same thing. In fact, Upanishads are parts of Vedas. Rig, Yajur, Sama and Atharva are the four Vedas. A Veda is divided into four parts, namely, Samhita, Brahmanam, Aranyaka and Upanishad.

***Nature of Hindu / Vedic Religion;***

Hindu religion is a "Code of Conduct", flexible and dynamic but with firm roots. The "Hindu Spirit" is based on

- charity and sacrifice
- No oppression, suppression, expansion and conversion
- Perennial Philosophy
- No time or space limitation: -Can be practiced by anyone at any time and at any place
- Not founded by a messiah
- Survived several thousand centuries.

**Overview *of Vedas:***

Sacred scriptures are classified into: -

**(A)** Shruti - for revelation of cosmic and eternal principles and processes, covering all facets of life.

Vedas: Viz: Rig Veda, Yajur Veda, Sama Veda and Atharva Veda come under "SHRUTI". And, Vedas are again classified into 'Vedangas', 'Upa Vedangas' and 'Upanishads'- which form several sub-sects amongst them like Vyakarana, Jyotisha, Arthashastram, Ayurveda, Dhanurveda, Taitriya and so on.

**(B)** Smruti: - for customization / localization of the eternal principles and processes for contemporary lifestyle and integrated welfare of the society. SMRUTI covers vast range of subjects – 'Aagamas', 'Darshanas', 'Puranas', 'Itihasas' and 'Dharma Shastras' – which form several sub-subjects like Shakti, Shiva, Vaishnava, Yoga, Mimamsa, Vedanta, Bhagavatam, Ramayana, Mahabharata, Bhagavad Gita, Manu, Yagnyavalkya and many others.

***The Vedas – origin:***

The Vedas are the First Scriptures , known as "Apaurusheya - Divine origin", are knowledge about Supreme Truth, are called "Shruti"-that which is heard, are teachings that were captured by Rishis from four directions and compiled into four Vedas, are "Aamanaayah"-passed on by Guru through 'Shishya-Parampara' courses.

The Four Vedas are compiled by the most revered sage Maharishi Vyasa (also referred to as "Veda Vyasar")

- Rig Veda is in prose form
- Yajur Veda is in the form of group of lines
- Sama Veda is in musical form
- Atharva Veda contains dialogues and prose.

Here, a brief look at the "Smruti-the Dharma Shastras", will enlighten us as to how MANU the author of "Manu Smruti", had dealt with the following subjects, centuries ago and which are relevant and widely used today:

Manu Smruti dealt with Law and Order, covering every aspect of life like

- o Inheritance (Transfer of wealth)
- o Marriage
- o Kingly rights and duties

- o Citizens' rights and duties
- o Taxation
- o Crime and Punishment

***Vedic mathematics, Astrology, Astronomy and Grammar;***

Vedic Mathematics are referred to as "Ganitam" which widely covers 'Arithmetic', 'Invention of Zero', 'Decimal System', 'Ekam, dasham, shatam, sahasram', 'Laksham, Koti' and 'Modern Numerals'. It is not surprising to learn that the subjects which are taught and practiced today, were clearly defined in the Vedic Mathematics. They are –

- Algebra –referred to as "Lilavati'
- Geometry – as 'Sulba Shastras'
- Astronomy – covering 'Suryasiddhanta', 'Aryabhatiya', 'Precision of the Earth's axis' and 'co-relating terrestrial occurrences with heavenly phenomena
- Principles of Vedic Mathematics are applicable even in modern day in the fields of architecture, planes, ships, vehicles etc.

The 'Limbs of the Vedas' are called the "VEDANGAS". There are six Vedangas:

- ✓ Shiksha (Phonetics)
- ✓ Vyakaranam (Grammar)
- ✓ Chandas (Meter)
- ✓ Nirukta (Etymology i.e. roots and origin of the words in Vedic scriptures)
- ✓ Kalpam (Rituals and times i.e. Calendar for social ceremonies, Panchangas, Almanac)
- ✓ Jyotisha (Astrology and Astronomy)

***Significance & features of the four Vedas;***

***Yajur Veda*** mainly deals with yagnas (yaj means Yagna). Explanations are given for procedures, rules and regulations, materials required etc. for the Yagnas. Yajur Veda also has details of 16 types of Samskaras, Mudras and Abhinayams (spiritual and dance) and creation of the Universe.

To enlighten further samskaras mean rituals, system, custom and procedures for pre-natal (e.g. Seemantham at the end of 6$^{th}$ month of pregnancy), Birth (e.g. Namakarana), First year (e.g. Anna Praasana, tonsure), Before ago 10 (e.g. Veda Aarambha, Upanayanam), Grihastha (e.g. Vivaha/Marriage, Vanaprastha/retirement, Sannyasa), Antyeshthi (Funeral rites and Shraddha).

These rituals are religiously followed by followers of Sanathana Dharma quite meticulously and as prescribed in the Yajur Veda, even today.

***Dhanurveda of Yajur Veda*** is significant even today with its details about Military, Astraas relative with fire, water, Naagaaastras, Brahmaastras, Garuda Vyuham, Administration and governance.

### *Gaandarvaveda of Sama Veda*

Gaandarvaveda of Sama Veda beautifully covers Music and fine arts, Vocal, Instrumental (Taala Vaadya), Dance, Rhythm (Taal and Jatis) and Temple scriptures. Main theme of SAMA VEDA is MUSIC. Seven 'Swaras' came from Sama Veda – Sa-Re-Ga-Ma-Pa-Da-Ni. Sama Veda is chanted in musical form with all 7 swaras. (Other Vedas are chanted with maximum 4 swaras). There are "Raags" (which are mainly born from these Sapta Swaras), which have the power to relieve us from headache and tension, even diseases, certain Ragas when sung with devotion can bring rainfall, and some Ragas combine to form 'Music Therapy" – often used by some in the field of medicine and music. Lord Sri Krishna in the Bhagavad Gita (Chapter.11) says, "Vedaanaam Saamavedosm" - I am the Sama Veda amongst the Vedas.

### *Arthaveda from Atharva Veda;*

Arthaveda deals with "Architecture" of temples and houses and "Vaastu" which is the 'science of ten directions and energies relative with five elements. In the Arthaveda, Manu's "Aaryadharma" describes the duties of a human being like Dharma, Artha, Kama, Moksha and Runas (indebtedness) of Deva, Pitru and Manava.

The Atharva Veda refers to elements of - Secret of life and moksha, Ayurveda, Surgery and even plastic surgery, magic and hypnotism and poison. Thirty two types of poisons are described. Sage Athri has described 12 types of clouds and their characteristics, 12 types of rains, 64 types of lightening, 33 types of thunder bolts. Maha Kavi Kalidasa has elements taken from Atharva Veda in his treatise "Megha Sandesha".

***Ayurveda*** (from Rig Veda and Atharva Veda) covers Medicine and Surgery, Herbal treatment from nature, treatment through diet and Physical Yoga and Pancha Karma Yoga. Pioneers of Ayurveda are Charaka and Sushrutha. Charaka was a practitioner of the traditional system of Indian medicine known as Ayurveda & authored 'Charaka Samhita." Sushruta was an ayurvedic surgeon known for his pioneering operations and techniques and for his influential treatise 'Sushruta-Samhita.' It was the main source of knowledge about surgery in ancient India.

### *Rig Veda*

Patterns of roles and prose forms and dialogues in a drama have their origin in Rig Veda. Integrated study of many important subjects like medicine, geography, astronomy astrology, boats and planes are covered in detail in the Rigveda. Healing techniques like acupuncture, acupressure, naturopathy, homeopathy, Mantras to cure many diseases, etc. are described in the Rig Veda. Besides, 'Geography in Rig Veda' covers detailed description of oceans, rivers and mountains.

In relation to Astronomy and Rig Veda, descriptions are made of rise, path and the effect of Sun on Moon and Earth, Movement of Earth around the Sun, Gravity being the reason for Earth to move around the Sun, seven energies of the Sun indicating the seven chakras in our body as seven colours of light (VIBGYOR).

Coming to "Transportation and Rig Veda", references are made about simple man driven boats. Chariot of Ashwini Kumaris which was probably a "plane with 3 wheels,' Pushpaka Vimana and Garuda Vimana among others.

### *Meditation & Yoga (Yog);*

In today's world of tension, busy schedules, sickness and health issues, human relationship, family issues, politics and national issues and so on, it becomes pertinent to know the basics of "Meditation" and "yoga (yog)'. Many people today are drawn into "Meditation and Yoga". Yoga is given prime importance and many nations in the world observe the International Yoga Day every year. Meditation is a medicine. It offers tolerance, patience and politeness. It destroys our negative energies (diseases). It increases memory power and sharp intuition. It changes one's life for better. Nowadays many corporate houses, companies, VIPs etc. seek advice and training on meditation and its practices.

Yoga (referred to also as "yog"). Patanjali Maharshi is the author of Yoga Sutras (194 numbers) which have references from Rig, Yajur and Atharva Vedas.

The Eight-Step Yoga (Ashtanga) are:

- Yama: - Self-control, abstention from vices
- Niyama: - Moral practices and discipline
- Aasana: - Postures for the practice of Yoga
- Pranayama: - Control of breathing and the body's vital energy.
- Pratyahara: - Withdrawal of the mind from sensory stimuli
- Dharana: - Concentration
- Dhyana: -Deep Meditation
- Samadhi: - The super conscious state of enlightenment.

It is in fact heartening to note that in modern day, today and in the 21st Century, yoga lessons, practices, sessions and demonstrations etc. have gained immense popularity. Lakhs of people have expressed relief and satisfaction from regular and sincere practices of yoga procedures and exercises (Aasanas) and have confessed to leading a healthy and better life too.

Conclusively, it is but sad to note today, that in our country – Bharat – the land of rishi munis, sages and saints, Vedas, scriptures, Puranas, Hindu Sanathana Dharma, rituals, temples and so on, there are vested interests who attribute words like "Myth & Epic" to the history of our great heritage. They work only to subvert the truth of 'Bharatiya Culture & Heritage'.

But these have not surprisingly diminished the interest, efforts and initiatives being taken by many reputed foreign scientists, researchers, astronomers and authors of heritage and history. Even NASA scientists have evinced keen interest in our Vedas and have expressed great surprise and awe to the observations and facts found in our Vedas and scriptures and defined clearly , centuries ago – like position of planets, space , Vaastu positions / architectural procedures, medicine and science, energy produced through yagnas and Agni, and many.

For instance, every year, the Hindu Almanac or Panchang or Calendar, for the next full year, is prepared well in advance. The

Panchang clearly specifies not only the day and date but also the defined time of planetary positions, effects of Navagraha's, good days and time, bad days too, festival days and important events. Above all, scientists are more astonished at the mention of even the precise time of the beginning, complete and conclusion of solar and lunar eclipses, in the Panchang, months before. Critical mentions and cautioning notes are also made much in advance (while preparing the next year's calendar), of calamities to follow like floods, earthquakes, cyclone etc.

Our temples of south India and some in the eastern parts too, have thousands of inscriptions, images, statues etc. depicting things and materials which are found today – like jewelleries, anklets, bangles, types of furnishings and many kinds of utility items, hair styles, attire, etc. Illustrations or tablet depicting scenes of our puranas, Dasavataram of Lord Vishnu, Ramayana, Mahabharata are vastly found in many temples. Some temples have awe-inspiring mysteries like steps resounding or producing the music of sapta swaras, intertwined chains made of thick black stones, cave temples made of huge single rocks, perfectly circled stone ball stuck in the mouth of a lion which can be rotated but cannot be taken out, and very many. Ancient munis and sages even knew the science of fertilization without a microscope. A 'more-than-thousand-year-old' temple in the south India, has the images (on rock /pillar) representing the development of progress of human embryo!! There are temples built along the seashore which have withstood severe storm, earthquakes and even the 'tsunamis' and that too for centuries! How?

In fact, foreign researchers and architectural experts themselves got amazed and astounded at how firstly such huge temples were constructed centuries ago, without even a basic construction material or an 'engine'. And, are awe-struck at many mysterious things and findings observed at each and every temple. Here too, we can write volumes. But what we would like to stress is that constructions of all these temples, architectural methods, Vaastu positions, science and engineering methods too and so on, are attributed or linked to "Aagama Shastras" prescribed in the Vedas. Like certain temples can even withstand severe strike of lightening and thunders, drive away satellites etc. And, today these are followed but given new twist as "modern engineering" or Vaastu technology, aided by many advanced equipment and materials!!

Finally, the need of the day, is to spread awareness about the importance and values of ancient Indian culture and heritage. We need to create an atmosphere which would motivate our young and educated youth to carry out research and unearth true and bare facts about our culture, heritage, civilization too.

Let us worship the Vedas and protect and preserve Indian culture & heritage. Lokah Samastah Sukhino Bhavantu - May Peace & Happiness Prevail!

# Timeless Love

*Meenal Moghe*

***Who is Meenal Moghe?***

*Meenal Moghe lives in Pune, India. She has lived in the USA, Europe and India at different points in her life. She has completed her Masters in Commerce, Diploma in Advanced French and Diploma in Creative Writing from Symbiosis College in Pune. She has published four stories in four anthologies- **'Aura of love'** and **'Share of Love'** under the Raindrops Publishing banner, as well as **'The Teacher I will never ever forget'** and **'Hat Tip'** under the Impish Lass Publishing house. Currently, she is working as a librarian in the French teaching institute of 'Alliance Française de Pune.' You may contact her at meenalmoghe@yahoo.com*

# Timeless Love

"One chai please" said Alex to the man selling tea on the road. Alex Parker felt like a genuine Indian drinking tea from the local chaiwala. India always fascinated Alex; the culture, the languages and the rich heritage sparked his curiosity. As he sipped the hot chai, he mused over how he got into this magical and mysterious land. India always held a special place in his heart ever since he and his parents took a trip to India.

Having been born and brought up in the suburbs of North Carolina, he was used to the American way of life but when he came to India, it was another world. The bustling energy of people, the sounds, the local vendors and the busy life captured his young mind. As a young child, the vibrant colors and various religious rituals made an impact on him. He even found the cows roaming freely on the streets particularly fascinating. He met a young boy named Suresh during his visit and there was an instant connection. They would write letters to each other for many years, describing their own way of life. Suresh had described how he celebrated the festival of Ganesh Chaturthi in celebration of the God Ganpati and along with one of his letters, sent Alex a small idol of lord Ganpati. He came to know later that Ganpati, also known as Ganesha, is an elephant headed God who removes all obstacles. Alex decided to keep the idol with him to keep him safe. Alex eventually became so enchanted by India that he decided to do a doctorate in Archeology with a specialization in Ancient Indian History. During his study, his University sent him on an educational trip to India. He traveled widely within the country. It felt like he connected to his spiritual roots after visiting Jaisalmer fort in Rajasthan, Meenakshi temple, cities like Varanasi, and Jaipur as well as the famous Ajanta and Ellora caves. He found the Khajuraho temples mystical with sculptured temples dedicated to Shiva, Vishnu, and the Jain patriarchs. It was an archeologist's dream come true to study the detailed carvings in these caves.

"Bees Rupaiya ho gaya bhai" said the local tea vendor. Alex was suddenly brought back to reality. The chaiwala was asking for Rs. 20 for his tea. Alex paid the man. Now, at the age of 35, Alex was back in India after 8 years. It felt it bit more crowded than before, but he loved the energy. Alex now worked for the California Museum in Sacramento, as head of the archeological department. The archeological department was planning an exhibit on 'Ancient Indian History'. The head of the museum sent Alex to the ancient Indian Harappan site, Rakhigarhi village in the northern Indian state of Haryana to study some artefacts from the Indus Valley Civilisation. The Indus Valley civilisation existed around the north western regions of India, from about 3300 BCE to 1300 BCE. In fact, the civilisation predated seventh millennium BCE in one form or another. The name had been derived from the discovery of the archaeological sites along the Indus River valley. The civilisation was known for its brick built houses and elaborate water supply and drainage systems. The Indus civilisation is also known as the Harappan

Civilisation. The large cities of Mohenjo-Daro and Harappa were part of the civilisation.

"Rickshaw!" called out Alex. Alex loved this Indian way of transportation. In fact, he enjoyed the little bumps on the road. He was off to Rakhigarhi village. He could feel the excitement building up inside him. What would he find? What mystery will he unearth? He closely held his Ganpati idol and prayed that he would find something amazing.

On reaching the site, Alex saw one young thirty something woman in jeans and a fitted shirt. She had auburn hair neatly tied back in a ponytail. "Hello, I'm Alex." She looked up from her clipboard and smiled.

"Ah. *bonjour*. I am Claudette. I represent the Louvre museum in Paris. I am an archaeologist from France. We are planning to create a display of ancient India in our museum. So, I'm here to dig for any artefacts that I can find from the ancient Indus valley civilisation" she said.

"I'm here for the same reason. I represent the California museum in Sacramento, California. If we work together, we can find a treasure trove of artefacts for our museums. I'm sure we'll make a great team." said Alex.

"*Mais oui*," said Claudette. "I'm sure we'll find a lot of interesting items which will give us a clue into how this ancient civilisation survived. I am interested in all ancient lost civilisations, but India in particular, enthrals me."

"Hmm." said Alex, "I have been enamoured by India since I was a child. I look forward to discovering more about ancient India."

"Let's first survey the land" said Alex. "So, we can map out where to start our dig. We can use both of our tools."

Claudette took out her surveying transit. It resembles a small telescope and is mounted on a tripod. It is used to map the area where the dig will take place. Alex and Claudette spent hours surveying the land until they found one section which looked like a good place to start a dig. "*C'est parfait*" said Claudette. She felt the site was perfect to start the dig. Alex had a book on the Indus Valley Civilisation.

"According to my book, we can find anything ranging from pottery to even ancient jewellery." They then divided the excavation site into squares, and then set up stakes and string to mark the squares. A coordinate was given to each square. This grid map will help them to record the exact location where each artefact was found. Alex was thrilled that they had found a good excavation site. The sun hit his head and he started sweating. He knew India was hot but today was a particularly hot day.

"*Il fait chaud*, it's hot", said Claudette.

"Yes", said Alex. But the heat didn't bother him. He was more interested in what ancient history he was going to unravel. Claudette was an attractive French woman, but he needed to focus on his work. He couldn't allow anything to distract him. India was like a cornucopia of ancient relics waiting to be brought to light. He knew there was a story behind whatever they found. They were actual people who lived their lives in another era.

Alex and Claudette started digging. A few hours went by and they could not find anything. Alex knew it takes a lot of patience and hard work to make a discovery.

"I've found something" yelled Claudette from the other side of the site. She held up an earthen pot. Alex immediately went and studied the pot. It was cracked in a few places but still in pretty good shape considering it was around 4,500 years old. Alex immediately took it in his hands and using his duster, dusted it off. Someone had probably used it thousands of years ago to carry water or cook a meal and now it was in his hands. A certain excitement and thrill came over him. He put the pot aside and with increased vigour started digging some more. He was certain that he was going to find something valuable. While he was digging, he hit upon something hard. "Claudette! I found something!"

Claudette rushed to his side. It looked like something white. After digging a little more, he decided to use a duster so he wouldn't damage the object. As he slowly uncovered the object, he slowly realized that it was not an object but a skeleton! It looked like a male. The male skeleton seemed to be holding on to a white object.

"Claudette, can you start dusting from that side so we can find out what this white object is?" "*Oui*," said Claudette and started dusting the white object. It was another skeleton.

"It's a female" said Claudette.

"This is amazing" said Alex.

“They appear to be holding hands.” said Claudette.

“Do you think they wanted to be buried together?”

“I don’t know” said Alex. “But I’m definitely going to find out. They were buried in a half-a-metre-deep sand pit. We will have to research the chronology and possible reasons behind the deaths. Let’s see if we can find any more clues to this mystery. Claudette, you start digging in that sector and I’ll start here.”

Alex was now determined to find out what exactly happened to these two people. Were they lovers? What was their story? Alex suddenly hit a rock. At least he thought it was a rock. After dusting the rock, he found out that it was a steatite seal.

“Claudette, come here! I’ve found a tablet!” He could barely hide his excitement. “It is written in Indus script, with symbols and images. Fortunately, I have studied how to decipher the Indus script. It is an ancient Indian script. One of the first forms of writing in India. The Indus Script combines both word signs and symbols with phonetic value. This type of writing system is known as “logo-syllabic”, where some symbols express ideas or words while others represent sounds. The early logo-syllabic scripts functioned like picture puzzles, based on the rebus principle. The Indus Script was generally written from right to left which is known as *boustrophedon* way of writing.”

“Well, what does it say?” asked Claudette anxiously. Alex carefully took the tablet in his hands. It had a rectangular shape. He dusted it and took out his magnifying glass.

“This is astonishing. It looks like a story written by someone. If I were to make a guess, I think this was written by one of the skeletons which we found.”

“Well, what does it say?” asked Claudette enthusiastically.

“There are no complete sentences, but I can make out the story from the images. I will translate it for you. Here is what it says

*“I, Head Priest Agastya am ruler of this land. I have plenty of gold and riches. Yet I have no one to share them with. I am a lonely king. Every day, I eat rice, lentils, bread and meat alone in my home. One day, I decided to go hunting for meat. So, I called my hunters and took my hunting tools. I rode my elephant into the forest. As I was going into the forest, I saw a beautiful young woman by the river. She had long flowing black hair and soft features with fair skin. She was draped in a light blue coloured sari. She did not have*

*many ornaments on her except for a few bangles. She was drinking water from the river. I was mesmerized by this beauty. After drinking the water, she went to the peepal tree and performed a detailed worship of the tree as the peepal tree is considered sacred. The sun hit her long dark hair and made it shine. I did not approach her but just watched her from afar. I have never seen such a beautiful woman. Suddenly, one of the hunters who was with me pulled me aside and told me that there was a deer on the opposite side of the river. I left the beautiful woman and went to hunt the deer. When I returned to the river, she was gone. After returning home, I ordered my servants to find this mystery woman. I prayed to lord Pasupathi to help me find this beautiful* woman. *That evening, I attended a social program where there was drinks, food and dance. After the food was eaten, there was a dance program. A group of women came out dancing in beautiful flowing saris and with veils on their face. When the dance started, the girls took off their veils and I could see that one of the girls was the same woman by the river! I watched her dance and after the program was over, I approached her.*

*"What is your name? You are a beautiful dancer." I said.*

*"My name is Myra" she told me.*

*"You are very beautiful, and I have fallen in love with you ever since I saw you at the river." I told her.*

*"I am the poor daughter of a snake charmer and you are the Head Priest. You are of high status. Society will not accept our marriage." she said.*

*"My love," I said, "I will not be able to live without you."*

*She looked at me and said, "I too have noticed you. You are strong and kind. I love you too."*

*After saying this, she ran away. I did not know that one of my guards was listening to our conversation. He told the whole village about us. The next day, I met Myra. I took her on a chariot ride through the village. "I love you" I told her. I then took out a gold beaded necklace with a green unicorn pendant and put it around her neck as a symbol of my love for her.*

*"This is beautiful" she said. I then gently kissed her. Suddenly, I felt our chariot had been hit by something. Myra was scared.*

*"What is happening?" she asked. I looked out and saw people throwing stones at us.*

*"How can you marry a girl of lower caste?" They yelled. "We will not accept her as our queen!" I immediately took Myra's hand and ran out of the chariot. We hid behind some trees.*

*"What can we do?" she asked. "We love each other but society does not want us to be together." "How can we be together?" I asked. "I want to be with you forever and the only way that can happen is if we die together and lay with each other for eternity away from all society. We decided that the only way to be together forever was to die together. We have decided to consume poison and lie here together forever."*

The writing ended at that point. Alex was shocked and almost dropped the tablet.

"Agastya and Myra are the skeletons which we found!" exclaimed Alex.

"*C'est magnifique*! That's amazing!" said Claudette. Alex was so overwhelmed with sorrow that the only way they thought their love could survive is if they died. But at the same time, he was excited to have found a piece of Indian history.

"Let's see if we can find something more." said Alex. He was now intrigued. Alex and Claudette started digging again. As Alex was digging, he hit some object. Excitedly, he sat down and looked at the object. It was a golden beaded necklace with a green unicorn pendant made of lapis lazuli.

"Of course," said Alex, "the unicorn was considered a prominent religious figure of that era." Alex's hands started shaking as he held the necklace. "Claudette, this must be the same necklace Agastya gave to Myra."

Claudette gently took it in her hands.

"This is incredible" she said. Alex felt tears streaming down his cheeks. "This is the symbol of their undying love for each other."

Alex suddenly hugged Claudette out of pure joy and gently gave her a kiss. "Agastya and Myra really stayed together forever just as they wanted..."

# The Rakshagarh Connexion

*Dominic Arivarasu Mathias*

***Who is Dominic Arivarasu Mathias?***

*Dominic Arivarasu Mathias, MA, BEd, MPhil (Eng), has been in the teaching profession for over 35 years and has taught in schools in Meghalaya, Mizoram and Arunachal Pradesh for 10 years before settling in Mumbai in 1994. Since then he has been teaching students of BCom, BA, BMM, BSc (IT), MBA as well as Junior Colleges in Mumbai. He has been the Chief Editor of his College and School magazines for two decades. He is a Moderator for HSC, BCom and BSc (IT). He has attended innumerable conferences and presented papers in over a dozen national and international conferences. A freelance writer, his letters and articles have appeared in every leading newspaper in Mumbai. Mr Dominic has won several prizes for essay and story writing competitions at different levels. He is a Master Trainer and a Mentor trained by the British Council. He is also a Moderator of CHESS (Continuous Help to teachers of English from Secondary Schools) programme of the Government of Maharashtra. Mr Dominic is a recipient of several awards for his contribution to education. He has also co-authored three guidebooks for Std XI and XII of Maharashtra State Board.*

*One of his stories was published by the National Open School (now NIOS) in its Supplementary Reading Materials in 2002. Three of his stories have been anthologized by The Impish Lass Publishing House, Mumbai*

# The Rakshagarh Connexion

There was a slight rustle: someone or something was obviously moving among the undergrowth.

'Who is there?'

No answer.

'Come out. Or else.... Come on, quick...' hollered Hanjo.

Slowly, with arms folded in supplication, a dark face emerged from the bushes hesitantly.

'Spare me, please. I mean no harm.'

Hanjo was shocked to see such a black and rugged face, and, more so, to actually hear it speak. It was not unlike that of a species of monkeys he used to hunt with his friends, but this had the semblance of a human being. If the 'face' had not spoken, he would have shot it with an arrow or pinned it with his bronze-tipped spear.

Shouted Hanjo: 'Who are you? Why are you hiding here? Where are you from?'

The Face gestured to him to give him something to eat and drink. Hanjo signalled to him to wait at a distance and kept a water skin and some meat on the ground and retraced a few steps. The man moved toward the victuals eagerly and emptied nearly half of the water first before gobbling the meat without even chewing much.

The man, who introduced himself as Khaba, was apparently part of a group of traders from Egypt and had been left behind when he went exploring the forests outside Harappa. He claimed that while he was bathing in a lake, the sight of a lioness with her cubs prevented him from getting out of the water. By the time he got out, hungry, it was dark, and he spent the night on top of a tree, lest he be attacked by beasts. In fact, he had spent a harrowing night on the tree due to the jackals that kept howling from the ground below. As the sun rose, he realized that the tree that had been his perch was a pear tree with tiny unripe fruits. He plucked a few of them and munched them so as to quench his thirst as well as hunger.

The crystal clear lake had a magnificent look from the tree. The wee ripples on the expansive surface moved in slow motion like miniature waves in an ocean. Set against the backdrop of steep mountains, the reflection of the verdant mountain on the placid water was a veritable sight to behold. It was a semi-natural lake of gigantic proportions between two hills – semi-natural because only one side of the lake had been hemmed in by a manmade wall. The architects had built it with much far-sightedness: several canals had been constructed to route water for irrigation, and there were outlets at the top of the boundary wall for draining the water lest it should overflow. However, a small portion of the wall on the extreme right seemed to be wet, exposing a fault in the construction, or it could be due to its age. The thick moss on the wall revealed it to be not less than half a century old.

Alighting from his post cautiously, Khaba walked towards the lake, scouting for a place to conceal his possessions, and to imbibe its pristine beauty. At the far end, he noticed a sprawling banyan tree and thought that it would be the ideal hiding place for his valuables. However, the rambling aerial roots left no space for digging, so he burrowed a ditch beside a fig tree, and interred two small but heavy bags, and covered the spot with a stone rolled from the adjoining hillock.

From here he could decipher what looked like the fringes of a town at a distance, towards the south, and started tramping towards it, following an animal trail: the meandering contours of the track debilitated him in the absence of food and drink. At long last, he felt relieved when he met Hanjo and his troupe of hunters. In order not to surprise them with his distinct facial features and complexion, he decided to hide from them and reveal himself by and by.

Hanjo wanted to take him to the Chief of the town but Khaba was scared that the Chief might hand him over to his Egyptian master who would certainly murder him since, he confessed, he had actually run away with some of his money. He requested that he be given a corner in the outskirts of the village and that he would remain there and serve Hanjo's father, since, having lived near a tributary of the Blue Nile, he was adept at cooking, fishing as well as farming. Khaba was introduced to one of the villagers who was warned to keep him incognito till the time was ripe.

Hanjo lived in the Upper Town of Harappa. The houses there were meant for the affluent ones while the economically weaker sections lived in smaller houses, mostly owned by their masters from the higher plains. Every house in the Upper Town was two-storied, with private bathrooms and concealed waterways that led to the common gutters. There was a flower garden adjacent to the house and a private area for kids to play. Behind the house there was an enclosure for poultry and a dog kennel for four dogs. At the far end of the house where the valley began its slope there were lodged over a hundred sheep and a dozen cattle. Two small hutments near the wooden gate served to accommodate the two servants who looked after the birds and animals.

While Hanjo's father, mother and his aged grandparents lived on the ground floor, Hanjo lived in the rooms above along with his sisters, Dasa and Aswa. He called aside Aswa and told her of his new discovery – the man and the money. Sensing the wrath of the Chief of the town, Aswa advised him to have nothing to do with Khaba and make him surrender. But Hanjo was keen on snatching the money pilfered by Khaba before turning him over to the Chief.

The next morning, when Hanjo went to visit Khaba after his brunch consisting of wheat cake, rice pudding and wild boar meat, the latter had already gone away to fetch fish from the lake. Khaba's host had served him a rice preparation garnished with local vegetables but Khaba insisted on showcasing his fishing and culinary skills.

Hanjo went looking for him near the lake on the higher plane but did not find him. For, with a view to securing the two bagful of gold coins that he had hidden under the fig tree, Khaba marched eastwards, surveying the locality. He came up to an under-construction walled barricade meant to block enemy's entry into the village. The walls were made of single burnt bricks held in place by clay mortar, interspersed with a pillar-like double bricked structure. He made a mark with a stone on the eighth pillar and proceeded toward the spot of the interment of the package.

Lo and behold, Hanjo was sitting with his friends in the shade of the same tree. Intrigued, he made obeisance to him and thanked him for sparing his life and accommodating him in the village. He realized, on discovering the arrangement of flat rocks under the tree, that it was the place where people relaxed before and after bathing in the river. Hanjo wanted to see the fish that he had caught. But he said that he had noticed some spotted deer grazing on the eastern side of the village and gave them chase but they were too nimble for him. He offered to join them for fishing.

Before they could venture into the lake for fishing, the sky suddenly became dark and it began to drizzle. The drizzle soon turned into a heavy downpour, and each one had to hasten towards their homes. The torrential rain continued non-stop for eight days, but providentially for the inhabitants of the township, there was an extensive drainage system that drained out the rainwater into a tributary of the Sarsuti River.

On the eighth day the lake where Khaba had gone swimming overflowed and the water in the canals was racing with the vengeance of a river hurtling down from the mountain. The Sarsuti River too was in full spate. Nevertheless, there was a lull in the thunder and rain on the ninth day. People started to venture out to gather food but found hardly anything of worth available as everything had been carried away by the fury of the rain gods: they needed to assemble at the village ground soon to placate the anger of the rain god.

Hanjo had planned to seize the gold from Khaba and hide it in a niche inside one of the drains in his room upstairs. Had he hidden it there, it would have been washed away since even the drains were being worked to their capacity!

Now that the rain had abated, he rushed to the house where Khaba lived in order to retrieve the gold coins before they got dispersed by the water. However, by the time he reached the lower village, it began to rain again. But the attraction of the gold took preponderance over the danger posed by the unprecedented rain, and Khaba and Hanjo hazarded into the forest, armed with a shovel each.

Braving the rain and storm, they managed to find the tree but the whole area had borne the brunt of the incessant rains. They began digging for the gold laboriously. The rain had loosened the earth making their task easier. They removed the stone kept over the bags, and as they caught hold of the two sachets, lightning stuck the tree and felled it into two. The tree collapsed on the embankment of the lake, breaking it with a thud. The duo did not feel the earthquake that preceded the breach on the embankment. Pieces of burnt bricks careered towards them, propelling them towards the village at the foothills.

The rupture on the wall became larger and larger, destroying the boundary wall, flooding the village and covering the houses with silt, stones and mud. The torrential rains and the flood fury did not subside for another four days, causing devastation to the whole town, not sparing even the people in the upper village. The earthquake had flattened the houses on the upper village, while the rain displaced every human being and flora and fauna.

* * * *

The following news appeared on the Indian Times newspaper dated September 08, 2028

***New Skull Discovered at Rakshagaon: The Harappan Conundrum has become Curiouser and Curiouser.***

*New Delhi September 8 (By our Special Correspondent)*

*The unresolved ethnicity conundrum of the Harappan civilization has thrown up one more puzzle with the discovery of a skull by two farmers at Rakshagaon last week. The ASI along with some eminent scientists and archaeologists have reconstructed the skull which have features different from those discovered so far in the Harappan region. The skull resembles that of a person of Egyptian origin!*

*Last week, two farmers of Rakshagaon chanced upon a few gold coins bearing some esoteric inscriptions, while trying to bury a bullock that had died of some mysterious illness. On finding the gold coins, the villagers foraged the area hoping to find more, even though they had been forewarned that any gold or artefacts found in the locality belonged to the government. However, they could neither sell the gold nor melt it without anybody's knowledge. The compunctions of their conscience got peaked when they stumbled upon a skull and a few bones scattered over there.*

*The ASI was excited as the skull found here was nothing similar to any discovered during the excavations since last century. It may be pointed out that as early as in 2019 a multidisciplinary team of 15 scientists from six different institutes of South Korea, UK and India had reconstructed the faces of two skulls from Rakhigarhi. The two settlers from Rakhigarhi appeared to have Caucasian features with hawk-shaped and Roman noses. Whereas, the reconstructed face of the Rakshagarh settler was oval shaped, with a sloping forehead and a long straight nose.*

*The correspondent of Indian Times reports that the discovery and their reconstruction have once again resurrected the question of the ethnicity of the people of the Indus Valley Civilization. More excavations, studies and proofs are needed before settling the question once and for all. Only time will tell when this enigma will be put to rest.*

# Section II
# Post Vedic Period
## *(1600 BCE to 600 BCE)*

The title itself is controversial as no one really knows when Vedas were composed or when the Vedic religion existed. I have used articles dealing with the great thinkers and philosophers of ancient times – the Buddha and Jina as the central theme for this part of the anthology. Orbs of Fire deals with one of the greatest universities of the time – Nalanda and the article describes the mundane with a subtle highlighting the period's greatness. The last article of this section deals with Jagannath Cult – one of the regional cults with origins in obscurity. Fits quite nicely into this period as it obviously post-dates the Vedic era.

There is huge amount of archaeological work done for this period. The use of Iron predates the Hittites and European Celts by at least two hundred years. Starting with the early Iron age, it was populated by the Black and Red ware culture. There is strong evidence of Vedic civilisation transforming into the Hindu religion and dynasties during this period. Gangetic civilisation was at its peak especially during the period of Painted Grey War culture and the beginning of the great Mahajanapadas.

The beginning of Sangam era is still shrouded in mystery. The tradition says that there were three Tamil Sangam's, the first one being presided by none other than Lord Siva himself. These Sangam's were more of a corpus of literature, mostly oral and to some extent written. The great classics of Silappadikaraam, Tiruppavai and Tirukkural comes from this era. The famed Kumari Kandam or the Tamil kingdom was said to be located south of the present tip of India and extending further than the present day Srilanka. The sea level rose by about 125 meters at the end of last glacial maximum – about 12000 year before present and it is believed that the Kumari Kandam with its civilisation and the first two Tamil Sangam's disappeared with it. Recent excavations have shown evidence of advanced civilisation dating back to the same period as the Harappans – third millennium BCE and it has rekindled the interest in this civilisation. However, there is no mention of the people of this culture in any of the Vedic scriptures except for the sage Agastya who makes a prominent appearance in the scriptures as one of the prominent family of priests. I have included the story from Sangam era in this section – a fascinating adaptation of Silappadikaram by Sudha Ganapati.

There is an article about the Jagannath cult included in this section as well. The origins of this cult are shrouded in mystery and there are some links with the Buddhist and Jain faiths. This was a period of the greatest thinkers and philosophers of ancient India – Panini, Patanjali, Baudhayana to name a few. Some of the works produced by these predate the widely accepted Greek and Roman theorists by several centuries.

# The Sangam Era:
# The Story of the Anklet (Silappadikaram)

*Sudha Ganapati*

***Who is Sudha Ganapati?***

*Sudha Ganapati is an Arts graduate from Mumbai University. She has been teaching at Children's academy, Malad earlier. A reputed school with branches in the western suburbs.*

*She is a reader of Sanskrit scriptures and is privileged to be a Judge at the annual Gita competitions held by the Chinmaya mission. Lately she has been contributing regularly to Impish Lass publications. Her article and poem have been published in the anthology, 'Emotionally yours'. Two more of her articles are lined up for publication.*


# The Sangam Era:
# The Story of the Anklet (Silappadikaram)


The port city of Puhar looked resplendent with rows and rows of shops lined up in the main street. There was a rich display of merchandise brought by traders from far and near, some of their own too. For this was the city of gold, the capital of the Chola Kingdom in southern India. Also, called Tamilakam, the Chola kingdom was known far and wide for its wealth, peace and prosperity. The king was benevolent, and abundance was apparent among the citizens, who practiced different professions for their living. There were craftsmen, weavers, sculptors, architects and traders. The land was lush with green paddy fields, coconut and areca nut groves. Spices like pepper and cardamom were grown and exported to neighbouring Srilanka and also as far as the Roman Empire. Art and literature flourished, and it came to be known as the Sangam age. Ships sailed the high seas from Puhar and brought back many riches that were sold in the markets.

Soft silk in various vegetable dyed hues, fine cotton cloth so light and thin that it could pass through a tiny finger ring, ornaments in various forms, jewellery delicately designed in gold and silver embossed with precious stones like rubies, diamonds, pearls and jade. They shimmered in the morning sunlight attracting many a buyer.

Kannagi the pretty maiden from Puhar walked alongside her mother admiring the wares. They were shopping for her wedding trousseau. She was the daughter of a rich merchant and her betrothed was Kovalan, a young merchant also from Puhar, who matched her in beauty and in wealth.

Kannagi was spoilt for choice in this bustling market but soon her eyes fell upon a beautiful pair of anklets, one that seemed to have been crafted by the great God Kuber himself. It was delicate and fine and felt auspicious. She was sure that it would bring luck to whoever who wore it. Kannagi's heart skipped a beat, "how I wish I could wear them for my wedding", she thought. Her mother quickly sensing her child's wishes, requested for the anklets to be sent to their home. The anklet was made of silver embellished with precious gems like pearls and rubies.

Kannagi and Kovalan were to be married soon after his return from a trade voyage he had embarked on, along with his father. His family was preparing for a grand marriage, a few days hence.

Everyone in Puhar looked forward to the wedding. There was rejoicing and celebration everywhere. Finally, the auspicious day dawned with ceremonial music wafting in the morning breeze. Kovalan and Kannagi in their wedding finery took the seven steps around the fire and repeated all the vows to solemnize the ceremony. The wedding concluded with the couple viewing the Arundhati star in the sky, which symbolises chastity, modesty and virginity. Kannagi was an embodiment of all these. Her parents were loath to be separated from her, but that was the custom and she had to go away to her husband's house. Teary eyed Kannagi bid adieu to her beloved parents, friends and relatives, and set forth to begin a new phase of life.

She soon settled down in the neighbouring province with her lord and master Kovalan, who was loving and caring. He was also competent and astute in his profession and his trade picked up well. The young couple gained the respect of all and many in the kingdom. They had many friends and some of them from the court too. Their life took on an exquisite turn of grandeur, magnificence and aristocracy. Kannagi was the happiest she had ever been, but little did she know that the very fate that had been so benevolent to her would soon turn against her.

One day they were invited to the royal court to witness a performance by the famous courtesan Madhavi. Their joy knew no bounds and thanked their good fortune as they read the invitation. Madhavi was famed for her talent and the couple were eager to rub shoulders with the aristocracy who would also be present at the performance. As Madhavi entered the arena specially erected for the event, she looked radiant, and captivated the audience with her striking beauty. Kovalan was mesmerised on seeing her. He just couldn't keep his eyes off her, watching her intensely. The couple returned home that night and Kovalan lay awake in his bed thinking of Madhavi, the dancer.

Kovalan was never the same again. He was lost and lived in a trance, hardly paying any attention to things around him, nor going to work, and Kannagi had to gently chide him and ask him to attend to his work. The next day he rose up early and got ready, Kannagi prepared his meal and as usual bid him at the threshold her right eye twitched. 'Very unusual' she thought but did not think much of it as she went on her usual chores.

That day, the path which Kovalan took, changed his destiny forever. Instead of going towards his workplace, he walked towards Madhavi's house. He knocked on her door thrice, the maid opened and asked him to wait while she informed her mistress. The musical sound of bells and rhythmic footsteps could be heard from within, Madhavi was practicing. Nevertheless, Kovalan waited patiently and he was finally ushered indoors and invited to her private quarters.

There was no introduction needed, an exchange of glance said it all. Madhavi was an entertainer and she knew, she had to look after the needs of her admirers. She took an instant liking to Kovalan, who grabbed the opportunity to fulfil his desires. There upon he was completely drenched in Madhavi's amorous desires and admired her skills in the art forms of dance and music. She impressed him immensely thus enslaving him into her fold.

Back home Kannagi waited and waited endlessly. The evening cast long shadows, but there was no sight of her husband. "Maybe he is busy with his work, or with a friend discussing trade or in some problematic affair which is keeping him away," she thought. She consoled herself and quietly went about her chores. But the evening turned into days, and days into weeks and it was nearly a month, and yet there was no sign of Kovalan.

One afternoon, she heard a knock on her door, which sounded very familiar. She rushed and opened the door to find Kovalan there, but before she could enquire about him, he thrust himself inside, and hurried out with the treasure chest full of cash and gold. Kannagi nearly fainted as her worst fears were confirmed. She had heard neighbours whispering that her husband lived with Madhavi, but she never believed those rumours. But now the truth came crashing down on her as she realised that her husband had abandoned her for the court dancer Madhavi.

After a few days she picked herself up, regained her composure and took a vow that she would surely release him from Madhavi's evil clutches. Kannagi immersed herself in fasts, puja and vrat. Her lonely days were spent in search of divine truth as she lived in austerity and undertook severe penance to atone the wrongdoings of her husband.

A period of four years elapsed. It was springtime and she could feel the gentle breeze caressing her tresses, the birds chirped beautifully, and the pleasant fragrance of flowers came floating in the air, when she heard footsteps near her door. She went towards the door, too afraid to hope, yet with a sense of anticipation. She opened the door, and silent tears escaped from her eyes, her prayers had been answered, Kovalan had come back to her. Kovalan too ashamed to enter, stood there with his head bowed down unable to meet Kannagi's eyes that were filled with tears and love for him. His relationship with Madhavi had soured and he had finally come to his senses.

Yet Kannagi welcomed him with all grace and dignity. Kovalan was overcome with remorse and guilt. He had lost all his wealth and felt morally drained. Kannagi gave him courage, strength and nursed him back to his original self. Kannagi had a strong conviction that God returns back whatever he takes.

Kovalan was overwhelmed with her affection for him and cursed himself for bringing so much distress on her. He realised that he had greatly wronged her, and he had no right to the sympathy she had for him. She, who was the embodiment of all that was pure and good, he did not deserve her. But all that mattered to Kannagi was that her beloved was back. She reassured him that all would be right, and that time would heal everything.

The couple decided to give a fresh start to their lives by leaving the Chola kingdom. They had heard of the kingdom of the Pandya's and decided that that would be an ideal place to start anew.

In order to erase the bitter memories of the past, the couple immediately left for Madurai, a city nestled on the banks of the Vaigai River in the Pandya kingdom. Once they reached Madurai, they rented a small house as advised by a friend and well -wisher. Kannagi carefully handed over one of her precious anklets from the pair bought for her wedding. She had safeguarded the jewel very dearly, even more than her life, as it was the most precious wedding gift given to her by her beloved mother.

It would fetch a good price and would help him start a new trade afresh. As he walked down the streets of Madurai, Kovalan felt uncertain of his future but Kannagi's love erased all these doubts. He made enquiries for a good jeweller and was led to the queen's jeweller's house where ornaments were made for the queen.

Reluctantly and slowly he drew out from his clothing, the pouch which contained the anklet. The jeweller saw it and thought the anklet looked exactly like the queens. He assessed its value and concluded that it was but a priceless and rare jewel. He was overcome with greed and a wicked thought crossed his mind and he worked out a sinister plot to trap Kovalan in a case of theft.

He would tell the king that this anklet, which was actually Kannagi's belonged to the Queen and that Kovalan had come to steal it from him (the jeweller). Thus, the jeweller stole the queen's anklet, kept it to himself, and replaced it with Kannagi's anklet, which looked just like the queens on the outside.

The vile jeweller took the anklet to the king, while telling Kovalan that he would sell it to the king and return with a good amount. Poor

Kovalan waited outside the palace in great anticipation. Inside the palace, the jeweller who had sold his soul to the devil, narrated his false story to king Nedunchezhiyan. He handed over Kannagi's anklet to the king saying that it was the queen's and the alleged thief who had come to steal it was caught and standing outside.

Now, the Pandya kings, were great rulers, just and well-known for their administration and trial by jury. Yet, due to a cruel twist of fate, king Nedunchezhiyan, neither consulted his advisors nor think much about the incident. Trusting the royal jeweller, he ordered the execution of Kovalan for stealing the queen's anklet.

The news of Kovalan's execution reached Kannagi, and her world collapsed around her. She could not believe her ears. Why should an innocent man be executed? Was the King so unjust to send a man to the gallows, who was new to the city and knew nothing about the law of the Pandya king? As she rushed towards the palace gates, she seemed possessed by a spirit within her. The courtiers at the entrance were taken aback when she called out to king Nedunchezhiyan and asked them where he was.

She was led inside the palace, where the king and queen were having an audience. 'Oh Raja", she cried out, "Where is your justice, fairness and integrity? Why have you killed my innocent husband who had come to your land, with one of my priceless anklets, to sell, and start a trade with the money"

King Nedunchezhiyan was stunned. "Who are you noble lady?" he asked.

With fire in her eyes, Kannagi replied, "I am the wife of Kovalan, from the Chola Kingdom, I've come for justice and I demand to know why my husband was executed so unjustly? I shall prove Kovalan's innocence, she said.

"How will you prove his innocence? Wasn't he the thief who stole the queen's anklet?" asked the bewildered king.

"The second anklet of the pair will prove his innocence," Kannagi cried out and so saying, she banged the anklet on the floor, with great force. The anklet broke open and rubies scattered from within it. She then demanded to know what was inside the Queen's anklet. Shaken to the core, the king replied that his Queen's anklets had pearls inside them. Now she asked the king to bring the stolen anklet which the jeweller had taken from Kovalan and had lied about its ownership to him. The queen in a state of shock, handed it to Kannagi.

Kannagi looked at the King and said "This anklet which is the first of the pair will decide and avenge my husband's death" and so saying she smashed the anklet on the floor and to the anguish of everyone present, precious rubies burst forth and scattered all over the palace floor. The rubies revealed the truth of the stolen anklet, which belonged to Kannagi.

Though, the queen's and Kannagi's anklets looked similar on the outside, they contained different gems on the inside. The queen's had pearls, while Kannagi's had rubies within.

The king realised his mistake and begged for forgiveness, but Kannagi was disconsolate with overwhelming grief and was unable to forgive him. She cursed the king and his Kingdom to be doomed and destroyed by fire. The city of Madurai burned and was destroyed by Kannagi's curse. With rage and fury, she stormed out of the city gates and walked and walked for many miles, until she entered the Chera kingdom. Here she unburdened her grief to a group of tribal women near the hills. As she gained solace and calm here, a bright light shone in the horizon above the hills and the people witnessed a flying chariot (vimana) descending down to the earth.

Kovalan emerged from it along with the heavenly gods and took Kannagi away, in the vimana.

This incident reached the length and breadth of Cheranad and the king's ears too. The king moved by Kannagi's chastity and devotion to her husband, had an idol sculpted in her honour and installed it at the sanctum sanctorum in a temple built by him. The temple built by the Chera king, 'Mangala Devi Kannagi' is in Idukki district, Kerala State, and is two thousand years old. Here Kannagi is worshipped as a goddess,

When the King and society failed a helpless woman in her quest for justice, the gods came to her rescue. Madurai was later rebuilt and reinstated to its past glory by succeeding Pandya kings.

*Footnote- The story is an adaptation from 'Silapathikaram' written by Illango Adigal, the ascetic prince, brother of the Chera king. Silappadikaram is considered to be one of the five great epics in ancient Tamil literature of the Sangam Era.*

# Jagannath Cult – the Synthesis of all Religion

*Sonali Sahu*

*Who is Sonali Sahu?*

*Sonali Sahu, with Masters in English Literature, is a creative and ebullient face in the arena of creative writing, who exquisitely writes poetry and works as an editor of the magazine 'WAVES'.*

*Her creative works are appreciated and followed by many of the literature lovers. She is presently a PGT (English) in Zee School.*

## Jagannath Cult – the Synthesis of all Religion

The people of Orissa owe a lot to Lord Jagannath. He is the Lord of the universe. About whom Vedas are silent. Sometimes people are puzzled about the mystery that surrounds the Lord. He is a great zero. you add zero with zero, the result is zero. you deduct zero from zero the result is zero. you multiply zero with zero the result is zero. zero is nothingness. It is also fullness. It represents the completion of a process. The Lord is omnipresent, omnipotent and omniscient. He is all pervading and he is the Lord of the Universe. Centuries of myths, legends and history have all blended into a grand composite culture centred round Jagannath, the Lord of the universe, one of the most revered and ancient of the deities of the Hindus pantheon. The origin and development or evolution of Jagannath cult is a great landmark in the history and culture of Orissa. The present Jagannath temple at Puri is one of the important centres of Vaishnavism.

The Purans and other ancient Sanskrit texts refer to the holy city Puri as Nilachala, Nilagiri, Niladri, Purusottama Kshetra, Sankha Kshetra, Martya Baikuntha. In Puri not only is the temple holy but to whole of its surroundings is treated as grand and splendid. The sea is Mohadadhi (the great ocean), the main road of the city is Bada Danda (the grand road), the offerings to the Lord Jagannath is Mahaprasad (the holy food) and the cremation ground is Swargadwara (gate way to heaven).

### *Jagannath as Tribal God*

The origin of the Jagannath cult is surrounded in obscurity. According to Sarala Das's, Mohabharat (the 15th century poet and scholar of Odia literature)- Krushna died of poisonous effect of the misdirected ground of Shavara, named Jara. When his dead body was cremated, all organs of his holy body defied the action of fire. It was therefore thrown into the seas by Arjuna. By a miracle, the divine heart had turned by that time into a blue stone. Jara worshipped it as Nilakandar with all devotion and after him his descendants did likewise.

Age passed away. Then king Indradyumna of Malava wanted to revive Vishnu worship in India. He sent messengers to the different parts of Odisha. One of the messengers named Bidyapati the Brahmin, after searching a lot came upon the Shavara village of Biswavasu. Biswavasu the Shavara chief made him marry his daughter Lalita. It was through her that Bidyapati came to know of blue stone deity (Nilamadhava at Nilakandar) of the Shavara that was secretly worshipped in the thick of two jungles. He also came to know from her that the piece of blue stone was really the heart of Lord Krishna. After this wonderful discovery, Bidyapati returned to Malava to bring down king Indradyumna to Orissa. But when he proceeded into the Jungle as guided by Bidyapati, he could not trace the blue stone deity in secret place. The God had disappeared. Next morning the stone image was found at the Puri Sea Shore but neither the king nor his whole army could lift it out of the water. But the Shavara headman and a Brahmin raised the deity with a touch from the water. Indradyumna got the sacred wood or Daru. So being persuaded by his queen Gundicha Devi, he requested an architect

(Biswakarma) for the construction of the deity. The architect agreed with one condition. He would construct the deity in a closed room and take twenty one days for conception. As the fifteenth day passed, the King and queen lost patience. At last the door was forced to be opened. The king was pleasantly surprised to see four incomplete deities. Those were Jagannath, Balabhadra, Subhadra and Sudarshan. Indradyumna constructed there a temple and made arrangement for the worship of deities. Considering from this point of view, Jagannath is a tribal or Shavar deity.

### *Jagannath and Jainism*

The Jain origin of Lord Jagannath is traced by several scholars. Jainism gave a great challenge to Vedic religion. Jainism had entered Orissa before 6th Century BC. It received royal patronage from Kharavela, the mighty monarch of the Chedi dynasty. Some features of Jainism are found in the cult of Jagannath owing to the popularity of Jainism in Orissa. Balabhadra, Subhadra and Jagannath have been regarded as the three cardinal principles of Jainism like Samyak Gyana (Right knowledge), Samyak Charitra (Right Conduct), Samyak Dristi (Right Faith) by Nilakantha Das (Great Scholar of Odia literature). The concept of Kalpa Tree in Jainism is regarded as the Kalpavata inside the sacred complex of Lord Jagannath temple at Puri. Kaivalya Mukti one of the tents of Jainism is identified with Kavalaya (Mahaprasad) of Lord Jagannath that offers salvation to man.

### *Jagannath and Buddhism*

There are a lot of literacy evidences of co-relation between Lord Jagannath and Buddhism. Lord Jagannath is a common epithet of Buddha. Sarala Das, the 15th century poet in his Mahabharat regarded Jagannath as an embodiment of Buddha. He wrote, "To deliver mankind Jagannath has manifested himself in the form of Buddha". Jagannath, Balabhadra and Subhadra represent Buddha, Dharma and Sangha respectively, that the Snana yatra (Bathing Festival and Ratha yatra (Car Festival) are of Buddhist origin. In Buddhism Dharma is considered as female and in Tri-Ratna, she is regarded as sister which is very similar to the worship of Subhada as the sister of Jagannath. At present an image of Buddha at Ellora is called Jagannath which proves

Jagannath and Buddha are identical. Jagannath is worshipped in Puri by the Odias as a form of Buddha for a long time. Jayadev in Gita Govinda also has described Buddha as one among the Dasavatara. Indrabhuti, the ancient Buddhist king describes Jagannath as a Buddhist deity in Jnanasidhi.

### *Jagannath and Saivism*

Scholar H. V Stletencorn opines that the predominance of Saivism in the religious firmament of Orissa over three or four centuries influenced a lot for the growth of Jagannath cult. He relates the worship of Shiva in his fierce aspect of Bhairva form and the sculptural representation of Ekapada bhairva in different temple walls brings a striking similarity with the image of Lord Jagannath. The existence of Shiva temples inside the premises of Jagannath temple at Puri is a pointer in this direction.

### *Jagannath and Sakti Cult*

Like Saivism, Puri was influenced by Sakti Cult. Sakti Purana and other Tantrik books mention the characteristics, features of Sakti faith in Puri including a few other places of Orissa. Tantric rites are found to have been followed. While Lord Jagannath has been described as Bhairab, Goddess Bimala established in the temple complex is being worshipped as Bhairabi. The rice offering in the temple become Maha Prasad only after it is offered before Bimala. This shows the Sakti influence on the Cult of Jagannath. Further the search of Daru for the Nava Kalevara of the deities of the temple of Lord Jagannath temple of Puri begins only after the worship of Goddess Mangala at Kakatpur and obtaining her divine order which suggests the Sakti influence on Jagannath Cult.

### *Narasimha incarnation and Jagannath Cult*

It is interesting to note that Narasimha the incarnation of Lord Vishnu has close link with Lord Jagannath. Narasimha emerging from a wooden pillar killed Hiranya Kashyapa. Likewise, Jagannath is mainly a wooden deity. For daily rituals Lord Jagannath is worshipped from the early morning to the end in Narsimha mantra and rites. There is also a mention in Purushottam Mahatmya of Skanda Puran that Lord

Bramha instructs king Indradyumna to worship Lord Jagannath in this mantra during navakalebara and isolate a stay for fifteen days on the eve of car festival. Seeing from a close angle one can clearly perceive that there is similarity between the square shaped head and round shaped eyes of Lord Jagannath and those of head and eyes of Narasimha. So, one can safely conclude that there is similarity between Lord Jagannath and Narasimha and idol of Jagannath has evolved from Narasimha cult.

### *Conclusion*

The significance of the Jagannath cult lies in the fact that it has absorbed all religion and all religious faiths within itself. Within it's all embracing fold, one can find the essence of the evolution of Indian religion and cult. Diversity in unity and unity in diversity became the character of Jagannath cult. The supreme God being one and same, Jagannath is the Lord of the universe.

Emerging as a deity of the primitives in dense forests, Jagannath stood to represent vedic Brahmanism, Jainism, Buddhism, Sakthism in various phases of time. Though in shape of wooden idols, Jagannath is that absolute being who is beyond description, beyond form and beyond comprehension. He is the saviour of all, irrespective of caste, colour or creed of man. In conclusion it can be seen that Jagannath cult has influenced immensely the social and political life of Orissa. The flag Nilachakra over Jagannath temple indicates the welfare and salvation of the downtrodden people. Tolerance, generosity, caste lessness and untouchability are the main characteristics of the cult of Jagannath. The cult of Jagannath is thus a gift of Orissa to humanity to satisfy its desire for spiritual, peace, social harmony and universal unity.

# Section III
# Ramayana Period

Ramayana is one of the two great epics of India and one of the longest literary pieces in the world. The controversies of whether it was based on a real characters and events and if it did, the period during which it took place rages on as we speak with a conclusion. There is no archaeological evidence for any of the events or characters found so far. There are no contemporaneous records for the events that took place in any of the cultures outside India. The dating of the epic goes from over 6000 BCE to around 1500 BCE and as recent as 600 BCE. While there is no archaeological evidence for any of the events or characters, there is evidence of the cities or places mentioned in the epic. Some of the major cities mentioned in the epic – Ayodhya, Mithila, Kaushambi date back to the middle of first millennium BCE and some even to the beginning of first Millennium BCE. However, sites these "cities" show evidence of small dwellings and basic living conditions. No sign of grandiose palaces and gardens described in the great epic. The controversy will continue until some archaeological or contemporary literary evidence is unravelled.

Sage Valmiki has shown his knowledge of the geography of the then India quite well. But the once the story moves to outside India, the accuracy suffers significantly, often completely wrong. He describes the scenery of travels quite vividly and should help us identify many of the places in the epic. The story itself should give us clues to the whereabouts of the actions. Let us look at the passages from the beginning to find clues.

Dasharatha is described as an emperor and king of Kosala. The Mahajanapadas – sixteen kingdoms - have been described quite well in both the Jain canon as well as Buddhist scriptures. Kosala was one of the kingdoms with Kosalapura or Ayodhya as the capital. At the time of the Buddha, it was ruled by King Prasenjit. Its capital was Ayodhya on the banks of River Sarayu. The river has been identified with the modern river Sarju or Gogra by F E Pargiter, the great orientalist during $19^{th}$ century.

Valmiki's travels with the two young Kosala princes – Rama and Lakshmana are well described. They are described as the sons of Emperor Dasharatha of Kosala with capital at Ayodhya on the banks of River Sarayu. Sarayu has been identified with the River Gogra of present. The city of Ayodhya defies experts so far despite extensive searches. The present day Ayodhya is unlikely to be the city of Rama as the archaeological evidence of the present city shows a primitive village dating to about $8^{th}$ century BCE. The Ayodhya described by Valmiki was a major city with palaces, orchards and big buildings.

There are at least four journeys described by Valmiki which should give us reasonably reliable clues as to the geography of the epic.

1. *Vishwamitra's journey with the two young princes – Rama and Lakshmana to his ashram and later to Mithila*
2. *Messengers journey Ayodhya to Girivraja to bring Bharat back*
3. *Journey of Bharata from Girivraja to Ayodhya*
4. *Wanderings of Rama, Lakshmana and Sita during their exile from Ayodhya to Lanka*
5. *Return journey via air from Lanka to Ayodhya of the heroic victors of the epic battle with Ravana*

The first journey describes Vishwamitra taking the two princes first to his ashram, Sidhashrama located between river Ganga and Sona. The ashrama located about a day's journey from the confluence of the two rivers was being attacked by the asuras/demons. They travel lasting four days takes them through the land between two provinces of Malava and Karusa. They initially walk along the banks of the river Sarayu before crossing river Ganga not far from the river Sarayu. Das and Griffiths consider Malava same as the Kingdom of Malaya mentioned in the Jain canon as one of the sixteen kingdoms. The Buddhist literature does not mention the Kingdom. Karusa does not get a mention in either of the Buddhist or Jain literature.

The route from Sidhashrama to Mithila takes them along the river Sona, across which they wade through. A journey of three yojanas from the crossing point they reach the river Ganga and cross over to the

Kingdom of Vaisali ruled by the King Sumati. They pass through the kingdom when they come across the deserted ashram of Gautama and Ahalya before reaching the city of Mithila. Cunningham identifies Vaisali as the current village of Besarh, which is still called by the name "Raja Baisal ka garh" (King Baisal's house). By the time of Buddha, Vaisali was being ruled by the Licchavis.

During the journey, Vishwamitra narrates the story of king Kusa, ruler of the kingdom of Vasu. As the river Sumagadha flowed through the kingdom, it comes to be known as Magadha during the Buddhist time. Magadha becomes a great kingdom and gets several references in both Buddhist and Jain canon. It is clearly identified with southern Bihar state.

Vishwamitra entertains the two young princes with the tales of building of four cities by the sons of king Kusa – Kusasmbi, Mahodaya, Pragjyotsa and Girivrija by Kusamba, Kusanabha, Amrutavaya and Basu respectively. Kausambi has been identified with the modern day Kosambi, Mahodaya or Kanyakubja with Kanauj and Girivrija with Rajagriha or Rajgir. The city of Pragjyotisa has not been identified even though there are some unproven contenders for the same. Vishwamitra also mentions the river Kausiki, which has been identified as the river Kosi, a tributary of river Ganga. Vishwamitra also talks about Kampilya whose king Bramhadatt marries the daughter of king Kusanabha. This has been identified with the town of Kampil in Farrukhabad district.

Archaeological excavations at Kosambi, about 56 kms southwest of Allahabad, have found bronze-age relics dating back to 2000 BCE at Kaushambi. Remnants of massive ramparts have been discovered around the ancient settlement stretching up to 6 kms. These ramparts are likely to date back to 1200 BCE. While there is no archaeological evidence for Mithila, the kingdom of Videha is believed to have straddled the Nepalese border with India around Janakpur district and Sitamarhi in north Bihar.

Archaeological digs in northern Uttar Pradesh, at Kanauj (Kanyakubj) have shown evidence of Painted Grey Ware culture dating back to 1200 BCE. We have to remember that these dates are being put back almost every year now with new discoveries and fresh digs. It is now believed that Painted Grey Ware culture is a remnant of late Harappan culture with significant correlations with the declining Harappan culture.

The next journey we should consider is the urgent travel of messengers from Ayodhya at the death of King Dasharatha and Rama is exiled. The kingdom is thrown into disarray due to lack of a successor to the throne. The messengers rush through the shortest route possible to the kingdom of Kekeya to bring Bharat back. Several places get a mention including Hastinapura, Pancaladesa, Kurujangala, Kurukshetra, Puri and rivers Sarasvati, Satarudra (Satadru) and Vipasa. Many of these places have been identified now. The Vipasa is the river Beas in the west, Rig Vedic Satadru is present day Sutlej and Sarasvati as the Gaggar-Hakra.

Hastinapura which plays such an important role in the epic Mahabharata has been identified with ruins discovered in the old bed of river ganga 57 miles northeast of New Delhi. Mr B B Lal discovered evidence of Painted Grey Ware culture at the site taking the city back to 1200 BCE. Kurukshetra is identified with the country adjacent to Thanesar west of dried bed of Drishadvati river. The messengers take seven days to do the journey in the epic. A simple logging of the journey by foot using Google maps shows it is possible to "walk" from Ayodhya to river Beas in 183 hours. The messengers would be fit runners who would do it in seven days due to the urgency of the situation.

Dasharatha marries the princess of the kingdom of Kekeya. Rigvedic Kekeyas lived on the banks of river Parushni. They are the direct descendants of Yayati's son Anu. After the Battle of Ten Kings (Dasharajna), the descendants of Anu migrate westwards. The name of the capital of Kekeya is called Girivraja. This causes some confusion as the present day Rajgir or Rajgriha has been identified as the ancient Girivraja, dating back to 1200 BCE. The present day Rajgir is in Bihar whereas the Girivraja described by Valmiki is somewhere west of river Beas (Vipasa). River Vipasa gets mentioned in Rigveda and has been correctly identified as river Beas. The great river Sarasvati had been considered mythical for a long time till recent satellite images of a vast riverbed traversing the Thar and Cholistan deserts, all the way from the Himalayan foothills to the Arabian sea. The dried bed has shown presence of water under the sand stretching up to 10 kms across in places. In the northern Rajasthan in Bikaner district the scientists have dug wells to find sweet water less than five meters under the sand. Excavations have now revealed several hundred archaeological sites along the dried riverbed dating back to mature and late Harappan phase – from third millennium to late second millennium BCE. Rakhigarhi near the confluence of dried bed of Sarasvati and Drishadvati is now known to be the largest of Harappan cities stretching over 400 hectares.

The third major journey we should consider is the route taken by Bharata back to Ayodhya. The many places and "tirthas" he visits on his journey taking seven nights cannot be identified with any certainty. Some of the place names in present day would take him way out of the direction of Ayodhya from Girivraja. The rivers Yamuna, Ganga and Gomati are the only ones which can identified with any certainty.

The fourteen-year exile of Rama describes his travels through most of the country south of Ayodhya and many places have been identified. The two rivers they cross, Tamasa and Gomati have been identified as Tons and Gomti rivers in Uttar Pradesh. After crossing the rivers, they come to the town of Srngaraverapura of Nisadas. This has been identified by Cunningham as present day town of Singor. After sending the faithful Sumantra back to Ayodhya, they are helped by Guha, the Nisada king to cross the river Ganga. They travel through dense forest to arrive at Prayaga, the confluence of Ganga and Yamuna. Prayaga is identified with the present day Prayag which is considered holy by Hindus everywhere.

They travel through the Prayaga forest and cross Yamuna on a raft to reach the Citrakuta where Bharata comes to visit them to beg Rama to return to Ayodhya. Citrakuta mountain has been identified with the modern Kampatanatha giri near modern Citrakut town. Mandakini river has been identified with the modern Mandakin river by Cunningham in his Archaeological Report.

Dandakaranya, the forest Rama was banished to has been identified with the entire stretch of land from Bundelkhand down to the river Krishna. Pancavati where they trio lived has been identified with the modern Nasik.

In this section we have a very interesting take on the antagonist, Ravana by Tarishi Chawla. He is by a common response defiled by everyone with the respect the protagonist Sri Rama carries with him. However, this article shows that not everyone ascribes to that view.

# Demystifying Ravana

*Tarishi Chawla*

***Who is Tarishi Chawla?***

*Tarishi is a freelance writer who loves to write about everything she can relate to. Bios, however, are an exception as they sound too pretentious and she wonders who reads them anyway!*

*When she isn't travelling the seas with her family, she can be found at home in Nooda, painting, teaching yoga and reading her favourite authors.*

*She loves to connect to her readers in a bold yet playful manner. The intent is to keep it light and entertaining and that takes care of the seven lines she was supposed to submit for this bio.*

## Demystifying Ravana

Gods, Deities, Super humans, Avatars.... they have many names. Call them what you will. They are the glorious winners of mighty battles where truth emerges victorious at the end. History you see, will always glorify the winner and for good reason. It is a very simple reason though.

It is the winners who write the books or get them written. The folklore has tales of the mighty conquerors and the musicians sing ballads in praise of the Victors. To do anything else obviously would mean certain death.

In a war, as they say, there is no place for the runners up. Far too much has been written of Gods and winners. What then of those worthy opponents? Doesn't every Krishna need a Kansa, Can Prahlad exist without a Hiranyakashyap and would a Durga be half as deadly without a Mahishasura? It is the joker you see that demands a batman and never vice versa.

The greatest epic of all time therefore needed a villain of supremely magnified power and strength. A character as mighty as the great Ravana. A driven, ambitious and deadly character who is larger than life.

A man who even at his deathbed had his conqueror begging for an insight into the deep knowledge he possessed. However, the God king was refused, on the simple account that he had made the request standing near the head of Ravana. The seeker needs more humility and should be standing near the feet. Ravana, was crystal clear in thought even at his deathbed and showed no fear pointing out the mistake of a man who is worshipped as a God. When Rama sent brother Laxman to stand near his feet and ask for the same knowledge, the request was granted with benevolence.

Such generosity in face of certain death leaves no doubt that the character was in essence Greatness. Further study however reveals that the greatness was coupled with genius.

The four Vedas are considered to be a vast ocean of knowledge, the mastery of one of these, it's said, makes a being superhuman. All four had all been mastered by Ravana. He was known as a Mahabrahmin as he had 64 different types of knowledge. He is the author of several books on topics which range from astrology to medicine. From ground politics to the complete esoteric...

There was little that he did not immerse himself into.

Extremely well suited for an emperor, he brought wealth and prosperity to his kingdom of Lanka. He is said to have had 10 heads which mean he could understand more, see more, feel more and know more. The 10 pairs of arms symbolise his prowess, his capabilities of doing more. No wonder he is worshipped.

Yes, this incredibly powerful, wise and strong ruler whose straw figure is blown to smithereens every year in North India, commonly thought of as an evil monster who kidnapped the wife of Lord Rama is also worshipped and celebrated in a lot of places.

"Ravan baba Namah" is a common chant in a 120 year old temple of Kanpur. In Jodhpur, Rajasthan, a sect of Mudgil Brahmins perform rituals and give alms in his name.

The Gond tribals of Maharashtra believe that Ravana did no wrong and worship him and his son Meghanad as Gods. In the South district of Kolar, "Lankadipati Ravana" is prayed to, during the harvest festival. In Mandsaur, Madhya Pradesh, the town of his wife "Mandodari" he is treated as a son in law. He is worshipped and respected for his unparalleled knowledge and his dedication to lord Shiva. Ravana is the embodiment of a multitude of virtues, even an exaggeration. Bravery, strength, courage, devotion and knowledge.

A couple of stories from the era give us a glimpse of this magnificent character. They say he was so enamoured by God Shiva that he took to tapasya and when the God failed to appear despite intensely long and severe worship which lasted for decades, he finally sacrificed his own head in dismay. The lord finally stirred and then blessed him with 10 heads. Hence the name "Dashanan" The ten headed being.

Another instance talks about how devout and fanatical worshipper Ravana was. Lord Shiva is frequently worshipped in the form of a "lingam". Ravana therefore wanted to possess the most majestic lingam in existence. After a comprehensive search he realised that the largest lingam was the mountain "Kailash" the abode of the God himself. Undeterred Ravana decided to carry the entire mountain to his kingdom. Unaware that Shiva and wife Parvati were atop Kailash at that moment, he started lifting it up. The mountain shook when Ravan started lifting it, Parvati stumbled. Thinking it was an earthquake, Shiva pressed his toe and Ravana was trapped underneath the mountain. Howling in pain, he uttered a cry (RAAV) that gave him the name "Raavan" On learning that the duo had been in residence atop, Ravana was full of penance and legend has it, that he used the nerves of his own body to create a musical instrument called a "Rudra veena" and composed and sang a beautiful and powerful hymn in praise of the lord.

The hymn called the "Shiva tandava stotram" is extremely popular to this day. Shiva was again enraptured by his love and devotion and blessed him, giving him a "chandrahaas" the invincible sword for a weapon and gifting a lingam called "Golinga" that he said was as powerful as Kailash. Ravana was permitted to carry it to his kingdom

Lanka on the condition that the lingam could not be put down the entire way and if it was, it would stay wherever it was put down.

Ravana, they say, thanked him profusely and proceeded to carry the lingam but enroute it was sunset time and he had to carry out his sunset prayer ritual. Lord Ganesha however did not want "Golinga" to leave India. Disguised, he approached Ravana offering to hold the lingam for the 10 minute duration of prayer. Ravana proceeded to start the prayer ritual, but lord Ganesha kept playing tricks on him by entering his mind and making him forget the ritual sequences repeatedly.

As soon as the designated 10 minutes were over, Lord Ganesha dropped the lingam on the spot where it remains to this day in a place known as "Gokarna". Ravana conducted his worship in a manner so austere with devotion so powerful that the Gods were forced to grant his boons on several occasions. He once asked for immortality and upon refusal he asked for invincibility in any battles against Gods, Gandharvas (Superhumans) and wild animals. He never considered humans a threat.

It wasn't the circumstances of his birth however that gave him an edge. His father was a sage by the name Vaishrava but his mother, Kaikeshi was a daitya (demon princess). A mixed race placed him at a major disadvantage, but he refused to be a product of circumstances. Instead he grew stronger and became the most powerful king of that time. He even mastered magical spells by staying with the glorious and legendary "Nivatakavachas" (Asura demons) for a year after not being able to conquer them. He is said to have acquired mastery in black magic, hypnotism, occult and mysticism. He is said to be the inventor of "Veena", the musical instrument. He was a lover of arts. He is the author of the Raavan samhita and He wrote seven books on Ayurveda.

The strong, powerful courageous man however did not believe in making friends. He was betrayed quite a few times in the story. He had once confided to his brother the secret that only the weapon of "Brahmastra" could kill him and that too if it pierced his navel. His brother turned against him and the rest as they say is history. Driven by lust, the man had 1000 wives. Another story says that when he was at the very verge of losing the war, He perpetrated a fire ritual that would turn the battle against him but it required him to stay in one spot throughout .

Ram came to know of it and sent the monkey army to dislodge him. After repeated failed attempts, they proceeded to drag his wife as a last resort. Raavan still did not budge until his wife shamed him by giving Ram's example for a man who was fighting a war for his wife while hers wouldn't move. Ravana moved, leaving the yagya ritual incomplete, which led to his losing the battle of Ramayana.

There is a story behind every story and when we talk about the great epics, there are generally several of them. What led Ravana to an end was that although he was a devotee of Shiva, He failed to imbibe any of the qualities that Shiva stands for. Ravana was besotted with wealth, moved by base passions and ruled by ego while Shiva is a God who treats demons, Gods and ghosts alike and as friends. A half man/half woman figure that show the degree of equality the God believes in.

Strength courage and wisdom are wonderful qualities but without love and loyalty, a city made of Gold can be brought down by mere monkeys. The epics frequently talk of the mind as being a monkey too. The stories of the epics can make one pause and look a bit deeper. The deeper we delve, the further we evolve. Ravana is deep delve into the nine facets of base emotions namely Anger, pride, Fear, Jealousy, Selfishness, Love, Ambition, Happiness and sadness. He is a man who is wise and wilfully chooses to "feel" and live every emotion in contrast to Rama who discards the nine heads and keeps Equanimity of the mind.

Neither has an easy life. Rama has to sacrifice the two people he loves most in the world in the name of dharma. He is putty at the hands of priests, rules and religion. His end is neither glorious nor happy. Ravana lives on his own terms and dies like a warrior. Ravana in essence lives the choices that he makes for himself as does Rama. The struggle between living a passionate and driven life versus a realised and stable life has been a perpetual struggle for humankind.

The epic of Ramayana therefore in essence is timeless.

# Section IV
# Mahabharata Period

Mahabharata is the second great epic of India. Said to be composed by the great sage Veda Vyasa. The composition has been dated to anywhere from early first millennium BCE to around 400 BCE. The shorter version consists of around 24,000 verses and called simply Bharata. The longest version stretches to over 100,000 verses making it the longest poem written in the world. It is four times the size of Ramayana and over ten times the size of Iliad and Odyssey put together.

The dating of the Kurukshetra battle of the epic conservatively put to around 10th century BCE. Yeoman work of the doyen Archaeologist, B B Lal has unearthed evidence of the city of Hastinapur dating to the period of Painted Grey Ware culture (1200 BCE to 600 BCE). His work has led many to believe the period of the epic to be around the beginning of first millennium BCE. Puranic genealogy however puts the period of the battle to be around 1000 years before Mahapadmananda (400 BCE) – taking it back to around 1400 BCE. There are some Indologists who place the battle to 7th millennium BCE based on some astronomical references. We must not lose sight of rational reasoning and thinking without becoming emotional in this regard. He metallurgy did not appear in the Indus valley till about late fourth millennium BCE as the beginning of Bronze age. While there is evidence of using meteoric Iron to third millennium BCE, Iron Age did not make its appearance in the Gangetic valley till about 1800 BCE. There are questions that cannot be answered for the heavy weaponry, chariots etc in the Kurukshetra war without use of any metals if it is dated prior to Bronze age.

The epic is a fountain of knowledge and advice, in not only day to a life but into royalty. It is particularly known for the advice given to Arjuna by his charioteer, Krishna on the battlefield and is now revered across the globe as Bhagavad-Gita. The content of this masterpiece is relevant today as it was thousands of years ago.

It is not surprising that we have the largest number of entries in this section of the book. There is a lot to be learnt from reading, listening and watching the scenes of the great epic even today. The Gits, as the Bhagavad-Gita is colloquially known, is taught and practiced across the globe and across all religions and races and creed. If there was one secular aspect of the great epics, it is this one.

Alapan Choudhury takes on the probabilities of how the famed city of Dwaraka might have met its end. Recent marine archaeology has shown evidence of two large cities – probably dating to the middle of second millennium BCE under the waters off Rann of Kutch a few miles from the seashore. The present hypothesis is that these two cities drowned when the sea levels rose after the end of the last glacial maximum. There is evidence of raise of over 125 meters in sea level – around 12000-13000 years ago. Alapan has used an article which surmised that a comet impact caused a tsunami.

Smitha Vishwanath looks at the inner battle of Dronacharya, a battle of greater consequence than that fought on the fields of Kurukshetra. The analysis is done with subtlety and finesse worth commending.

Meghna Dinesh Karkera asks to look at another controversial figure in the great epic – Duryodhana. Was he as bad as he was made out to be? She has used flash backs effectively to give us the underlying love and hate between siblings which all of us could relate to. Very interesting take.

Dr Aparna Bagwe has chosen the story of the life of Karna – a man born with a disadvantage and grows up to be an epitome of sacrifice. He does make the final sacrifice for his friend. She has weaved the story of the entire epic based around the story of Karna.

The story of Uloopi is one of the sub-plots within the great epic not many people might have heard of. Dr Smitha Chatterjee has done yeoman service to this often neglected part of the epic. It has been handled with the care and finesse. Without losing the central plot of the epic itself.

# An Untold Tale from Dwaraka

*Alapan Roy Chowdhury*

***Who is Alapan Roy Chowdhury?***

*Alapan Roy Chowdhury is currently studying in New Zealand. With a passion for teaching, he has worked as a lecturer of English in India previously. History is one of his foremost passions too. His research articles on Literature and History have been published in several magazines and journals. Alapan loves composing poems, some of which have also been published. He has edited a bilingual little magazine too.*

*The story is an imaginary account of what might have happened in the last days of Dwaraka. The idea that the tsunami which engulfed Dwaraka was caused by a comet impact, is derived from Bibhu Dev Misra's article 'The Comet impact in The Indian Ocean that may have submerged Dwaraka'. The link to the article is here: https://grahamhancock.com/dmisrab12/*



# An Untold Tale from Dwaraka



A son had returned to his still-prosperous city after trading for several months. But the city did not welcome him with a happy state of affairs. After entering the city, the people he met on the streets exchanged half-hearted smiles with him, while others did not. Several people didn't even notice him. Something was not right! He moved towards his home with anxiousness only to find his family safe and sound, still. However, all was not well. The society had degraded; the bloody civil war had killed many of the city-dwellers; the beloved King and other important personalities had died too. And now there was a new danger knocking at the door...

After exchanging deliberate smiles, the confused son asked, "Pitashree, is there anything wrong? Why are they panicking?"

"We were worried, Putra! It is good that by the grace of Varuna, your boat has brought you home in time."

"Yes, but... Then, are we all going somewhere?"

The father replied with a sigh, "Yes, dear. The Maruts are angry. The Muni has predicted that the wrath of the Devas is going to engulf our beautiful city."

"What! How is this possible? And, what if he is wrong, Pitashree?" the son asked, while trying to be a bit optimistic.

"It is true that even revered Munis could make mistakes. But don't forget that he follows the teachings of Maharishi Parashara. So, our people have faith in his confidence." the father asserted.

The son could only utter, "Is there no way to protect...?" His words seemed to dry up in his throat.

The father perhaps gave it a thought, and said, "Umm, we are left with no other option! There are many things which are beyond us, Putra. This is one of those. We have to move to higher grounds for the time being. Then... Let us see what the great Arjuna decides."

But would that keep us away from the Maruts?" the son replied, with a hint of fear on his face.

"According to the Muni, yes. An ominous dhumaketu is approaching Prithvi Mata. Dyaus Pita would see the dance of the Maruts in few days' time. This would eventually upset Varuna Deva."

"Maharishi Parashara says, two dhumaketus appeared in the days of Manu. This was followed by the Pralaya which destroyed all creation, as we know."

"Yes. But is this a new crisis that we are facing?"

"No dear," the father explained, "itihasa says, there was an old city on this very land. It was flooded by the sea, and all was lost! I think Kusasthali was its name."

"Oh, that is terrible! This land is really cursed." the son stated with an air of sadness.

“No no, Putra. It is not a curse. It has been thirty-six years since the devastating Bharata war, when Mata Gandhari had cursed our old King. My Guru says these events are actually associated with the change of the Yugas. The Dwapara yuga is ending, and the Kali yuga is knocking at the door.”

“Oh, Pitashree! Destiny is chasing us like a tiger, it seems, and is planning to crush us at any cost!”

“We never know... It acts in apparently unexplained ways.”

“It has only been a few months since I had to leave home after the cremation of our near and dear ones who fell prey to sheer mindlessness.”

The father looked pensive, as the son continued, “Before leaving for Ahichhatra, I had heard that our King believed that the deaths were a result of the curse. To add to that, his own accidental death- it has added to our misfortunes. How could such a personality be killed by a mere hunter’s arrow? That is unimaginable! Bala Deva is no more. Pradyumna too... The pillars of Anarta are falling apart. Oh! Has the new king been coronated?”

“No, not yet. The wounds of the Bharata war have become fresh again, Putra! In this darkest hour, we needed him the most. We miss our deceased King, and we are still mourning the irrevocable losses. It takes time, Putra.” the father’s expression changed while saying this, and the eyes got slightly wet.

“Understandably... Their pyres are still warm. And as if all this was not enough- now..., now we have this...! Might this also be one of the effects of Queen Gandhari’s curse?”

“No, I don’t think so... Well, but... Who knows...! Who knows?”

“But why did she curse our King, when all that her sons suffered was due to their Karma?”

“Putra, remember she is a mother.”

“Hmm, I can understand her feelings...”

“Have you faced such a situation before?” the son asked, suddenly changing the course of the conversation, as his eyebrows highlighted his curiosity.

“Yes, when I was a child... Well, you know that Indra Deva had helped the Pandavas, and they turned Khandava forest into the magnificent city of Indraprastha you see today- everyone knows that. But there was a great flood in Gokul once. Indra was angry with us- he had unleashed great storm and rain! A holy hill named Govardhan had provided us shelter during that calamity."

The son didn't say anything. He was lost in his own thoughts, seemingly. After a few seconds of pause, the father added, "The great King had always been our saviour, as you know. He advised us to worship Govardhan and Go-Mata instead of Indra, since Giriraj Govardhan used to nourish our cows with his bounty, and the cows were our source of livelihood. This annoyed Indra, the people thought." While he was speaking, a few teardrops started rolling down his beard-covered cheek.

"Pitashree, I have never been to Gokul! I have only heard stories from..." the son said and tried to remember something.

The tears became prominent as the father's voice broke, "Hmm, that is sad. I wish I could..., we could. Even I have not been able to visit, not even after Jarasandha's death."

"Please don't cry Pitashree. Please don't..." the son said and tried to console him with genuine concern.

After his father had regained his composure, the son inquired very softly, "But why did he attack Mathura in first place?"

The father continued with a broken voice turning into normal, as he said, "He was Kamsa's father-in-law, and wanted to exact revenge! But it is natural that you, belonging to this generation, don't know such details. With the support of our people, the god-king had killed the tyrannical Kamsa. But Jarasandha and his allies posed a bigger threat to Mathura after him- they wanted to slaughter every single citizen for supporting Kamsa's killer! Anyway..."

"Pitashree, I cannot stand the thought of leaving my golden Dwaravati forever! This is my place! It is in my blood; in my thoughts when I stay away for months! I had left with a sore heart after the war and the King's demise, only hoping that things would be better when I return." the son delivered the words in a single breath.

"I can understand your feelings, my dear. I feel the same way too! It will not be easy. We must leave in order to live. If we live, we could gain all that is lost." The son was observing the uncertainty in his father's eyes as he spoke. It was reflected in his speech too as he tried to say, "I know. But... But..."

As the son's sore heart was at a loss for words, the father came to his rescue saying, "But just think of the nomads. They never have a fixed home... I know you are not used to that kind of life, and neither am I! Perhaps that is natural- may be, that is how it should be. Maybe?"

His mind was convinced, but his heart was not when he answered the rhetorical question, "Perhaps…"

Before the father could say anything else, the son asked in a heavy voice, "What are Yugas, Pitashree?"

After a long pause, the father started explaining the Yuga-cycle to his son, when a soldier arrived at the door. He announced that the late King's close friend Arjuna had arrived to save the citizens from the impending peril, and he would address them shortly. Thus, he had requested at least one member from every family to be present at the Samiti today.

The father returned from the Samiti when the son was feeding their pets. Upon seeing him, the son welcomed him with an artificial smile, and asked the wise man calmly, "What happened at the Samiti, Pitashree?"

The father spoke in a matter-of-fact tone, "We are moving to Indraprastha. Arjuna said in agreement with the ministers that we are going to take the land route and avoid water bodies. People are being warned to stay away from the seas, rivers and lakes on certain days of the coming week. The exodus begins with the first light of the sun exactly after seven days."

"And what about the Dwarkans who are still in far off places?"

"The ministers have already dispatched the messengers and some of the troops to such lands... Even before you arrived. They will escort those rishis, traders, tourists and…, and representatives to Indraprastha, in turn informing the kingdoms which are still unaware of the danger." This time he was a bit positive in his response.

"But in case it becomes impossible for them to retreat towards Indraprastha..." the son was going to ask automatically.

"Then they'll be taken to other safer places, hopefully... I know, Putra, you are thinking that we might not reach all the people, or some of them might still fall prey to the Maruts."

After a quick sigh he resumed, "Yes, that is true. Also, there are men who cling to their territories, no matter what, while few others might die on duty. But that is how it is, Putra! That is how it is."

Nodding unconsciously, and then quickly shifting his thought, the son asked, "We need to dismantle our boats, don't we?"

"Umm hmm and turn them into carts for the time being. We don't have much time, and the distance is huge, the journey difficult. We must make the carts as tough as possible. But... Leave it,"

Turning his face away from the son, the old one said, "The Muni has prophesied that the Maruts might hit some parts of the lands as well. This raise concerns even if we leave Dwaraka safely. Arjuna has an alternative route in his mind that might keep us away from their rage. He has selected it after having a long and thorough discussion with the general, and the ministers. We have faith in him, as he has vowed to look after us."

The son had that aura of optimism on his face while saying, "I hope we could at least be able to reduce the losses if we move out before the Maruts strike. Won't we?"

The father replied without looking at his son, "Sure. But we have women, children, and the old- that includes me. We need to pass through forests, and even enemy territories."

The son smiled a bit as he noticed that his father was observing the animals. The father smiled a bit too, this time facing his son. But his eyes didn't go with that.

Now looking at the animals, the son started speaking, "Forests are okay. But would the enemies try to harm us during this emergency?"

"I have been around for quite some time. I have also seen the Bharata war, Putra; and we have seen the intra-city war. We might trust animals, but not humans!"

After some moments of silence, the father resumed, "Our people have become pleasure-loving, Putra. Excess pleasure is also an enemy."

"You are right, Pitashree."

The disappointment was evident on his face as he said, "You know Putra, we used to be hard-working people once."

"Hmm. Srishti is so strange. The hard-working become pleasure-loving. The rains come from above, and so do the dhumaketus. We are so dependent on Varuna in every way, and still men must flee from rivers every now and then. However, this is no flood; this is going to be a Pralaya!" the son pondered.

"Change is the only constant thing. You see, these days the mighty Saraswati Mata enters Patala at some spots and re-emerges from there at others. She is no longer free-flowing like she used to be in our ancestors' times." the father stated.

After a brief look at the setting Mitra, the wise one said, "Let us keep our fingers crossed. They say the dhumaketus are inauspicious. If that is true, Putra… Even if we escape unhurt with our possessions, can we escape the ultimate doom? Then there is the curse of Mata Gandhari which is beginning to bother me."

Following his father's words of concern, the son added, "If I am not wrong, it had bothered the wise King ever since the end of the Bharata war."

"The King was not a happy man in his final days, and that was not pleasant at all."

"How could he be? He was sad at the degradation of the Dawarakans. Moreover, he was deeply saddened by the fratricidal killings in which he also lost his own son, to add insult to injury! His life-long companion left his mortal frame too."

"I feel sorry for him, my Putra. I really feel sorry for him!"

They leave for the city of Indraprastha as planned. After travelling for many yojanas they entered a region infested by barbarians who had a world of their own- these fierce bandits were the outcasts of Dwaraka only. The time was ripe for them to avenge their banishment, and they didn't fail to make good use of it when the Dwarakans were passing by a forest.

It took a few moments for the escorts and the refugees to realize what had happened. But soon enough they understood that they have been ambushed.

Arjuna tried to stop the attackers by announcing that it is unethical to take advantage of such a critical situation, but they paid no heed to his words. The Pandava and Dwaraka troops accompanying the refugees were no match for the booby traps and guerrilla fighting techniques of these forest-dwellers- they knew these parts better than them.

The now old Arjuna put up a tough fight but failed to protect them. His life was spared because the bandit-leader thought that it would be more humiliating for him to live with this scar of defeat than to die at the hands of his henchmen. Many were killed; the women were abducted, and the wealth was looted. As a result, the refugees were split into multiple groups, only one of which reached Indraprastha.

The father was badly wounded in the skirmish. The son somehow managed to escape the pandemonium while carrying his father on the back of one of their pet bulls. Separated from every other group, the son moved to an apparently secure location where he halted to treat his father with the medicinal leaves from nearby trees. Panting, he spoke to his father, without receiving any response from the veteran. He tried to bring animation to the body, but all his efforts went in vain. He even checked whether the father is unconscious or not.

Some harmless animals were looking at the father-son duo from a distance- perhaps they didn't expect human presence. Mitra was setting fast, but time had already stopped for the son. He was sitting still in front of the mortal body of his father. Suddenly he stood up in grief-mixed rage, and looking at the sky, roared like a lion scaring away the deers, "Hey Maruts! Why do you script the end of every Yuga such cruelty? Why? Last time…" He continued, as his voice choked at times. His words were being echoed by the hilly landscape; but was it heard by the Maruts as well?

The gods he was addressing, appeared high above him, and started throwing their arrows towards the crust. One of those hit the spot where the son was standing, creating a big crater. They had answered him.

Dwaraka was also submerged by the great cataclysm that triggered dust clouds, earthquakes, tsunamis and climate change. It led to the collapse of the contemporary cultures making way for a new Yuga. Nonetheless, the story of Dwaraka has survived to this day. We are still living in the Kali Yuga. The lost mythical city is nowadays regarded as the 'Atlantis of the East'.

Perhaps no one knows what happened to the ones who were away from Dwaraka at the time and were expected to be escorted by the messengers and the troops. They never reached Indraprastha. So, did they survive and settle in foreign lands? Did survivors like them become the pioneers of later civilizations? Perhaps…

# The Last Days of the Battle – A Mythology

***Smitha Vishwanath***

***Who is Smitha Vishwanath?***

*Smitha Vishwanath embarked on the writing journey in 2016, with her personal blog, https://lifeateacher.wordpress.com, while still working as a banker. After having worked for almost two decades in senior roles in the banking industry, in the Middle East, she quit and returned to India in July 2018. Since then, she has actively participated and won in several poetry writing competitions. Her poems, articles and quotes have been published in various anthologies. She published her first book of poetry in July 2019: Roads – A Journey with Verses*


# The Last Days of the Battle – A Mythology


The sky is black as if a veil of death hangs over the city. The eerie silence of the night is broken only by the blood-curdling wails of widows and the injured. The breeze carries with it a concoction of smells - rotting flesh and burning wood from pyres. The battle for the day is over, but it rages on inside me and refuses to be doused.

I toss and turn on the hard wooden cot; questions that I have asked myself several times since the beginning of the war, hound me again. Why? Why am I here? Why did I agree to fight this bloody battle? Why did I not leave when I finished my duty as a teacher to the Princes'?

'Obligation!' I say to myself.

*"Is it that or is it a father's greed?"*

A voice within me asks. I had learnt to subdue and ignore the voice, since a long time, but it had started finding its way out lately.

'No! I did it for Dharma alone,' I am convinced.

*'Dharma' is a word that has made a fool of the best of us. Do not speak of 'Dharma.'*

*Every great warrior here believes he is a hero – doing what he was born to do – to bring righteousness on this earth. There is no greater lie. Every man here has his own agenda. Some fight for honour and some for pride; but most fight for vengeance.*

*The poor soldier alone is righteous, for he fights because he has no choice.*

'I too am duty-bound to the throne – I have not forgotten my past. I too am a victim, a slave of the Kingdom of Hastinapur!'

An old memory comes back to me now- the memory of Dhrupad, my childhood friend - the memory of us in the ashram - playing with cowrie shells and collecting gooseberries. My heart grieves.

If only Dhrupad had acknowledged my friendship none of this would be happening. How could he forget all those years of togetherness when he became King? How could he break his word? When I had no money to buy milk for my only son, Ashwatthama, I went to him for help, as he had promised to help me if the need arose. But Dhrupad who was King now, belittled our friendship and embarrassed me before his entire court. He said that I was a fool to even call him a friend; for how could a poor Brahmin like me be a Kshatriya's friend?

When Bhishma appointed me as a teacher to the Princes' of Hastinapur, I should have forgiven Dhrupad and moved on. But I chose not to; I trained Arjun and asked him to capture Dhrupad, as my gurudakshina. Arjun succeeded. I did not want to hurt Dhrupad. I wanted to remind my friend that I was no lesser than a Kshatriya when it came to the knowledge of warfare. But my actions angered him. And he took an oath to kill me. This battle became a ground to make his wish come true.

But now my friend lies dead with thousands of others; killed by my sword. A Brahmin's sword.

I never wished to kill him, but he was on the other side, against Hastinapur; the kingdom which gave a poor Brahmin and his son a great deal of respect, wealth and honour.

This is my truth. This is the only truth. Therefore, I'm here. The air is still. My head hurts with the lack of sleep. I remember seeing

Arjun today. For a fleeting moment, it seemed as though he too were looking at me. I thought, if only I could have fought on the side of the Pandavas. I turned away, unable to meet his eye. I had murdered his son the previous day. The boy would have been the age of my grandson- if I had one.

I had heard Arjun's cry, in the dead of night on seeing Abhimanyu's lifeless body. I had seen the look in his eyes – of anger, pain and bitterness. I had heard Yudhishthira telling him how guilty he felt for death of the young boy – that Abhimanyu had entered the Chakravyuha to save him - and how he had been brutally killed; that one of the murderers was I; Dronacharya!

Arjun's horror-filled eyes looked at me and asked one question, *'How could you?'* as I paid my last respects to the departed soul.

I wanted to tell him that his son had died a brave death – a warrior's death. I wanted him to know that I had felt my heart swell with pride, seeing the boy's courage and skill - that I had felt deep sorrow that I had not taught the young man- that I had also felt a pang of jealousy that there was a better teacher than me – the one who taught the young boy. And after all that I thought of how I shut out all thoughts and shot the first arrow even as Abhimanyu reminded me that he was unarmed. I had said, 'All is fair in war!' and released my arrow again. But the boy's eyes showed no fear until the end.

'Is it the fear of death that makes me question my actions?'

That cannot be. I am not afraid of dying. I have fought many wars for Hastinapur.

*How do you say you fight for obligation then? You have paid the kingdom of Hastinapur, multiple times and brought much glory to the kingdom. You said that yourself now. Why do you not walk away from all this? This is no place for a Brahmin and for one who is a teacher to both the warring sides.* It was the voice again.

As Commander of the Kaurava army, I must fight and destroy the enemy. The enemy has no face. I must overpower the voice, which is becoming a nuisance. I must rest now. I have a war to win tomorrow. This is no time for repentance or regret. But sleep evades me. And questions swarm my head. An hour later I am still unable to sleep. The faces of those I have killed swim before my eyes. Voices of the dead and the living ring in my ears – shrieks, conversations and questions.

"He's eighty but he fights like sixteen," I had heard one foot- soldier say to another earlier in the day. Those had been his last words. Oh God! I have not even spared those weaker than me.

'He's invincible; Guru Drona' I heard Nakul tell Sahdev. I had been close enough to strike them down, but I did not. Duryodhana chided me when he got to know, later that day. I did not offer an explanation to Duryodhana, despite the provocation. I remember the look in Karna's eyes.

Why do I remember it? *Amongst every single person fighting this war, Karna, is the most righteous. He alone is fighting with no agenda, no selfish interest. He fights for obligation, for friendship. Karna has proved to be more of a warrior than you.*

Karna is far more righteous than Yudhishthira, whose love for gambling, is the cause of this war, I thought. I had to agree with the voice on Karna being the most righteous.

The responsibility of this destruction is entirely Yudhishthira's to bear; not mine.

I must have dozed for an hour or two. I do not know. But when I woke up, I saw the sky was a pale, watery blue as if the Gods had been crying all night. I tried to shut my eyes again but the voices in my head grew louder.

"*Whether the war is because of you or not does not matter. You broke all rules of war.*" It was the voice again.

*"Fighting late into the night after sunset, killing irrespective of rank, hatching a plan to kidnap Yudhishthira, setting up a strategy to distract Arjun and Krishna so that the plan could be put in action and killing Abhimanyu when he was unarmed."*

*Did not Karna tell you, "It is dishonourable? You must not resort to it. Yet you carried on."*

"All's fair in love and war," I had replied to Karna, shocking him into silence. Victory must be achieved at any cost. Rules are meant to be broken. Karna's eyes had held an expression that I couldn't read. Disbelief mixed with scorn. Or was it shame – of knowing me? Duryodhana had laughed, happy with my response.

"Was it honourable when Draupadi laughed at me, when I fell into the pond, my friend? Was it honourable when she asked you, who your father was at the Swayamvar? There was nothing honourable about it. Guru

Drona is right. We must fight. Everything is fair in war!" Duryodhana reminded Karna. Ashwatthama, my son had looked at me, pride in his eyes and affection; for me. He was laughing too. I had felt elated.

The soldiers' voices made its way into my tent, an incessant buzz; telling me that it was time to rise. I thought of Bhishma lying on a bed of arrows. The Pandavas had not spared their grand-uncle, who had cared for them when they were young. 'Everything is fair in war,' I convince myself again.

'I will do my duty, my dearest Bhishma, I make this promise to you, today,' I think, putting on my armour.

Did you not say that I must fight because we – you and I are also responsible for all that is happening. 'Because we remained silent when we should have spoken. Because we did not harness the reins of the ponies in our care. And because we sowed the seeds of difference by loving one more than the other –and because we allowed them to commit one mistake after another and did not stop them.'

I do not agree with you, dear Bhishma, regarding the responsibility. How can a petty Brahmin like me be responsible for this Great War? But I will fight, though our reasons are different as are the rules we fight by.

The sky is an orange–crimson and mirrors the ground below. The conch is blown to announce the start of the day's battle. I stand on my chariot surveying the land before me – where warriors have been engaged in a bloody battle since the last fourteen days.

Swords strike, maces clash, blood spills like water; the sound of trumpets, conchs and battle cries fill the air.

'*We will never win if we don't kill him,*' I hear someone say, as I rage forward, destroying and decimating everything in my way; I cannot be sure whose words they are. When I turn to look, I see Krishna and my favourite student looking in my direction. Arjun looks worried but Krishna's lips shows the hint of a smile.

*'Krishna! How agitating it is to see him smiling now!'*

Something tells me that today will be the last day of the battle. It is the inner voice; again.

My heart aches looking at the carnage around me. I ignore it.

A bead of sweat trickles down my head, making its way down my face.

If today be my last, then I must kill as many as I can; of the enemy. I decide to use the Brahmastra. I invoke the divine weapon against the Pandavas foot-soldiers. The weapon that has been bestowed upon me on the condition that it will not be used on any ordinary warrior. But I use it. I do not know why. I do it even though I know I am wrong. *Sometimes one makes mistakes knowing fully well that it is a mistake and that the consequences will be irreparable. That is man's biggest weakness.*

The heavens bellow. They plead with me to retract the weapon and remind me of the blunder I have made. I relent to the Gods' and retract the weapon but do not change my decision to kill as many people as I can. Something at the back of my head tells me that my end is near. I hurl forward on my chariot and pulverize everything ahead of me.

I race, annihilating everything until I hear the words, 'Ashwatthama is dead!' My charioteer brings my chariot to a halt. I feel the jerk.

My mind tells me that the words are not true. But a father's heart is stronger than the rational mind. I order the charioteer to turn the chariot towards Bhīma who is beating his chest and guffawing. Ashwatthama- my son! My only son - slaughtered to death! I cannot breathe.

How had Bhima managed to kill him? Had the power of Shiva, which my son was blessed with, not been enough to save him?

My mind warns me, *'It's a war tactic. Just like you used the Chakravyuha to kill Abhimanyu. It is a lie. Do not listen. Remember everything's fair in war.'*

I ignore the warning. My eyes search desperately for Ashwatthama. I do not see him. *Ah!* I see Yudhishthira.

"Is Ashwatthama dead?" I ask Yudhishthira who is honest to a fault.

"Ashwatthama is dead," he says, his eyes, looking down.

He says something more, but the sound of trumpets and conches drown the rest of what he says. Or is it my own ears that shut down after hearing what I feared? I have lost all will to live, let alone fight. All that I have ever done has been for my son, I think. Without my son, duty has no meaning to me. It does not matter to me who wins or loses or why the war is being fought. All I ever wanted, was to see my only son happy. How many times had I thought of leaving but I was scared after Karna's coming, if Duryodhana would side-line my son? So, I stayed on, to make sure Ashwatthama was fine. But now he lies dead, with all others killed on this battlefield.

I wish to see my son one last time. So, I step down from my chariot and walk across the battle-field towards Bhīma, even as I hear Karna's voice in the distance, warning me, not to get off the chariot.

"Where's Ashwatthama? I ask Bhīma, ignoring Karna. How did you kill him?"

"With my mace"

"Where is he?"

"There- in a pool of blood and there lies his head," Bhima says, pointing to the royal elephant, Ashwatthama; who he has beheaded with his mace.

I turn to Yudhishthira." You lied to me!" I scream, but my voice is drowned by the other sounds in the battlefield.

"I am unarmed." I tell Bhīma. "It is against the rules of war for you to fight me now. Let me go back to my chariot and we can fight; like true warriors."

"The future will call you a coward, Bhima."

"Did you not think of that when you attacked our son, Abhimanyu, Guru Drona?" Bhima asks me with a sneer.

They watch me – the brothers' -Arjun, Bhīma, Yudhishthira, Nakul and Sahdev but they do not kill me. There is a hint of that smile again on Krishna's lips.

I see Drishtadyumna, the commander of the Pandavas army - my dear friend, Dhrupad's son - Draupadi's brother- my student - heading towards me to fulfil the purpose of his birth- to avenge his father- and I know my moment has come. I kneel on the ground and look up at the skies. The clouds have covered the sun. The sky is scarlet. I think I will be spared after all. It is sunset. But I have done away with the sunset rule, since I took over as commander, three days' ago. I have done away with all rules.

I see Eklavya standing in front of me, giving me his right hand – the one without the thumb – to help me rise. The clouds move away from the sun. The light blinds me. Is that a peacock feather I see on Eklavya's head? It is Krishna!

Am I hallucinating? My mind is playing games with me. Or is it a lack of sleep that is making me delirious? I am exhausted. An exhausted warrior is as good as a dead warrior. I must focus.

"You are allowing them to kill me by lying to me. How is that fair?" I ask Krishna, who looks ten times his size. I must control my mind.

"Don't talk of fairness, Guru Drona. You have never been fair – neither to Eklavya whom you did not teach and yet asked him for gurudakshina when you realized he was better than Arjun nor to Karna. Your obsession to make your word come true - that Arjun would be known as the greatest warrior is the cause of this war. If you had allowed Karna to participate in the contest on the day the greatest warrior was to be declared without asking him about his birth, he would not have been under Duryodhana's obligation and Duryodhana would never have mustered the courage to fight this war. You are as responsible as Yudhishthira and Bhishma, for this bloodshed."

It is Krishna. He is not smiling anymore. Then Drishtadyumna's sword touches my neck. I feel a sharp sting. I feel light. I remember no more.

# The Villain

*Meghna Dinesh Karkera*

***Who is Meghna Dinesh Karkera?***

*Meghna is an MBA graduate working as an HR. A Mumbaikar at heart she currently resides in Hyderabad with her Husband.*

*An artist by nature whether it be with the paintbrush or the pen.*

*She is a day dreamer and strives at looking at things from a different perspective.*

# The Villain

There she stood drenched in Sushasana's blood. The blood that was supposed to quench her thirst for revenge. But Bheema could see it in her eyes. It was not working.

Suyodhana breaks down looking at his baby brother's distorted body. Bheema had squashed him like a ripe Pumpkin. His ears deafened by the screams of the battlefield. He could hear Sushashan shouting, seemingly like yesterday.

"Higher Bhaiyya, higher"! shouted Sushasana. Suyodhana climbed higher to get the juiciest Mangoes for his brothers and his little sister who was collecting the mangoes in the frills of her skirt. Suyodhana looks down at his brothers feeling proud of the height he had attained. Sushasana's face went pale. Before Suyodhana could know why, he felt a jolt on his head, and he falls. Groaning in pain he looks and sees a huge body standing over him with the sun at its back.

"A girl should be inside the Palace premises playing with dolls and not climb trees" mocked Bheema. Bheema was not yet done with Suyodhana but was stopped by a hoarse voice reprimanding him.

"You are a son of a slave, do not tell me what to do!" Bheema said hesitantly. "Perhaps Bheeshmapitamah would want to know about this then." said Vidhur. Bheema fled! Suyodhana could see the hurt in his uncle's eyes at Bheema's words and wanted to hug him. But his uncle never allowed him to do that. He wondered why?

At sunrise in Guru Drona's class, Suyodhana yawns at his Guru's bragging about Arjuna's archery skills. He sees Arjun pull his arrow towards his target; Suyodhana froze. His target was a harmless tiny bird of flesh and blood. Suyodhana closed his eyes and prayed, which was answered by a sound of a large thud. A tiny road urchin had managed to break into the palace. "Who was that scoundrel"! barked Guru Drona. "running around and polluting the holy grounds of Hastinapur"!

The Pandavas grabbed their weapons to get the rangy kid – to impress Guru Drona. But he escaped like the wind. At sunset, all the would be warriors of Hastinapur returned to their Royal chambers. Suyodhana however could not get the kid out of his head wondering why he risked his life. He saw a shadow coming towards the scattered ripened and wasted mangoes lying in the corner of the Palace grounds. It was him! Suyodhana caught his hand. It was fragile, he was afraid he might break it. His body was dark, his ribs could be counted. Suyodhana could see his heart pounding under his skin that looked like a piece of rag. He picked up the fruits and handed them over to the boy-

"What's your name"?

"Eklavya." the boy whispered and sprinted.

At a distance, Guru Drona gives Suyodhana a disgusted look – A prince making friends with a Shudhra. A long lecture from Bhishma Pitamah was awaiting in the palace.

Entire night Suyodhana wondered, if there were more like Eklavya under the rule of Hastinapur. Was it not Dharma of a king to take care of his subjects? But he was never trained about this in Guru Drona's class. Why he wondered? As he grew up such questions clouded his mind and for which many of the times he was laughed at. Also, for being a child of a Blind King - Dhritarashtra.

His only comfort was Shakuni Mama. He was the only one who managed to answer all Suyodhana's questions – in his own ways. Some of which he could not understand. Shakuni was like a substratum to his meaningless floating life. Shakuni always told him to beware of the politics being played at the palace; while he himself was seen rolling the dice, while his presence always bothered Bhishma Pitamah.

Once he heard Guru Drona lashing out at Yudhishthira

"You are the next King of Hastinapur! Practice harder!"

Suyodhana felt his heart turn bitter. Wasn't he supposed to be the next king after his father? He was the eldest son of the present King of Hastinapur. He grew up listening to his father and Mama preparing him to be the next King. One fine day his Aunt turns up with five cousins who were not even the biological sons of Uncle Pandu. How could they be the next heirs? Was this justice?

His mind never got tired of his own questions. One day he sat beside his mother and asked, "Maa do you love Pitashree, to have decided to blindfold yourself for him?" The satin ribbon covering Gandhari's eyes grew damp at her child's innocent questioning.

He grew up with the same people but developed a different concept of Dharma. As and how he got closer to the reality of world, his beliefs grew stronger. He realised the injustice done to his Mother and the Blind warrior – his Father Dritharsahtra.

On the day of Martial arts exhibition, Arjun was being hailed as the best Archer in the whole of Bharat! His pride was brought down in no time by an anonymous Archer, a disciple of the great Parshuram himself.

"Which Kingdom do you belong to asked Bhishma Pitamah?"

"I am a son to a charioteer; I am not a prince Sir." came the reply.

Arjuna's face lit up! The crowd condemned the low caste. Was credibility not Kshatriya Dharma thought Suyodhana. And he did what was right to even the scales in Karna's favour he gifted him the kingdom of Anga! The Pandavas were favoured by majority, but Suyodhana still kept going, giving it a tough fight. His belief in Self-righteousness became deeper with time. To stand and fight against those who demeaned his loved ones. Fight for rights – come what may.

It was Panchalii's Swayamwar, while the whole of Bharat believed who was the eligible Groom, Suyodhana still accompanied Karna.

"Stop! Screamed Draupadi. "I would never marry a Sutaputra! You may leave".

Later the same Draupadi agreed to live happily with her five husbands under the same roof, as it was Dharma to follow the wishes of her in laws and Husbands. Was discrimination a part of Kshatriya Dharma too? wondered Suyodhana. And where was the love? He married Bhanumati and pledged that he would love her and only her for the rest of his life. To protect her and give her everything that could make her happy. While Polygamy and Polyandry was a thing – Like his cousins followed.

During a game of dice, when the Pandavas lost everything to the Kauravas reluctantly Yudhistr traded his wife Draupadi like a sickle and the brothers did not object as it was against the Dharma to object the elder brother. Was it Kshatriya Dharma to trade a woman of your life who was their love and responsibility (A property). While Kauravas played well as the enemy, true to their nature.

"Napunsak" roared Draupadi disrobed! "This Sabha is Napunsak."

Suyodhana's eyes lit with fire, looking at the helpless woman who insulted his father – the Blind King and his dear friend. He invited her to sit on her lap – wanted her to feel what it means to be demeaned.

"I would not tie my hair unless I bathe with your blood", she cursed Sushasana; who had dragged her by the hair to the open Sabha! However, it was her dharma to still stay by her husbands' side even after whatever happened. There she stood drenched in Sushasana's blood - the blood that was supposed to quench her thirst for revenge. Not pacified. It would not be difficult to understand why.

The Pandavas looked down at the crying Suyodhana- "Choose any of us and defeat him, and we shall consider that you defeated us in the battlefield today".

"Bheema", shouted Suyodhana loudly and unflinchingly;

"I chose Bheema".

Best in mace, a good fight went on between the two, until Bheema attacked Suyodhana's thigh – Which was against the law of the battlefield. On his death bed Suyodhana roared, "I was righteous, a good friend, a loyal husband and a terrific enemy".

"Above all I was a good King. Can you say the same about yourselves?"

With a smile he left the world. Little did he know that after his so called defeat in the battle of Dharma he would be defamed as Duryodhana, the Villain of Mahabharata.

# The Tragic Life of Karna

*Dr. Aparna Bagwe*

***Who is Dr Aparna Bagwe?***

*Dr. Aparna Bagwe has a Ph.D. in Applied Biology and, till October 2018, was a senior Scientist with the Tata Memorial Centre, Mumbai. She has a flair for writing, excels at editing, is passionate about nature and wildlife photography, and has travelled extensively within and outside the country. She used to be an active blogger on Rediffiland, and, in recent years, her writing has appeared in her Centre's house magazine, in newsletters and websites of professional societies, and on several online literary platforms. She has won several awards for her writing as well as photography in online literary and photography groups respectively. Some of her poems have been included in three anthologies published over the past year. She is presently an Administrator of the Asian Literary Society.*

## The tragic life of Karna

***Prologue***

She stood, hands raised in supplication to the glorious morning sun, as its gentle rays and the soft breeze played with her curly, jet black hair. After saying her special prayers, she sat down under the mighty Parijaat tree, by the gently flowing river. Listening to the chirps and twitter of the birds sitting on the branches above her, she sang to herself in a sweet melodious voice and collected the fragrant, orange stemmed, creamy white blooms strewn on the grass all around her. Using a gossamer thin thread, she strung them into a delicate chain and placed the chain atop her head. She felt so at ease with the elements, eyes shining with an internal spark, as her dimpled cheeks warmed slightly remembering the previous night. He had come down to Earth from the heavens above and spent the night with her. She was still unsure if it was a dream, but it was a night Kunti would never forget. Her secret tryst with the handsome Sun God himself!

### *Background*

Kunti was the daughter of the King Surasena of the Yadav dynasty. The sage Rishi Durvasa had once visited her father's palace and, pleased by her conscientious care giving, he had granted her a mantra (invocation) that could draw any God to her. Her union with the Sun God led to a pregnancy that she kept secret, and, upon the birth of a boy child, she placed him in a basket that she released into the river Ashvanadi. Before letting go of the child, she had noted the glow from a golden chest plate (kavach) and ear lobe decor (kundala) and the resemblance of his feet to hers. Floating down the small rivulet into larger tributaries that finally merged with the holy river Ganga, the basket reached the Anga kingdom and was discovered by Radha, the wife of charioteer Adiratha. The childless couple were thrilled at this find and adopted the little baby. This is where the story of Radheya (son of Radha) an alter name of our hero Karna (named for his ear lobes) began. His adopted father worked in the court of King Dhritarashtra, the ruler of the Kuru kingdom whose capital was Hastinapur.

### *The curse of being a Sutaputra*

The young Karna stood out because of his prominent kavach kundala but faced a lot of ragging and insults from other children and adults as he was called a sutaputra - a lowly charioteer's son. From childhood, he had dreamed of wielding a bow and arrow, and waited to grow up to become a warrior. He knew in his guts that this was his calling, what he had been born for. However, when Karna approached his father Adiratha, he was gently dissuaded from this pursuit because, in those days, a son had to follow his father's profession and could not aspire for anything higher. Karna however could not stem down his dream and decided to find a teacher on his own.

Having heard of Guru Dronacharya, a renowned teacher of weaponry in the kingdom, he sought to be his shishya (pupil). It was there that he met Duryodhana, the eldest son of the Kuru King. After some time, the guru got to learn that Karna was the son of a charioteer and not a Kshatriya as he had thought and threw him out of the school. Karna felt deep shame and his blood boiled at the insult. He then approached Guru Parashuram, another great teacher of the martial arts in that region. This time he kept quiet about his origins and was accepted for training. Over the years, he underwent gruelling training in various martial arts. He excelled at most of them and stood out in particular for his skills of archery. This is where he met another student Arjuna, the third son of King Pandu who had married Kunti. There was tremendous competition and rivalry between these two great trainee archers. Once while practicing archery, Karna's arrow accidentally hit a cow and killed it. The cow's owner who was a Brahmin cursed Karna saying he would be also killed by an arrow when he is at his most helpless.

As was customary in those days, the pupils stayed in the Gurukul during their training, and helped the Guru in various chores. One day as Guru Parshurama was taking his usual afternoon nap, with his head resting on Karna's lap, a huge wasp landed on Karna's thigh. So as not to disturb his Guru, the young Karna did not shoo away or swat the wasp. The wasp bit into and even burrowed into the wound it had created on the young lad's thigh. Despite the terrible pain and bleeding, Karna held himself still and did not move because he did not wish to awaken his sleeping Guru. When the Guru felt warm blood flowing on to his shoulder from Karna's wound, he was startled and woke up. Upon seeing what had happened, the Guru instantly understood that the boy training with him could only be a Kshatriya because only a Kshatriya could withstand such terrible pain. He realized that Karna had lied to him about his origins in order to train with him. Mad at being taken for a ride, the Guru cursed Karna that, although he has learnt the use of the toughest weapons from him, he would lose all knowledge about how to use the weapons when he needed it the most.

Deeply hurt by what had transpired, Karna left the Gurukul and returned home. He related everything that had transpired to his father Adiratha and asked him, "Father, you are a Suta – a charioteer. Why did my Guru call me a Kshatriya?" Adiratha revealed to Karna that Radha and he were not his biological parents and related the circumstances of finding him, explaining that they did not know who his real parents were.

### *The roots of life-long associations and enmities*

Karna's friendship with Duryodhana, the eldest son of King Kuru developed slowly around then, and, with the passage of time, they grew to be close friends and confidantes. Recognizing that Karna was a great strategist with tremendous native intelligence, Duryodhana started seeking Karna's advice in vital matters. For the first time in his life, Karna was treated as an equal. Taking cognizance of the fact that Karna was not being given due respect by others and could not participate in various archery championships against Arjuna and others because of his caste, Duryodhana bestowed upon Karna the title of Angaraja, king of Anga land, thus anointing him equal to a Kshatriya. Karna never forgot this great act of his friend and, from then onwards, he stood steadfastly with Duryodhana in all his actions. Karna stayed loyal to his friend till the very end of his life!

In the meantime, the negativity kept building up between Karna and the Pandavas – in particular, Arjuna. It was during the exile of the Pandavas that the swayamwara (championship between suitors for the hand of the princess) of the Kshatriya Princess Draupadi was held. Arjuna and his brothers arrived disguised as Brahmin mendicants. Karna too was one of the contenders for Draupadi's hand, and he objected to them because he felt that only a Kshatriya could vie for a Kshatriya princess. In the wrangling that ensued, harsh words were exchanged. Karna was the first one to succeed in lifting the heavy gold bow, aim at the fish's eye seeing just its reflection and hit its eye. Despite that Draupadi insulted him in front of all saying she would not marry a sutaputra, and instead chose Arjuna as her suitor and, with much fanfare, her hand was given in marriage to Arjuna and his four brothers. Karna never forgot this insult, and, from that time, he treated Arjuna as his sworn enemy.

The Pandavas had built a beautiful new palace at Indraprastha and invited the Kauravas for a visit. They entered one of the huge halls in the centre of which there was a beautiful carpet. It looked very beautiful and realistic, and Karna stepped on it to walk ahead. However, the carpet was an illusion created over a water pond and, as he stepped on it, he slipped into the water. Draupadi who was watching the incident while hiding behind a pillar, laughed out loudly at him. Karna never ever forgave her for one more deliberate insult.

The most infamous incident of the epic Mahabharat however is when the Kauravas invited the Pandavas to a game of dice. Shakuni mama (maternal uncle of the Kauravas) was a very nasty person and master of deceit. He wanted the Kauravas to win at any cost and cheated in the game of dice. It is said that, during the game of dice, it was Karna who constantly told Duryodhana not to let deceit enter the game but to play the game fair and square. However, so hell bent were the Kauravas to win at any cost, that they did not listen to Karna and cheated in the game goaded by Shakuni mama. The Pandavas kept losing and were incited to keep playing and losing their money, their land etc until they had nothing left but their own persons. At that point they were incited to bet on their wife Draupadi. They lost that last game too and had to forfeit Draupadi. After winning Draupadi, they dragged her into the hall. In the great excitement at winning, they lost total control over their humanity and morality, and attempted to disrobe Draupadi in the court before all those who were present. She pleaded to everyone there to help her, but no one (not even Karna) came to her help. It was the great Lord Krishna who saved her by magically conjuring yard upon yard of sari around her so that she was not exposed. This terrible incident left a very bitter taste in the Pandavas about all the Kauravas, with Karna firmly on their side.

### *The great war of Kurukshetra*

Over a period of time, matters came to a head, and the internecine rivalry between the Kauravas and the Pandavas reached such a level that war became inevitable.

Karna was famous for his generosity. Everyone knew that if anyone asked him for anything at noon, the time when the Sun was at its peak, he would unhesitatingly give whatever was asked in alms. In fact, it is said that Lord Krishna had warned Karna that someone was going to try and trick him out of his armour in order to weaken him. Taking advantage of Karna's generosity, Lord Indra (who was Arjuna's father and firmly on the side of the Pandavas) approached Karna in disguise at noon. He asked Karna for his kavacha kundala. Karna was so generous that he immediately cut out both from his body and gave them to Lord Indra, despite recalling the prior warning and also knowing that he would be totally unprotected without the armour.

The Kauravas appointed Karna as the lead warrior from their side. But Bhishma who was leading from the Pandavas side refused to engage in battle with a sutaputra. Even at that critical time, Karna was insulted for the accident of his birth and kept out of the battlefield. It was only after Bhishma was killed, that Karna was sent in to fight. Karna was a very brave warrior, skilled in weaponry and a great tactician. After his entry into the battlefield of Kurukshetra, he started decimating the opposition quite rapidly. This was a long drawn out war of a kind not seen ever before. During this war, greatly advanced weaponry and strategies such as use of the chakravyuha (maze) were brought into play. There was massive loss of human life on both sides, with the Pandavas and Kauravas losing parents, uncles, brothers, sons and close relatives.

Coming back to our hero Karna, it is said that he came to know of his true parentage rather late in life, when he was already firmly committed to be on the side of the Kauravas in the Kurukshetra war. He first learnt of it from his true father Lord Surya dev, the Sun God himself, who appeared before him one day and told him the significance of his kavach kundala that were placed on him for his protection. The second learning came to him from Lord Krishna who tried to move him out of the war games telling him that he was Kunti's son and should be fighting alongside the Pandavas. However, Karna refused to ditch his lifelong friend Duryodhana and go to the side of Pandavas. The third revelation took place one night, during the battle of Kurukshetra. In those times, the battle used to end at dusk and both sides used to retreat to their own camps to rest and recuperate. One night, Karna received a very unusual visitor. Kunti, the mother of the Pandavas, came to meet him and revealed to him that he was her eldest son whom she had had to abandon soon after his birth. She revealed to him the story of his conception through union with the Sun God and begged him not to kill Arjuna as she wanted all her five Pandavas to live. Even at that tough time, he showed great generosity and promised her that he would not kill her sons.

Soon came the day when the great rivals Karna and Arjuna came face to face on the battlefield. The weather was stormy that day, as the Lord Indra was ensuring torrential rain in a bid to support his son Arjuna. On that day, it was as if all that fate had in store for Karna came together in a set of great coincidences. Karna's chariot got mired in the wet mud of the battlefield. Usually when such incidents took place, both sides ensured a pause in fighting and waited until both the warriors had a level playing field again. However, when Karna got off his chariot and bent to lift out the chariot wheel from the mud, Arjuna shot an arrow at him and killed him instantly.

### *Epilogue*

Thus, ended the life of the great warrior Karna - the first born son of Kunti, the elder brother of the Pandavas! Due to the unfortunate circumstances of his birth, he was disowned by his natal family, and grew up under the support provided by the Kauravas who as time went by became the sworn enemies of the Pandavas. Through no fault of his, he had to bear a lot of insults and suffering throughout his life. Just before the war, taking advantage of his great generosity, his protective armours were snatched away from him. His own mother used feminine tears to secure the lives of her sons. Despite knowing the outcome, he promised her he would not kill any of them, and lived to his word, sacrificing his life.

Perhaps that is the reason why, even today - so many millennia after the epic Mahabharata was enacted on the Indian diaspora, people still hold Karna in great reverence. He may have suffered a lot during his very troubled life, but his name lives on forever as a great warrior, a very intelligent and generous person and one who proffered total loyalty to his friend.

# Uloopi, the Snake Princess and Wife of Arjuna

*Dr. Sujata Chatterjee*

***Who is Dr. Sujata Chatterjee?***

*Dr Sujata Chatterjee is a postgraduate in anaesthesiology from Tata memorial hospital, Mumbai university. She is an author by passion. She has authored 3 books flights of fantasy, a collection of short stories and looking through the prism, a collection of 17 motivational poems and waves of fortune, an anthology of emotional poems. She has also co-authored 15 more books, which are in the process of publication. The book speak your mind is dealing with the current problems of India, which is going to the prime minister Narendra Modi. The book jamboree jubilation, which is a book on various religious festivals of India, is an eBook. Broken bits of the moon are a book which is based on various stories and poems based on the moon.*

*She is also the winner of shonghoti sammanana award, awarded by the hello Kolkata team. She has been honoured by a winner gold medal and a certificate from national book honour awards. She is one of the 100 inspiring authors of India awarded by the Indian awaz team. She has been selected as one of the top 50 influential authors awarded by the spirit mania. She has been awarded the women empowerment award by the media house hello Kolkata. She has been also awarded the swami Vivekananda excellence award, by the seva youth guild for her contribution towards English literature. Her book looking through the prism and flights of fantasy were selected for the Delhi world book fair, both 2018 and 2019, Chennai book fair 2018 and Kolkata international book fair, 2018 and 2019.*

*Dr sujata has also passed journalism from Delhi school of journalism new Delhi. She was a regular contributor of the column, the patient I can never forget, in the fortnightly magazine, the women's era.*

# Uloopi, the Snake Princess and Wife of Arjuna

Once upon a time, many years ago, Arjuna, the Pandava broke a vow. For this offence, he had to go on an exile for twelve years. Accompanied by the Brahmanas, he set out from Indraprastha, his capital. His first halt was at Gangotri, the source of river Ganga.

"Where will we go from here?" asked the Brahmanas.

"I will visit the holy places of the land," declared Arjuna.

Wherever he went, Arjuna performed the fire sacrifice. He looked upon this as his sacred duty. Sometimes, a fire sacrifice continued for many days. One day, as, usual, Arjuna went to bathe in the Ganga before beginning the sacrificial rites. As he was about to step out, he was pulled down the water, as if by a spell. He felt helpless and could not move a step forward. The Brahmanas, rushed forward to his rescue. But when they reached the spot, Arjuna had vanished from the sight.

Arjuna was dragged deep down into the river, till he came to a beautiful palace. He saw himself, lying down on an exotic golden bed. Slowly, amazed, he got up from the bed. He started to roam about in the palace in awe.

"I wonder, where I am, and to whom this palace belongs?", he wondered in silence, till he reached a spot where there was a sacrificial fire.

"Ah a sacrificial fire! Perhaps it is meant for me," he ruminated.

Unseen by Arjuna, a lady was watching him. Arjuna sat before the sacrificial fire and performed his rites with devotion. After finishing his rites, he lifted his eyes, only to see a beautiful maiden before him.

"Who are you?" he asked.

"I am Uloopi, the daughter of the Snake-king, Kauravya. You are in the underwater city of the Snake-people.

"Why have you brought me here?" he queried.

"Because I love you. Please make me your wife." She replied

"How can that be possible? I am an exiled prince." Exclaimed Arjuna.

"It is the duty of the prince to relieve the distressed." Replied Uloopi. "If you do not agree to my proposal, I shall surely die."

“My sacrifice at the Gangotri is incomplete,” replied the prince.

“I shall take you back tomorrow. But please be with me today.” She replied passionately.

Arjuna was touched by Uloopi’s pleadings.

“I shall do what you wish, dear one,” said Arjuna.

Throughout the hours of his stay, Uloopi looked after his needs with tenderness and care. Next morning, as Arjuna woke up, he was greeted by Uloopi.

“You have saved my life. I am grateful to you, my beloved husband. I shall take you back, as I promised.” Said Uloopi.

Uloopi led Arjuna back to the spot from where her magical powers had drawn him.

“He will soon forget me,” thought Uloopi.

As Arjuna emerged from water, he turned around to see that Uloopi had disappeared, unable to bear the grief of parting.

“Where is she? Where has she gone?” mused Arjuna.

The moment Arjuna appeared, one of the Brahmanas who had accompanied him, came forward and asked him, where he had gone to and what had happened. After telling them in brief, what befell him, Arjuna completed the fire sacrifice. Then he makes a decision. He told the Brahmanas to stay there if they wished. He intended visiting the holy places in the east.

And thus, leaving the Brahmanas behind, Arjuna went eastwards. After a long journey, he reached Manipur. As he wandered on, he came upon a palace. He entered the palace gardens and suddenly stopped on seeing a handsome girl.

“Is she Uloopi?” wondered Arjuna.

He went closer still. “No, she is not Uloopi. Who are you, fair maiden?”, he asked.

“I am Chitrangada, the daughter of the King of Manipur.” She replied.

Then Chitrangada suddenly turned her face, blushing.

“What power is it that draws me towards her?” wondered Arjuna. “I shall seek to speak to the king.” Decided Arjuna.

Later, at the court, Arjuna introduced himself, as a Kshatriya and sought Chitrangada’s hand in marriage.

“Who are you, O valiant one?” asked the king.

"I am Arjuna, son of Pandu," he replied back.

"Arjuna, the Pandava! You shall certainly marry my daughter; but she is my only child. The son borne to her must become my successor and rule my kingdom after me." said the king.

"It shall be as you wish, O king," said Arjuna.

Meanwhile, Chitrangada thought that how fortunate she was to marry, Arjuna, the great Pandava.

Arjuna married Chitrangada and lived happily with her at Manipur. Months later a don was born to them. Chitrangada named him Babhruvahana. Arjuna then, said that it was time for him to continue his pilgrimage. Chitrangada coaxed him to stay with her for some months more, until Babhruvahana was one year old. Arjuna then left Manipur. Meanwhile, Uloopi had been very unhappy since she parted from Arjuna.

"Arjuna does not love me. Therefore, I don't want to go to him." She thought. "But I can spend my time with Chitrangada and Babhruvahana, whom he loves."

Uloopi decided to visit Chitrangada. After changing her form by her magical powers, she visited Chitrangada and introduced herself as Uloopi, the snake-princess and her co-wife, Arjuna's wife.

Seeing Babhruvahana, she took him in her arms and asked him his name.

"I suppose this is our son." Said Uloopi. "He will become a valiant prince and unequalled king of Manipur,".

She soon took leave of them and promised to come to visit them often. Chitrangada welcomed her with great pleasure, addressing her as her sister. As Babhruvahana grew up, Uloopi true to her words, often visited him. She had a great influence in his growing up. She told him tales of his father, Arjuna and convinced him to practice archery and become a great hero like his father. She told him to concentrate in his work like Arjuna. Uloopi told him stories about Arjuna's achievements. He was specially amazed at Arjuna's prowess of hitting the eye of the fish by looking at the image below. Babhruvahana became a fit successor after the death of his grandfather and became the King of Manipur. Uloopi continued to visit Manipur and related him Arjuna's news by means of her magical powers. She told him that he lost his kingdom to the Kauravas, his cousins in a game. She also told him that Arjuna was preparing for the battle against the Kauravas and it was time that she left.

Meanwhile, at the battle of Kurukshetra, Arjuna, shielded by Shikhandi, showered a volley of arrows on Bhishma, the commander of Kauravas. Bhishma fell wounded on the arrows. All the celestial had gathered in the sky to witness this battle. Among them were the Vasus, the brothers of Bhishma.

"That was unfair. Arjuna should be punished.", they replied. The Vasus went to Ganga, their mother and asked her to put a curse upon Arjuna, who had sinned.

"He must go to hell, when he dies," they proposed. Ganga complied to their wishes.

Uloopi, unobserved heard everything. She thought that Arjuna did not deserve this fate as worst sins have been committed on the battlefield of Kurukshetra. She went to her father Kauravya for justice, who assured her not to worry. Kauravya propitiated the Vasus, who enquired about his boon that he sought. Kauravya asked for the curse on Arjuna to be lifted. The Vasus replied that the curse would be redeemed, if Arjuna was killed in the battlefield by his son, Babhruvahana.

Kauravya came back to his daughter and told her about it. Uloopi was dismayed and reflected that when the time came, she had to be present on the battlefield to save her husband.

Meanwhile, the Pandavas won the battle of Kurukshetra, against the Kauravas, and Yudhishthira, the eldest of the Pandavas was crowned the king. Soon after, Yudhishthira decided to perform the horse sacrifice. When the horse for the sacrifice was selected, he told Arjuna to protect the horse, as it wandered over the whole of the earth. If any king stopped the horse, he would have to fight Arjuna. If the king permits the horse to roam in his kingdom, he would acknowledge Yudhishthira as his superior. The horse was let loose and Arjuna was prepared to follow it. He followed the horse to many kingdoms, as it wandered at its will through various kingdoms either winning or vanquishing allies for the Pandavas.

At last, the horse arrived at the kingdom of Manipur. Arjun reflected that it was a great kingdom and his son was the king. He hoped that his son would fight him like a true Kshatriya.

But Babhruvahana came forward to welcome Arjuna.

"Father, I am proud to be your son. Welcome to my kingdom." He said.

"O king! This is not proper. You have failed in your duties," exclaimed Arjuna. "I have come here as the protector of Yudhishthira's horse. If you don't fight, you will be called a coward."

Babhruvahana was stunned by his father's words. How could he fight his own beloved father?

Then Uloopi arrived on the scene and urged him to fight his father as it was the righteous and dutiful thing to do.

Babhruvahana thought for a while. He decided to fight his father to win back his respect. He put on his armour, mounted his chariot and drove up to the sacrificial horse and had it seized by his men.

"Seize the horse of Hastinapur," ordered Babhruvahana.

"Ah! my son! My worthy son," mused Arjuna.

Arjuna checked the advance of Babhruvahana. Babhruvahana sent an arrow which pierced Arjuna through his shoulder. Weak with pain, Arjuna rested a while, leaning against his bow, looking almost dead. Then his strength came back to him and he praised his son.

"Now face my arrows and fight without running away." He challenged his son.

But Babhruvahana's arrows, cut Arjuna's arrows into bits. Arjuna cut off the standard on Babhruvahana's chariot and killed his horses. Infuriated, Babhruvahana got down from his chariot and fought Arjuna on foot. Arjuna attacked him relentlessly, till blinded by rage, Babhruvahana shot an arrow straight into Arjuna's heart. Arjuna dropped dead on the field. At the same moment, partly through exertion and partly through grief, Babhruvahana fell, down unconscious. All this while, Uloopi watched the entire scene, calm, unperturbed, a picture of serenity.

A messenger ran to Chitrangada with the news of Arjuna's death and swooning of Babhruvahana. Chitrangada turned paled and asked to be taken to the battlefield. At the battlefield she cried with remorse and when she came to her senses, she saw Uloopi.

"O Uloopi, I know you are devoted to our husband. Yet I do not find you grieving!" she said in anguish. When Uloopi showed no sign of emotion, Chitrangada went to Arjuna.

She coaxed to Arjuna to rise and follow it to the other kingdoms and to protect it and follow it to the other kingdoms. She had set it free. But she found that all attempts to revive Arjuna failed, so she turned to Uloopi. But Uloopi remained unmoved. Chitrangada, commented that if Uloopi did not do anything, she would give up her life. Saying this she sat at Arjuna's feet. Just then, Babhruvahana regained consciousness. He reproached himself, that his mother Chitrangada, who was brought up in luxury, was sitting on naked earth beside his dead father and it was he who killed him.

Then his gaze fell on Uloopi. He accused her to be hard hearted, as seeing her husband dead beside her did not melt her heart. By killing Arjuna, he had done as she had wished, but for him there was no redemption. He would sink to hell, as he had sinned in killing his own father.

Uloopi heard all the accusations in silence. Babhruvahana, stricken with grief told Uloopi that he would follow his father.

"I shall starve myself to death right here on the battlefield, next to his father. Rejoice, mother! Your son too shall die before your own eyes." Said the prince remorsefully as he sat next to his parents. Uloopi watched the three of them.

"It is time I acted," she mused. She closed her eyes and thought of the gem of the snake- people, which could revive the dead. The gem, the most precious possession of the snake people came sailing through the skies and dropped into her palms. Uloopi went to Babhruvahana and told him to rise, as Arjuna had been killed for his own good. She told him of the curse of the Vasus which could be lifted only if he was killed in the battlefield by his son. The words of Uloopi did not console Babhruvahana. Then she handed over the gem of the snake people to Babhruvahana and asked him to place it over the wound of Arjuna, who would arise alive, as valiant as before.

Babhruvahana was delighted and did as he was told.

"Dear mother, how could I have ever doubted you?" he said. "I am ever grateful to you.". He went up to Arjuna and placed the gem on his chest, where the arrow had pierced him.

Arjuna woke up rubbing his eyes, like the one who was fast asleep. He saw Babhruvahana, looking at him in wonder.

He embraced his son and said, "My son, I am proud of you. Your valour is unmatched."

Only then did he notice Chitrangada and Uloopi. He turned to Babhruvahana and said,

"What are your mothers doing on the battlefield?"

Babhruvahana bowed his head respectfully and said, "Mother Uloopi will explain everything."

Uloopi told Arjuna about the curse of the Vasus. Arjuna hearing all this then said,

"Beloved wife, I am indebted to you, both for this life and for the life here after."

Thus, Uloopi's dream of winning Arjuna's life was fulfilled.

# Section V
# Mahajanapadas and the Mauryan Empire
## *(600 BCE to 185 BCE)*

This period is probably the earliest in ancient Indian History with literary as well as archaeological evidence. There is mention of the rulers of these kingdoms in the contemporary literature as well. A period of great scientists and philosophers and the birth of the two of the leading faiths – Buddhism and Jainism. There were sixteen kingdoms spread over the northern part of the country with large cities, fortifications and paved roads. Many archaeologists consider this to be the second urbanisation period after the great Harappan urbanisation during the third millennium BCE. It corresponds to the Northern Black Polished Ware period. Fist coinage also (Gandharan coins – punched mark coins) appeared during this period. Other kingdoms such as Kosala, Magadha, Surasena, Avanti, Panchala also introduced their own punch marked coins during this period. Introduction of emperors or *chakravartins* with Bimbisara in 544 BCE set the tone for the future of India and brought together a conglomerate of entities into one country, at least in the north west. His successor, Ajatasatru expanded further and gradually the sixteen Jana padas started to shrink in number as the Aryan empire started to grow with each emperor.

This is considered to be a watershed in the long history of Indian Subcontinent with several sects and faith coming out in revolt against the established Vedic/Hindu religion. This is also in all probability the period during which Vedic religion transformed itself into the Hindu religion or faith as we know of it today. Many experts believe that this was the period when the final version of Manu smriti was composed and brought in the different *Varnas* and differentiation of different groups of people which is clearly absent during the Vedic period. Great thinkers the Buddha and Mahavira established their following. Panini, probably the greatest grammarian of all times is dated during this period. It saw the birth of Magadha empire which in turn led to the birth of the great Mauryans and the Ashoka that we all know.

Gandharan culture saw some of the most beautiful monuments and fortifications built around this period. Greek and Macedonian influence in these are evident in the Gandharan monuments even today. It was towards the end of this period – 326 BCE to be exact, when Alexander of Macedonia brought his massive Greek ad Macedonian legions to the northwest of India. He was repelled by the great Nanda empire and retreated soon after only to die on his way back to Greece.

It was Chandragupta under the tutelage of Kautilya or Chanakya, who unified India further and expanded the kingdom into a truly great empire. Kautilya's Arthashastra is considered one of the masterpieces of statecraft even today and it should not surprise anyone if some of the major Ivy league universities still quote his work. This was also the period of one of the greatest universities of ancient world – Taxila (Takshashila) – archaeological remnants still a poignant reminder of what wars can do to a great civilisation. Chandragupta defeated the Greek satrap, Seleucus and ended the Seleucid rule set up by the receding Alexander. He thus extended the Magadhan empire westwards over the Indus into the Oxus and beyond. Arachosia and Gedrosia (of Bactria Margiana Complex) came under the Magadhan influence during his time. Several Greek ambassadors resided in his court and diplomatic relations with far flung countries of east and west established his place in the world stage.

The Mauryan empire was established towards the end of Magadhan era by Chandra Gupta Maurya and expanded to some extent by Bindusara. Chandragupta used Magadha as the centre to spread his empire across all the borders. It was left to his grandson, Ashoka to take the empire to its limits – extending from Balkh in the west to the southern tip of the sub-continent. He was ruthless in his conquest and did not take retreat as an option. It was probably the largest empire in the world at the time extending to over 5 million square kilometres in area. Ashoka's capital was at Pataliputra, present day Patna. While Chandragupta embraced Jainism as the national religion, Ashoka followed the Buddha. During Ashoka's reign, after the Kalinga war, Buddhism expanded beyond the boundaries of Mauryan empire at the time.

Ashoka turned from an almost despotic and cruel ruler to an example of what a memorable ruler could be – with compassion, respect for law and kindness as the centre of his rule. He set out his edicts across the land, mostly as stone inscriptions for everyone to read. Most of the edicts were written in Prakrit used by the common man as well as Greek and Aramaic in the western satraps.

We have an excellent account of the period straddling both the Magadhan and Mauryan empires by Mr Saumendra Nayak. He is an excellent storyteller and take you back thousands of years with his visual descriptions. It has a personal touch to the story which makes it endearing as well informative. I am not sure how many of the readers have read "*Amathya Rakshasa*" by *Kavi Kalidasa*. If you have, you will find that this article – *Vishkanya* - is equally interesting.

# Vishkanya

*Saumendra Kumar Nayak*

***Who is Saumendra Kumar Nayak?***

*Saumendra Kumar Nayak is an Author, a Poet and a guest faculty in Management institutes.*

*His debut Novel* ***"Forever & Beyond"*** *has earned great accolades and response from readers across many countries and featured in "Guardian weekly" as one of the interesting fictions to read on 'Romantic Suspense' in first Quarter of 2017. His recent Novel* ***"Don't wake me up, Please"*** *is selling quite successfully across geographies. Some of his poems in different anthologies were appreciated much among readers. With more than a decade of corporate experience in field of Marketing and Sustainability, he is currently associated as a Strategic Advisor with Ernst & Young.*

*As a visiting faculty in Management Institutes he loves to interact with youth while delivering lectures on Marketing, Agriculture and Sustainability.*

## Vishkanya

I looked at the small open window on the left side of my bed through which I could still see the yellow dazzling moon which was about to vanish from the dark sky along with its friends, the stars. It was the darkest night giving its way to the wee hours of early morning twilight conditions which was about to wake up the day with a frightening news that would deliver a cascading series of consequences. A cool breeze entered the room fluttering the transparent curtains of the small window and touched my half naked body giving me goose-bumps while reminding me that this is the last twilight that I should enjoy. It brought calmness to my mind bringing in a sense of satisfaction to have served the final purpose of my life. I might have been born with a different purpose, but this was the intent with which I was brought up.

Beside me lied the naked body of a great king who had shaken the reigns of the Magadha empire and helped in the dethronement of the mighty and truant king Dhanananda, thus bringing the end to the Nanda dynasty in the history of Magadha. He is king Parvatak whose body has turned pale and bluish, muscles contracted and lost its flexibility becoming stiff. Froths which came out his open mouth have settled as white linings around his chin. There was no sign of life left in him as I cannot see his chest moving up and down as an act of breathing.

I pulled myself closer and concealed my scantily clad muslin textured soft body under the warm tiger hide blanket to feel warmth from the cold breeze of the morning hours. While doing so, I smiled at the accomplishment of my life's mission.

"Who am I?" "What was my life's mission?"

I am not a normal girl nor was bred to be one since my childhood memories made me reconcile those earliest impression of my very existence. I didn't have any memories of my parents. It might have been erased from my mind even before I grew conscious. I grew up in a dark secluded cave secretly away from the society in a forest along with snakes. I never have any memory of a family which I find very strange when people talk that everyone loves each other in a family. My only companion in those dark woods were the deadly venomous snakes and few other girls like me. We never had a name; we just had a number assigned to us which kept on increasing gradually along with the level of venom content in our blood. We were referred to by that number only. Our lives were meant to be sacrificed and the maximum age of life expectancy from us was 30 years. Living beyond that was never anticipated nor a desire. The only desire for us since our mind has gained consciousness was to achieve a good target that would accomplish our mission.

"Were we faithful to a person or to a nation?" we never had such questions in mind nor were we allowed to carry them? Those were considered distractions from our mission. We were never tortured anytime physically nor compelled to do anything except those moments of devouring poisons for the first time.

In fact, we received all kinds of treatment to make our bodies the most beautiful one with an unmatchable attractiveness among all women. I have seen my small body with its tiny and lean limbs turning up into a sexually attractive body of a woman with every perfection right from my head to the toes under strict vigilance and guidance of those charmers who made us as if invincible weapons to kill someone at the only strike that we could get. I have seen my rough, matte dry hairs turning into long dark silky thick and bouncy tresses which were dense and dark enough to hide any secret. The skin that was once dry in childhood has turned out to be as soft as butter which would take your fingers in when pressed hard on it. Eyes have turned themselves into dark bluish charmers who once marked its victim would never let it go. Those lips which were once cracked and chapped had turned into thick soft velvety petals which were very lethal but would attract anyone for a sweet bite of a nectary death. An unblemished face as if carved out of a piece of pure milky white marble by the best sculptor on the planet. Well-formed round and firm breasts, narrow, thin and curvy waistline, plantain stalk-like slender thighs and very attractive fingers and toes as if some goldsmith has worked on it with much frailty and fineness. Every part of the body was so full of vigour and resplendent with the glow that defines youth. It was difficult to say if my touch was more lethal or my look as it would pierce the heart of anyone from a distance without even noticing that I have marked my victim.

Now one would wonder what the use of such a beauty is, if someone is to live in darkness secluded away from the society for years together. We were meant for it. Under this soft and attractive skin flew the most venomous blood of hundreds of poisonous snakes. We were fed small quantities of poison everyday. Initially out of every 100 girls like me, only 5 would survive after being fed with small doses of poison. Slowly as the level of poison in our diet would increase many would fall sick and die eventually. Only those handful of girls who would succeed in surviving through all these would finally be groomed into enchanted but lethal beauty called 'Vishkanya'.

Any Vishkanya like me would never have a family nor any intimacy towards anyone in the society from where they were completely cut off. We were only awaiting that glorious moment where we would materialise the purpose of our life and would kill the target before our life come to an end. We were nurtured for a single attack to inject the venom onto our prey and whether we are successful or not our life would come to an end the next day.

But out of my own curiosity I kept a track of the most happenings during the turmoil of the politics of Magadha and the change of reigns from Nanda to Maurya dynasty. By enquiring from anyone possible I always remained inquisitive of the actions of the Kautilya, Acharya Chanakya as I knew that he was the centre of all actions happening in the political arena of Magadha. It was a known fact that Acharya Chanakya was the mastermind behind dethronement of the tyrant king Dhanananda and placing Chandragupta Maurya on the throne of Magadha. Any Vishkanya was forbidden to keep a track of the happenings in the society or politics so that they do not develop any kind of emotion for their target. We were not allowed to think logically or develop any sentiment or emotion for anyone.

But in spite of all these forbidden cautions, what kept me hooked to keep a track of the scenario is the high level of intellectual war between Amathya Rakshasa and Acharya Chanakya.

Acharya Chanakya who was once insulted and humiliated in the court of King Dhanananda, vowed to get rid Magadha from the tyranny of Nanda Dynasty. King Dhanananda ordered his soldiers to grab and behead this ugly looking brahmin who dared to raise his voice against him. But Acharya was fortunate enough to get help and shelter from Prince Parbat, one of the sons of king Dhanananda, whom he promised to help in seizing the throne of Magadha in exchange for the safety of his life. Then finally he was able to escape from the palace through a secret door and made his way to the jungle with the help from Prince Parbat.

There he discovered a charismatic child with exceptional leadership skills and great sense of judgement. This child showed extraordinary talent of bravery and intelligence to win the heart of Acharya. Acharya Chanakya had 2 options before him. He had options of Prince Parbat who helped him and saved his life and Chandragupta, whom he found in the forest but with extraordinary talent of bravery and leadership; out of whom he had to choose one as the successor of king Dhanananda. He decided to train them both with skills of martial art, warfare and diplomacy.

But finally, he had to make a choice which seemed tough under the burden of help from prince Parbat. So, he decided to try them both in terms of intelligence and duty. He tied woollen amulet around the neck of both. One day he asked prince Parbat to remove the amulet from Chandragupta's neck while he was sleeping with a condition that it should not break, nor would he wake up Chandragupta. After trying for few times prince Parbat gave up accepting his failure to remove the amulet under the given conditions. Then one day he asked Chandragupta for the same task of removing the amulet from the neck of prince Parbat without waking him up or breaking the amulet. Chandragupta came back to his guru with a smile of success on his face and the amulet in his right arm and the head of prince Parbat in his left arm. Acharya was startled at the first sight of the cut head of prince Parbat in the hands of Chandragupta, but again in the very next moment he found himself relieved from the burden of the favour which was making him reluctant to accept Chandragupta as a more eligible heir to the throne of Magadha.

Acharya Chanakya secretly raised an army along with the support from his protégé Chandragupta Maurya by using the gold that he had hidden in the forests and by motivating the captured soldiers of war from different kingdoms. Then he started attacking Pataliputra, the capital of Magadha several times only to face defeat from the hands of the mighty army of King Dhanananda whom even the military might of "Alexander the great" also feared to encounter. One day while passing by a village he heard a mother scolding his son for burning out his finger after trying to eat his food from the centre of the hot bowl. She advised him to eat first from the periphery of the dish which would have been cooler and then slowly progress towards the centre which would become less hot eventually. This strikes the mind of the genius Acharya who immediately understood his mistake of attacking the capital, Pataliputra to face the mighty Magadhan army head-on. Now he started attacking the peripheral parts of the kingdom which made the mighty army lose its confidence and made several mistakes in the warfare strategies.

Acharya and Chandragupta also went to Himavanta kingdom in the north and made 'Mettikaya'- the treaty with its ruler Parvatak whom they promised to give half of Magadha once they are able to defeat king Dhanananda. With help from king Parvatak, Chandragupta's army marched towards the capital city of Pataliputra and were able to defeat and kill king Dhanananda. Although the enemy was defeated and killed but the battle was not yet over. It was the prime minister of the Nanda dynasty, Amathya Rakshasa who declared his diplomatic and guerrilla warfare to avenge the death of king Dhanananda and started conspiring to kill Chandragupta. Acharya Chanakya and Amathya Rakshasa were equally talented to continue the struggle against each other for a much longer time. But although Amathya was looking for a revenge and was conspiring to kill Chandragupta, Acharya had other intentions. Although he was trying to counter each attack of Amathya and save the life of Chandragupta but at the same time did not want to harm Rakshasa as he knew that Rakshasa was very faithful and loyal to the kingdom and was most deserving man to hold the position of the prime minister. Hence, he wanted to convince Rakshasa for continuing his loyalty to the throne with Chandragupta on it just as he was loyal to the Nanda dynasty.

In the meanwhile, he started facing the opposition to create one great kingdom of his dream where he had dreamt of "Akhand Bharat"- one nation. This opposition mainly came from king Parvatak and his son Malayketu who had helped him in dethroning the Nanda dynasty from Magadha. Mettikaya – the treaty said that the King would ascend the throne of Magadha which would be divided equally but there was no mention of the heirs to the throne in case of the King's demise. The discontentment lead by the delay in dividing the kingdom grew the anger of both Parvatak and his son Malayketu on Chanakya and King Chandragupta.

Rakshasa knew well about the discontent of Malayketu and was looking for an opportunity to divide and rule. Chanakya although aware about the intentions of Amathya Rakshasa, was unable to do anything regarding it as he had dreamt of 'Akhand Bharat'-a greater kingdom of one nation being ruled from Magadha and dividing it would destroy all his desire and dream for good. He also knew well that if Rakshasa would have no support from Malayketu, then he would have no choice but to surrender.

Then Amathya Rakshasa who had been desperately looking for an opportunity to strike Chandragupta after his repeated failures in attempt on the life of the new king ordered me to be used as an undeterred and unbeaten venomous weapon. I, like any other Vishkanya, who had been groomed for the final and only strike of their lifetime, happily accepted the offer as now I knew whom I was going to strike before I am dead.

I was transported from the darkness of the cave to the glitter of the palace of Pataliputra. Arrangements had been made for me to perform a well-articulated seducing dance in front of the new King and his guests. While performing along with other women on the floor of the palace, I could see the smiling face of Acharya Chanakya who just arrived during the dance. From the expressions on his face, I could gauze that he seems to be aware about my lethal intentions. This made me a little scared not because of the threat to my life if in case I get caught, but because I won't be able to fulfill the purpose of my life and then my life and all its penance would be an absolute waste. But Vishkanyas are also trained on various other aspects like stress handling and how to conceal their emotions of any kind so that it doesn't appear in the facial expressions. I continued my dancing as if there is nothing to hide and nothing to reveal and hence nothing to get caught.

My target was clear, and I slowly started approaching king Chandragupta on his throne during the performance of the dance. When I was about a couple of feet away from the king, a loud voice stopped the dance and ordered me to freeze my feet to the ground. I closed my eyes for a moment knowing that the end of my life has come in the voice of Acharya Chanakya. When I opened my eyes, I saw the face of Acharya Chanakya gleaming with confidence and a cunning smile that was glorifying his diplomacy for which he had earned the name Kautilya. Before I could think or say anything, he ordered me to escort king Parvatak to the royal guest chamber. From the smile and confidence on his face, I could clearly say that he was sure of the intentions of my presence in the palace but did not stop me as he had something else in mind which seemed to be more lethal than the venom flowing under my skin.

I smiled, bowed and walked king Parvatak to the royal guest chamber. Now here I am sitting beside the corpse of king Parvatak on the soft bed in the royal chamber. Like most of the Vishkanyas, I would have ended my life immediately after the purpose was achieved to escape from the tortures after being caught. But this is my curiosity about politics, diplomacy and specifically the actions of Kautilya, which gave me a desire to stay alive to know the reason behind Kautilya's decision. He could have easily captured and commanded my killing thereby failing the purpose of my life. But his cunning smile revealed that he had other intentions in mind.

A sudden knock on the door shook me up from my reflecting thoughts where I was lost and brought me back to the real situation. I stood up beside the bed and started to clad my bare body with not just my silken clothes but also the gorgeous looking ornaments as I knew my last journey to free myself from the shackles of life was about to begin. The knocking on the door grew from a whispering tap to a loud banging breaking the silence of the calm morning. I stood still, completely dressed up before the door, waiting for the soldiers to break it open. Then there was the final bang with the heaviest possible force shattering the heavy wooden door into few pieces. I stood still with a calm face waiting for the soldiers to come and grab me.

It seemed they had come prepared. They chained me, held me tight by my neck with a long iron frame which seemed to be a precaution taken against the bite of any Vishkanya. With an anticipation that they would directly take me to behead my head, I uttered just one name "Acharya Chanakya".

I was least expecting my desires to get fulfilled when someone among the soldier whispered, "Acharya Chanakya is expecting your presence, immediately". My heart was filled with happiness and my eyes with tears of content. I walked happily without the soldiers having to drag me on the floor. I was made to kneel on the floor of a dark chamber and was shackled firmly. After a few moments of waiting in curiosity and anxiety, finally someone entered the room with a small flame in hand. It was Acharya Chanakya. He asked the guards to stand outside, shutting the door firmly behind him.

I could not have been happier and was unable to control my tears which rolled down my cheek. I didn't remember when the last time it had broken the confinement of my eyes and rolled down like this. These were the tears of happiness to see someone in front of me whom I had been following my whole life.

Before I could open my mouth to utter a word, Acharya stopped me by the gesture of his arm.

"I knew the purpose of your presence even before you arrived at the palace".

"So why didn't you stop me?"

"Sometimes you don't have to stop an arrow from your enemy to protect yourself. Rather you can redirect it at someone else who can emerge as a more potent enemy of your enemy"

I could see the cunning smile on his face which confirmed of a more lethal mind in action under the clean shaved head. I knew well that he might have already planned many things which would result as a cascading consequence when this news would break out.

He came closer to me without the fear of approaching a Vishkanya and whispered in my ears,

"You fulfilled my desire of 'Akhand Bharat', and I do not have to divide the empire of Magadha. You have also given me the reason of turning my enemies against each other. I cannot reveal anything more than this. This is the principle of politics which says never reveal till done".

I desired to touch his feet and he denied saying that he cannot take chances although he knew very well that I would never harm him. He blessed me from a distance and called the guards ordering them for my immediate execution before the sunrise. I touched the dust from the floor after he left the chamber and moved my palm full of dust over my head as a gesture to salute this seasoned statesman.

[* Chanakya used the news of king Parvatak's death in the hands of Vishkanya sent by Amathya Rakshasa thus turning Malayketu against Amathya Rakshasa thereby breaking any chances of a treaty between the two. Chanakya's spy Nipunaka was able to possess Rakshasa's signet ring which slipped from the hands of Rakshasa's wife, whom Rakshasa had made to stay secretly with one of his good friend Chandandasa, the chief of the jeweller's guild. After capturing Chandandasa, Acharya Chanakya declared to execute him in public thereby forcing Amathya Rakshasa to surrender in the court of Chandragupta Maurya.]

***Saumendra Kumar Nayak***

# Section VI
# Imperial Kanauj
## *(300 CE to 1018 CE)*

This is a period which saw the rise of several empires as well as decline of some. Historians consider this as the classical age of Indian history with the establishment of Gupta empire to the time when the last King of Kanauj, Yashovarman died. Kanauj dates back, archaeologically, to Painted Grey Ware period (1200 BCE) and has been continuously occupied since. The Guptas were probably the greatest of the several empires that ruled Kanauj (340 AD to 600 AD). There was the rise of imperial Pratiharas in the west, Palas in the East, Satavahanas and Cholas in the south to name a few. Cholas in the south rose around 300 BCE and came to a peak during the 9$^{th}$ century AD with a golden period of Chola dynasty which extended its influence beyond the borders of Indian subcontinent over the waters to the east – Indonesia, Malaysia and even parts of Thailand. Imperial Kanauj existed in continuity under one or other empire until it was captured by Mahmud of Ghazni in 1018.

Satavahana dynasty does not really fall into this period as it ends by breaking up into several smaller kingdoms towards the latter part of 3$^{rd}$ century AD. It is now considered by many experts that Vikramiditya was not necessarily a single king or emperor, but a combination of multiple entities – similar to the great Manu or even Moses of biblical history. The Sanchi Stupa was embellished to large extent by one of the kings of Satavahana dynasty. In Ananta's epic poem, *Vicharita,* Salivahana is an adversary of Vikramiditya of Ujjain. Dr Rajeshwari Rapata has brought out the conflict of different varnas or castes that was at the forefront through out the era with significant persecution rampant.

The Cholas can be traced back to 4$^{th}$ century BCE, but the chola empire did not flourish till about 9$^{th}$ century AD. During the period of Raja Raja Chola the empire extended to include almost the whole of peninsular India as well as most part of Sri Lanka – 11$^{th}$ Century

AD. They were great temple builders and have left an amazing legacy throughout the southern India of massive stone temples of uniquely Cholan style. Rajendra Chola had extended his empire into the Northern India – to conquer Orissa and marched up to river Ganga. They were not only builders of huge temples, but also water canals for irrigation. They were probably the best sailors India ever saw with a navy to match any other in the known world of the time. Ankita Chakraborty has written an excellent fictionalised account of the life during the Cholan times in her story "Fierce child of Patteswaram". It is pleasant to see that the emotional side of the past, often neglected, has been brought out so well.

Any section of Kanauj cannot be complete without a story about the Palas. They were in prominence in northern India around 8th and 9th century AD. Pala emperor, Dharmapala built the Vikramashila university as a competition to the famed Nalanda and did go on to become one of the greatest universities until it was destroyed by Bhaktiyar Khalji in 1193. Som Shubra Karmakar has in his article, Orbs of Fire, brought out the greatness of the knowledge reared in the university in a rather entertaining article.

Advaita philosophy can be rather dense for mortals like me. Modern scientists have been looking at the non-dualism ever since the discovery of quantum particles and physics. Eminent scholars like Schrodinger have tried to explain the non-dualism using experiments, but it still evades the grasp of common man. Description of the "God Particle" (Higgs Boson particle) in 1964 and its eventual discovery in 2014 has accelerated the research into this aspect of quantum physics. Scientists like Ervin Laszlo have gone to great lengths looking at consciousness and non-dualism not just in living beings but in the cosmos as well. It should not come as a surprise if this was described in the Mandukya Upanishad thousands of years ago. Adi Shankara dissected out the Upanishad and explained the Advaita philosophy long before any of these scientists, in the beginning of 9th century AD. Adi Shankara does not need any introduction – one of the trinities of probably the greatest philosophers India has ever known. Bhagvati Ramakrishnan has taken a look at his life and his philosophy and tried to explain the Advaita philosophy to us commoners and succeeds eminently in doing so.

# The Royal Throne of Victory

*Dr Rajeshwari Rapata*

***Who is Dr Rajeshwari Rapata?***

*Adorning several feathers in her cap and a versatile personality, Dr. Rajeshwari has vast experience in teaching as an approved Principal, Hospital Administrator, Professor (HOD) Anatomy, by MUHS, Nashik.*

*Her expertise includes Homoeopathic consultation, Academics management, Counselling, Hospital Administration, Training and Internal auditing for NABH.*

*She is an assessor, examiner, paper setter, convenor, centre observer for conduction and assessment of theory and practical exams at Maharashtra University of Health Sciences (Nashik).*

*It takes a great courage when you marry against your community wishes especially when you are an apple of the eyes of your parents and relatives. Yes, both me and my soon to be spouse were in the same situation. He was from a potter community, me from a brahmin community. I was fifteen and it was all a fairy tale for me.*

# The Royal Throne of Victory

This charming prince came to claim my hand for marriage. My parents and me were affirmative. Then came the opposition from some of our friends and relatives. He went back to our native place a small village at Anantapur in Andhra Pradesh to convince them but all in vain. He went to his village head desperately and explained his perplexed situation. The village head knew his family members very well. He told him a folklore about Salivahana descendent Mysore

Maharaja and his throne which belonged to King Vikramaditya who was killed by King Salivahana in the war.

This story enlightened him with the information that he belonged to the Salivahana caste and in Telugu, also called as Kummara (Potter) (Kumhar) (Prajapati). This folklore readily convinced his family members that Potters, and Brahmins can marry in each other's family and it will result in a hybrid offspring just similar to the mighty king Salivahana.

***The story goes this way…***

King Salivahana defeated the great King Vikramaditya in the battlefield. His throne which was buried for many years was found by the one of the Vijayanagar kings and it passed on to the present royal Wadiyar family, said to be the heirs of the Salivahana dynasty. None of the heirs can sit on the throne more than ten minutes and it emits heat till the seated person sweats, gets exhausted and has to leave it soon.

The Golden throne also known as Chinnada simhasana or Ratnasimhasana is made of fig wood and embellished with gold, silver, ivory and precious stones. It has ten steps leading to the seat with astadikpalakas, the deities of eight directions, It is said that after winning over vetal, As King Vikramaditya ascended each step, the astadikpalakas again asked him questions, validated him as the king and then let him sit there.

The Royal seat is called the kurmasana, the hand rests are made of half elephant and half lion and the back seat is made of artwork. In the centre, there is the Goddess Chamundeshwari with Goddesses Lakshmi and Saraswathi on either side. The main Royal seat is supported by horses in jumping pose and adorned by Brahma, Vishnu and Shiva figurines. The lions as the sign of victory are placed and on the three sides there are carvings of two horse, two tigers and four swans. The back rest has the royal emblem and the inscribed quote 'Satyamevoodharaham' meaning 'I shall uphold the truth always.' Therefore, it was a throne which was truly said to have passed from the Satyuga as the title Satavahana claims. Shalivahana or Satavahana was a legendary emperor associated with many stories from southern Andhra region to northern Jat region of India. The only ruling family of south India, who also ruled some parts of northern India. They held a long ruling tenure in Indian history.

***The Birth of Salivahana.***

There was a very learned Brahmin and a warrior called Naga Raja who belonged to the Naga Dynasty. (This explains the reason why this name is more common in our family)

The astrologers told him that he will be blessed with a son with star Rohini in the month of Chaitra on Friday who will become the greatest king of Indian history and this can happen only if he meets his wife on the prescribed night after twelve years.

So, he went on a pilgrimage for twelve years and when he was about to reach back on the said time there were sudden floods which made him stop at Kotilingala village situated at the shores of river Godavari. He took shelter at a potter's house and told him about his problem. The potter had an eligible widow daughter who was willing to bear his child. He then spent the night with her, and she bore him a son who was named Salivahana.

Salivahana was extremely intelligent and inclined towards pottery. He started making dolls of soldiers, cavalry, infantry, chariots, weapons and behaved like a king among his people.

He used to sit underneath a tree where he could solve all the conflicts of the villagers and render justice. He broke up the gangs that robbed traders' caravans. He grew up to be a wise young man and King Vishwa Natha Raja appointed him as his second minister. Salivahana stopped all the taxes which were paid by King Vishwa Natha Raja to King Vikramaditya.

King Vikramaditya was enraged and sent his emissaries for tax. He refused and asked to defeat him if they wanted the taxes. King Vikramaditya with his large army marched towards the kingdom of Vishwa Natha Raja. Shalivahana sprinkled magical water on his dolls and thousands of them came alive, pounced on the armies of Vikramaditya and finally he was killed by a mud arrow which cut off his head and fell amidst his queens who cursed him that there will be only one last male offspring in each of the generations in the paternal lineage which will end the family tree. (This seems to be true and confirmed as per the family tree of the Salivahana community).

Afterwards King Salivahana ruled for a long time over Ujjain and created a prosperous kingdom which was continued by his successors. This became the Salivahana or the Satavahana Dynasty. The Salivahana

Era was established by the ruler Sri Goutamiputra Satakarni one of the descendent of Salivahana family. The shalivahana Era, also known as Saka era, is used in the Hindu calendars, Indian calendar and the Cambodian Buddhist calendar which is used by Telugus, Guajarati's, Marathi's, Kannadigas and Konkani's in India. King Gautamiputra Satakarni is credited for initiation and establishing of the Shalivahana era officially on his ancestors' name "Shalivahana" The founder of the Satavahana Dynasty, to celebrate the victory against Vikramaditya in the year 78 A.D.

### *The Etymology:*

According to Neelkanth Shastri, in the first half millennium BC, the basic changes started in the languages of the Indo Aryan cultures. The Indo Aryan, Ancient Dravidian and Kol languages were intermixing and there were many new names originating misleading the lineage of the dynasty. There was a close relation with Horse in all the lineages and was found in the excavation reports of Mahurjhari and surprisingly the salivahana, satavahana or sadavahana have originated from Nagas of Megalithic culture who were warriors and skilled horse riders and had a great importance of horses.

Satavahana also means Son of a horse in Munda language, Likewise the word has many meanings such as Hundreds of Elephants, hills, swords, Chariots etc. Finally, the story ended with a flamboyant royal feel running in my prince charming's mind and he cheerfully headed to his house and convinced his family members. They all agreed, and It was a happy beginning in 1985.

### *The learning:*

During the time of First Veda, Rig Veda period, there were no gods neither Brahma,Vishnu & Maheswara. Only the God Prajapati was considered as creator of the universe. But later the vedic period, the Prajapati was replaced by new gods i.e The Trinity of Shiva, Vishnu and Brahma. At the coming Atharva Vedic period the concept of Hiranyagarbha (golden egg) & Prajapati was change into Brahmand (cosmic egg) & Brahma concept. In earlier vedic period there was no caste system in Hindu society. Everyone could become Brahmana by attaining Brahman (one ness) knowledge.

This is clear by the following hymn:-

***The Atreya smriti 141-142***

*janmana jayate shudrah*
*samskarad dvija ucyate*

*vedapathi bhaved viprah*
*brahma janati brahmanah*
*One is a Shudra by birth*
*By observing Sanskara one becomes a Dvija*
*By studying the Vedas one becomes a Vipra*
*One who knows Brahman is a Brahmana*
*Om Tat Sat !!!*

***Rajeshwari Rapata***

# Orbs of Fire

*Som Shubhra Karmakar*

***Who is Som Shubhra Karmakar?***

*Som Shubhra Karmakar was born in Kolkata and now lives in Mumbai. As a child he discovered his love of reading from his mother, late Ms Bharati Karmakar, with classics of Tagore, Premchand, Tolkien, Dickens and such others. His father, Mr Rabindra Nath Karmakar, encouraged his love and appreciation for performing arts. He is an alumnus of Jadavpur University (Dept. of English) and has completed his M. A (English Literature) & M. Phil (English). An avid philatelist with a passion for Indian art, Som also loves photography. Deeply interested in history, archaeology, aesthetics and writing, he hopes to collaborate some day in bringing his passion for history and culture to a wider audience. Currently he is working as a language trainer with a well-renowned book publishing company. In his free time, you would find him enjoying a graphic novel.*

# Orbs of Fire

Our tale unfolds on a beautiful autumnal evening. The sky had smeared itself with the magenta shade of fading sun. In the waning dusk, the silhouette of a Buddhist monk stood out sharp against this roseate skyline. He stood motionless, saffron robe gently billowing in the wind. The twilight breeze carried with it many soft lilting voices that pulsated out of the main sanctum and prayer hall. It was time for the vespers at the sangha.

Abruptly, the lull spell of the evening quietude broke as unfamiliar hollers cut across like discordant notes. Atiśa Dīpaṃkara looked up towards this source of cacophony. His curious eyes narrowed towards the north gates where gradually a din was building in momentum that soon was threatening the peacefulness of the place. The din had startled birds in their nests across the groves around the university campus.

This Vikramashila University and its walled campus with its viharas or monasteries was the world renowned beacon for disciples of education. Close to the present Bhagalpur district in Bihar, Vikramashila along with Nalanda, was one of the two most important centres of learning in India during the Pala Empire in the late 8th or early 9th century. The academia was spread across a thousand hectare of land with lush green groves, votive stupas, temples, monasteries encircling the central prayer hall. The university housed hundreds of learned scholars who were responsible for educating thousands of students who had come from the far reaches of the Indian subcontinent. Vikramashila had a more clearly delineated hierarchy with resident monks (Bhikkhu), professors or teachers (Upādhyāya or Āchārya), senior and junior scholars (Mahapaṇḍita & Paṇḍita), six gate scholars (Dvārapaṇḍita; one each for the Eastern, Western, First Central, Second Central, Northern, and Southern Gates) and the abbot (Adhyakṣa). And above all of them was the Maha Āchārya, Atiśa Dīpaṃkara. Born in Bengal, Atiśa Dīpaṃkara's fame surpassed everyone as a polymath, scholar, educator and the Buddhist monk who was responsible for the spread of Buddhism into Tibet & Nepal. Eager students as far as from China and Tibet travelled to gain tutelage under him.

As we return to the events unfolding before us, we see the sexagenarian scholar standing upright; his senses alert. He saw in the fast-approaching evening spots of light accumulate one by one like fireflies in the field. But these were no harbingers of peace. Instead, he knew these to be man-lit torches that foretold of some bad omen. His years of experience had clearly made him distinguish the tempest that was accumulating to break itself on this tranquil oasis.

The uproar of many human voices was gradually growing in intensity like the angry sea threatening to engulf this retreat. Even from this far he sensed the scuffles, abuses and retorts that was violating the genuflections, pleas and reasoning. By now many students and acolytes had left their daily prayers as curious faces peeped from the viharas and prayer-hall. Even in this fading light, Maha Āchārya could read panic in those curious faces as they looked towards the growing unrest.

Suddenly Atiśa's hawk eyes saw a familiar figure detach itself from the dark mass of bodies engaged around the Northern gates. The young monk was approaching him with quickened pace and stumbled few times before he reached the footsteps leading to the open-terrace where Atiśa stood. He could now clearly identify the nervous Tathāgatarakṣita, his bhante (fellow monk), who came running out towards him. There was urgency and fear in the young monk's footsteps that skipped the terrace steps in twos and threes to approach where he stood.

The cool, calm voice of Atiśa greeted the panting monk:

"Evening, bhante! May Lord Buddha give you peace. Now, now; calm down and tell me what brings in the Chedi army to our peaceful doorstep?"

It took a second for Tathāgatarakṣita to get over his shock as to how Maha Āchārya knew about the marauding militia forcing itself inside their estate. But he knew he was standing in front of none other than Atiśa Dīpaṃkara; the dynamic lamp-holder. Nothing escaped his sharp intellect as he knew everything that transpired within the university campus.

Tathāgatarakṣita pointed with his trembling fingers at the source of the upheaval and exclaimed:

"Mahātya! King LakshmiKarna Dev has entered our campus seeking asylum while fleeing the pursuing Magadha army and is now disrespecting his terms of sanctuary. His boisterous army has already forced open our granaries and stores and have started to loot our resources. While few of our younger novices tried to calm them, the belligerent mob had beaten them and are now threatening to raze our lyceum into dust."

For an instant Dīpaṃkara's docile eyes lit up with pain and remorse for the victim and the feeble. His mind went back to the train of thoughts that was fleeting across him as he was peacefully watching the day's end before this pandemonium. How immature these kings are! Brute strength may be the weapon of terror for the powerful, it is peace that will always conquer the hearts of all. He quickly looked at Tathāgatarakṣita and directed him in his gentle yet stern voice:

"Ask our senior monks to go to the mango-grove where King LakshmiKarna has set up his temporary tent. Tell them to invite him and convey my humble request to join us here."

But Tathāgatarakṣita did not get a chance to take the steps; for soon Atiśa saw a procession coming up towards the flight of steps. He recognized the royal Chedi insignia at once soaring among the clustered group of discernible heads. Soon King LakshmiKarna's bilious figure outlined behind his circle of bodyguards; who was followed by some foot soldiers and his ministers; while a handful of sangha seniors came meekly behind in the tail-end of the queue. Atiśa had heard of the sly character of the gluttonous king; so, he was not surprised to see a mixture of shrewd lascivious eyes set in a toad-like contour of the king that clearly betrayed his lust and greed. The king, seeing the young monk cowering in front of him, roared:

"You, there! How dare you defy my orders and not hand over the keys to my general when he asked for them?"

Atiśa's voice addressed the king:

"Apologies your majesty; but my sangha-brother Tathāgatarakṣita was acting on my instructions."

King LakshmiKarna, now suddenly aware of this stranger, looked up and asked in annoyance:

"And who are you?"

The reply came crystal clear:

"I, O king, am a humble monk here at Vikramashila and have taken the responsibility of looking after the lives of who reside within these walls. I am the Maha Āchārya and I welcome you and your small contingent here amidst our peaceful haven"

A moment's pause, and the king's arrogance turned swiftly into stunned reverence as he looked up towards this man in the humble monk's attire as he exclaimed:

"You are Atiśa Dīpaṃkara! Forgive me, I mistook you for an insignificant tutor."

Atiśa smiled, and in his honeyed voice he replied:

"Your Majesty, no living being is insignificant here within these sacred walls. We strive constantly to maintain peace in the name of Lord Buddha and to assist every person to walk with our teachings and actions towards the path of the Enlightened One."

The Chedi king started to reply with irony in his sentence:

"Ahh, yes, I know. Your university here is renowned across four corners of Aryāvarta as the true seat of peace studies ..."

"....and so, your Majesty came to test our tenacity by bringing in his army to our humble congregation.", finished Atiśa, with a hint of wit in his words.

King LakshmiKarna's toad-like face suddenly turned crimson in growing rage. While he stammered to befit a reply to this, he caught the impudent young attendant suppress a smile. How dare he? The king knew how famed this meagre monk's reputation was and so decided to turn his wrath instead on the disobedient junior.

"I, I,...I lost my calm when this disrespectful junior of yours refused sustenance to my hungry army", stammered the king.

Atiśa knew very well why LakshmiKarna had taken sanctuary here. While the king's plan of a guerrilla attack on Magadha had backfired and he was forced to flee from the pursuing enemy, the sly king knew very well that taking sanctuary within these safe walls of Vikramashila would stop their pursuers from entering this hallowed ground. However, the king was wrong in taking up the sangha's peaceful existence as their show of weakness; for as long as Atiśa was in charge, no living being could face injustice within these sacred walls. He looked straight into the eyes of the king who seemed to cringe at the heart-piercing stare of the monk. Without changing his peaceful tone, Atiśa spoke:

"Your Majesty, as Lord Sakyamuni is our witness, let me tell you this: None shall go hungry or empty-handed out of these walls. We quench the thirsty mind with free knowledge; the hungry soul with peace and the stomach with our grains and fruits. Don't you hear the chants reverberating all around?

*Buddham sharanam gachaami*
*Dhammam sharanam gachaami*
*Sangham sharanam gachaami.*

Then tell me this: why are your armies breaking into our store-rooms and granaries when they have already been satiated? Why are your foot soldiers' man-handling our senior monks who have rushed to stop the unruly horde? Why did your personal guards advanced to take Tathāgatarakṣita prisoner when he politely refused your demand for alcohol and meat? Did you ever give it a thought? And to top it all, by instigating all this, you are in fact defying the very rules of sanctuary that you have invoked while taking shelter amidst our serene sanctum"

Alas, these earnest denunciations of the king's spineless act fell to deaf ears. Atiśa saw in vain how LakshmiKarna threw back his head in shameful mirth and roared loudly in unabashed laughter. However hard he tried to reason with the king, LakshmiKarna guffawed his plea as mere harmless words, dismissing it saying he cannot call back his men who needed some distraction.

The senior monk was familiar with King LakshmiKarna's reputation as a bully and tyrannical king. Atiśa was now indeed in a fix. If he did not put a stop to this, right now, LakshmiKarna will end up believing their non-violence way as their weakness. And to that, Atiśa was not at all ready to let his peaceful stance be labelled as cowardice. The reputation of the whole institute was now at stake.

He looked up at the glowing orb setting on the horizon in helplessness and suddenly his mind found the solution. Why did he not think of it before? This would not only put a stop to this rowdy mob but will also ensure no bloodshed within these sanctified enclosures. While the king was busy repeating sardonically the monk's words to the delight of the assembled group, who sycophantly giggled along with the king, Atiśa quickly called Tathāgatarakṣita and hurriedly whispered to him some quick instructions. The king and his retinue failed to see the change in the young monk's expression which turned from fear to confusion and then to wonder and finally to a jubilant smile. He quickly moved out of sight, beckoning the small flock of cowering monks at the end of the queue.

King LakshmiKarna looked up, teary-eyed after so much of laughter, to Atiśa. His mouth, still bursting forth with disgraceful giggle, looked at the calm yet determined face of the senior monk. Maha Āchārya Atiśa Dīpaṃkara waited patiently for the laughter to die down, and then asked, in his discreet tone:

"Your Majesty, I ask you, one last time, will you please refrain your men from defiling our peaceful haven?"

"No, I will not", came the arrogant reply.

"Then you leave me no choice."

"OH, yes, reverend Maha Āchārya! Let us see too how much strength your sangha has that can only hold dhamma in the name of Buddha! Bah, humbugs!". Another bout of shameful heehaws.

Atiśa took all this disgrace in his stoic glance and just raised his hand as if in benediction. This was the signal. King LaksmiKarna Dev saw a serene smile of calmness spread across the monk's face as he raised his hand, as if to bless all around him. And suddenly the vihara reverberated by loud bangs and flashes of light and explosions near the unruly imperial mob.

That very instant bedlam broke loose among the king's men. The assembled royal men were startled by the unexpected sight and sound as smoke engulfed the throng of the impatient Chedi army. The king and his entourage saw their men ran helter-skelter in confusion. These startled onlookers perceived whizzing orbs of glowing sun-like spheres bursting from nowhere in between the gathered militia.

Soon the belligerent soldiers were lost in a cloud of smoke and utmost chaos. The king looked in utter disbelief as his men dashed towards the exit gates as their confused mind was unable to comprehend the origin of these sudden sorcery.

What can this be? Did these Buddhist monks held dark and supernatural forces in their power that could command the elements? How can there be thunder and lightning when no clouds covered the heavens? This bizarre occurrence happening right in front of the king's eyes had completely baffled his senses.

This was perhaps the very first display of the powers of gunpowder on Indian soil. It was only a few days back that Atiśa Dīpaṃkara had just been introduced to this Chinese pyrotechnic marvel. The missionary convoy from Tibet had got few of these wonderful globes as a small token of gift for him with a humble invitation to him to visit their Himalayan kingdom. These 'Orbs of Fire' are but samples of the modern wonder of alchemy that the Tibetan king had sent along with his humble request to grace his court with Maha Āchārya's enigmatic presence. The Tibetan entourage had explained how these spheres were used to amaze the crowd during ritualistic gatherings. Atiśa Dīpaṃkara too was astounded at first during its first display. He had accepted these gifts with gratitude and had never thought till now to use their powers.

However, his mind now was quick to estimate the power of these wonder orbs. He quickly thought of these as the fitting solution to his present predicament. While he contemplated as to how to stop this locust army from pillaging his sangha, his eyes were drawn at the fiery solar ball setting in the West and he remembered those 'Orbs of Fire'.

He had quickly explained his plan to Tathāgatarakṣita who was to pass-down unnoticed from the king's view and assemble his few fellow monks and tell them to install themselves silently in the gathering darkness, each holding out these fantastic orbs. Just when they would see Dīpaṃkara's signal, they would throw these simultaneously around the assembled army without any of them injuring a single man. The plan was to just startle them with the loud bang, the sudden flash and the engulfing smoke. And the plan worked!

King LaksmiKarna Dev, bewildered, scared, lost and flabbergasted at these never-seen-before explosions, turned dumbfounded with just these three words to the Maha Āchārya: "Witchcraft! Help! Please!!"

His men had now fled in fear of the sorcery that just took place within the university premises. They shall never again set foot here. His army gone, the king now looked helpless and powerless in front of this enigmatic man. His mind was still trying to comprehend how tables were turned without even any clash of metal? LaksmiKarna had anticipated the mighty scholar to plead in front of his military strength and accept his superiority. He was almost jubilant thinking of the humiliation of this trivial scholar. His mind was still grappling to come to terms with his sudden turn of fortune. How can this man win? This weak, old, senile scholar whose only strength were words and books? How?

And so, on a beautiful autumnal evening some eleven centuries before, Maha Āchārya Atiśa Dīpaṃkara became part of the legends in the canon of history as he found a solution to disarm men without bloodshed. All that was needed was trust in Lord Buddha, your belief in peace and his dynamic 'Orbs of Fire'.

**Note**: While Atiśa Dīpaṃkara, King LaksmiKarna Dev and Vikramashila University are historical, the character of Tathāgatarakṣita is my own creation. Further, I must admit of lifting this incident from an episode in Saradindu Bandopadhay's historical fiction "Tumi Sondharo

Megh" (inadequately translated, 'You Are the Evening Cloud'). I have taken the liberty of eliminating many characters mentioned in the original novel; adding new ones and setting a dramatic scenario to give it a more fast-paced appeal. While there is a mention of the incident in the novel, I have used my skills of translation and transliteration and combined them with my imaginative skill to give colour to this piece. All deserved credit should go to the novelist for bringing to us this amazing episode. It is my earnest desire to translate, someday, this breath taking historical romance to bring it to a wider readership.

***Som Shubhra Karmakar***

# The Story of Jagadguru Shankaracharya and the Adwaita Philosophy

*Bhagvati Ramakrishnan*

***Who is Bhagvati Ramakrishnan?***

*Bhagvati Ramakrishnan is a postgraduate in English. She is an educationist and started her career as an English and humanities teacher. She has been an examiner for the S.S.C Board and later worked as a moderator for the examinations.*

*Bhagvati has worked with students, writing scripts for plays and directing them. She has also worked on scripts for mono act plays based on history. She has taught history to school students at the S.S.C level. She has a deep interest in Indian history and culture and is in the field of new research.*

*Bhagvati has retired as the Head mistress of a reputed school in Mumbai.*

# The Story of Jagadguru Shankaracharya and the Advaita Philosophy (788 to 820 CE)

I have been bold enough to choose the story of the great Guru, Sri Shankaracharya, of the eighth century, born some one thousand four hundred years ago in this great land of India. Buddhism was already on the decline then and there rose in India this colossus of intellect who brought about a great revival of Hindu thought and philosophy. Of course, whether I've done justice to his greatness, you'll know by the end of this article.

Before I proceed further, I would like to embark on a little story.

Once, after a dip in the pure and holy waters of the Ganga, (It was really pure during those times!) Shankara and his disciples visited the holy shrine of the very famous Kashi Vishwanath temple. As they were returning through the narrow paths of Kashi, they came upon a huge, grimy looking, Chandala who almost blocked their path. He had an odour filled, not so clean bag slung on his shoulder, probably containing some meat. He also had four dogs walking along side. On encountering the Chandala, Shankara entreated him to move away from his path. The Chandala stayed where he was and spoke thus: 'O holy man, what should I move? This body made of flesh and blood or the everlasting aatman? What should I get away from? This body (pointing to himself) from that body? (pointing to Guru Shankara) This Consciousness, from that Consciousness, which are but one?

What is the difference between a Chandala and a high born like you? Your Reality and my Reality are the same. The Chandala had actually spoken about Non-dualism or Oneness of the Aatman. In fact, he had explained the philosophy of Advaita. Shankara was so stunned and pleased with the Chandala's explanation that he fell flat at his feet and prostrated in front of him. He realised this was none other than Lord Shiva. The four dogs were in fact the four Vedas! Lord Shiva blessed Shankara and the Manisha Panchakam, a hymn of five verses explaining the Advaita Philosophy was born.

Now I shall take you back to the beginning of Shankara's story. Down south, at Kalady, in Kerala, there lived a pious Namboodari couple, Shivaguru and Aryamba. They lived by the banks of the Poorna river, a tributary of the Periyar. They were childless and often prayed to Lord Shiva, especially to Lord Vadakunnathan, at Thrissur. In the end, their prayers bore fruit and they were blessed with a baby boy whom they believed was an incarnation of Lord Shiva himself. So they named him Shankara. Shankara was a brilliant child prodigy. He lost his father at a very young age and was brought up by his mother. At the age of eight itself he had mastered the Vedas, the Srimad Bhagavatha and of course the Bhagavad Gita.

Shankara was inclined towards sanyasa right from the young age of eight itself. However, his mother refused to give him permission for the same. One day, the young Shankara was taking a bath in the river Poorna. His mother arrived there and was shocked to see that a crocodile had caught hold of her son! Shankara requested his mother that if at all he had to die, then he would do so as a sanyasi. His mother acceded to his request, and the crocodile immediately gave up its hold and released Shankara! Thus, the world was blessed with a great Guru to be!

Shankara soon set out in search of a Guru. While travelling towards the north, he came upon a learned scholar, Shri Govinda Bhagavadpada. This scholar had the great Shri Shri Gaudia Bhagavadpada, the great Advaitin as his Guru. The learned man enquired about the young sanyasi.

Shankara then answered in verse explaining the Advaita philosophy. The Guru was so impressed that he immediately accepted the young sanyasi as his disciple. Shankara learned many things from his Guru, at the banks of the Narmada, at Omkareshwar. Govindapada then asked Shankara to write a commentary on the Brahmasutras and propagate the Advaitha Philosophy all over the land. The Brahmasutra was an Upanishad, and Shankara became famous for the brilliant commentary that he wrote at the behest of his Guru.

At this juncture, I would like to explain in brief, the ancient wisdom of the Hindu philosophy. The Vedas are four in all and are named as the Rig Veda, the Yajur Veda, the Atharva Veda and the Sama Veda. These Vedas are a timeless corpus of Hindu literature. In fact, they are the pillars of Hindu philosophy.

We also have the Upanishads, which are placed at the end of each of these Vedic texts or in some cases even in the middle. They are called as Vedanta, the essence or the great fountainheads of knowledge. They form the highest and the timeless jewels of wisdom of the Vedas. There are many Upanishads. However, Shankara chose about ten of these Upanishads and wrote brilliant commentaries on them. Some of the Upanishads that he chose are: the Ishopanishad, the Keno Upanishad, the Katopanishad, the Mundakopanishad, the Mandukya Upanishad, the Taitreya Upanishad, the Aitreya Upanishad, the Chandogya Upanishad and the Brihadaranyaka Upanishad.

For a student trying to study and understand Vedanta, Shri Shankara wrote what is known as the Prakarana granthas or the introductory texts. These texts form the stepping-stones to study and understand

Vedanta, which is a philosophy appealing to the intellect. Some of the main Prakarana texts are the Advaitha Anubhuti, Aathma Bodhanam, Kevaloham, Manisha Panchakam, Prashnotra Ratnamala, Sadhana Panchakam, Tathva Bodhanam, Sanyasa Paddadhi, Vedanta Kesari, and Viveka Chudamani.

There are more but those listed are some of the majorly well known Prakarana texts, which later help us to go for higher learning in Vedanta; just as a student entering college from school needs special help for his higher studies. Shankara also wrote some beautiful lyrical hymns or Stotras. The stotras of Shankara include the famous Bhaja govinda Stotra, the Shivanandalahiri, the Annapurna ashtakam, the Harimede, the Dasashloki, the Krishnashtaka, the Manikarnikashtakam, the Gangashtakam, Kanakadhara stotram and the Maya Panchakam. Some of these hymns are as useful as the Prakarana granthas to understand Advaita.

Shankara's Upadesha Sahasri is considered as his most original philosophical work. Here, I must make a special mention of the Drig Drisya Vedanta. It's a very small work and written in such a clear, lucid, logical and dramatic manner that I urge all new students to go for this piece of work to easily or better understand Advaita philosophy. There is a commentary of a commentary and translation into English by none other than the monks of the Ramakrishna Mission. It clearly illustrates the meaning of the Advaita Philosophy.

Now, what Advaita taught, was that all individual souls, called atman are not different from the Ultimate Reality called the Brahman. But our ignorance does not allow us to understand this and makes us feel separate from the Ultimate reality. To propagate Advaita, Shankara engaged in a series of debates with prominent Buddhist and Hindu scholars. Notable among them was his debate with Mandana Mishra who believed in the philosophy of Purna Mimansa. Mimansa was based on ritualistic practices.

Shankara defeated Mandana Mishra in the debate which lasted for many days. Finally, Mandana Mishra accepted the Advaita Philosophy. Shankara then established the Sharada Peetham at Sringeri, in Karnataka, the Dwarka mutt in Gujarat, the Govardhan mutt at Puri in Orissa and the Jyotirmath in Uttarakhand in North India. Shankara also established the Shanmata tradition of Hinduism, which includes

Shaivism, Vaishnavism, Shaktam, Kaumaram, Ganapatyam and Sauram.

The monastic order of those times consisted of trishul or trident holding sanyasis. While Shankara is credited with starting the Dashanami, a new monastic order of a single staff renunciation. The following mutts which have adhered to this tradition are – Bharati – Sringeri school, Saraswati-Kanchi mutt, Thirtha- Dwarka mutt; the other monasteries include Giri, Puri, Vana, Parvata, Sagara, so on and so forth.

All these names are traceable to the Ashrama system of Hinduism and Vedic literature. Adi Shankara had a number of disciples who were scholars in their own right. Famous among them was Padmapada, also called Sanandana who wrote the text Atma Bodha. The other disciples were Sureshwara, Tothaka, Prithvidhara, Bhodendra, Bramhendra who authored their own works on Advaita.

Here, I would like to mention a few words about Tothaka, one of Shankara's disciples. Shankaracharya had met him at Sringeri and accepted him as his disciple. His premonastic name was Giri. The young disciple had a lot of respect and 'Shradha' for his guru, He would offer all the services to his guru like washing his clothes at the river, collecting flowers for his pooja, cleaning up the ashram, so on and so forth. On one such day, Shankara was about to begin his class on Advaita Vedanta. However, Giri was busy with all the regular chores. The Guru waited for his disciple to join the class. At that time, another disciple, Padmapada who was proud of his intellect was annoyed with Giri's late coming. He told the Guru that teaching Giri was the same as teaching a wall as Giri was so dumb. But Guru Shankara was so touched by Giri's sincerity and devotion that he wanted to reward him for it. He mentally blessed and granted Giri complete knowledge of the Shashtras. The enlightened Giri returned to the ashram singing verses in praise of his Guru, just created on the spot, at the spur of the moment. It was in the Tothaka metre made of eight stanzas and later called 'The Thotakashtakam'. Thus, the humble Giri became famous as Thotakacharya. Later, he was made head of the Jyotirmath Peetham, in modern day Uttarakhand.

Every verse of this ashtakam ended thus, '*Bhava shankara deshika me charanam*', meaning 'O Shankara who is the realized master, be my refuge!' Adi Shankara is believed to have left behind his mortal body at the young age of thirty two, at Kedarnath. His disciples last saw him behind the Kedarnath temple, walking on towards the Himalayas, until he was seen no more.

There are many traditional biographies written about this famous Advaita Philosopher. They are called Shankaravijayams. Some of the main ones are, Madhaviya Vijayam authored by Madhavacharya in the 14th century. The Anandagiriya Vijayam by Anandagiri. The Chidvilasiya Vijayam by Chidvilasa. Out of these, the Madhaviya Vijayam is most widely and popularly accepted. Finally, I must admit to using many Indian and Sanskrit words in my article. Any story or article written in English in India, is bound to have a smattering of words from other Indian languages, considering that ours is such a vast country with so many beautiful languages that we absorb and intersperse our own language with it. I would like to pay a tribute to this Great Guru Shankaracharya by ending with these famous quotes that form the essence or gist of the Advaita Philosophy;

*Prajnanam Brahma – Consciousness is Brahma – RigVeda*
*Aham Brahmasmi – I am Brahman – Yajur Veda.*
*Tat Tvam Asi – That thou art. – AtharvaVeda.*
*Ayam Aatma Brahma – This Self is Brahman – AtharvaVeda.*

I conclude this article here and hope it has been interesting and informative to all readers, especially to those who are students of India's glorious history and her philosophy.

***Bhagvati Ramakrishnan***

# The Fierce Child of Patteswaram

*Ankita Chakraborty*

***Who is Ankita Chakraborty?***

*Ankita Chakraborty- Doctoral Research Fellow with focus on South East Asian Studies. Have MPhil degree in Foreign Policy Studies and Masters in International Relations.*

*Also studied Indonesian Language and culture in Semarang State University in Central Java, Indonesia.*

*Author of one self-published book and have also contributed several articles and stories in various websites and also in anthologies for several publishers, also contributed article for Indonesian Embassy in New Delhi E brochure.*

*Have immense interest in Indian History, Indian culture and South East Asian culture and linkages to India.*

# The Fierce Child of Patteswaram

This is a work of a fiction, it's a narration of a very old above 80 years old Meena Amma, who had once served as the caregiver of Royal Price Maduranthagan, Who later had come to be known as Rajendra Chola I, and one of the great King of India who had not only expedite but had also spread India's culture Indochina states or present day South East Asia. Meena Amma had devoted her life serving the little Price, and when He was set out to conquest, she went out of Royal Palace of Patteswaram to live in a small hut in seclusion. She narrates some of her early days and memories with the little Prince's childhood when a surprise happens to her. Story depicts the little Prince kind and tenderness towards every people.

## I
### *Somewhere in Patteswaram*

"I was sitting on the balcony of my tiny mud house, lighten the diyas, whispering the name of my Lord, the Lord Shiva, when I heard some victory possession outside my house, I have no strength left on my leg and I am bend from my shoulder, still I walked hurriedly to see the matter; when my neighbour Sita had stopped me told me, that I should not walk or work much in this age and should rest. I told her, that whenever I heard some victory possession I wish to run to see the glimpses of my little Madura, he may have grown up big now like his father and must have forget me, but I will never forget him, as He is still a child to me, He is like a son to me. I had seen him growing in my hands, fallen asleep in my lap, how I could forget those days and the little child." Sita continued, "it is not your Madura, the possession is for the victory our beloved Raja who had conquered a large part across the ocean and now our country's name will be echoed there."

"Little did she know that I had once served the Royal Palace and nursed the little Prince in my own hand. I was the chief maid to my beloved Queen Thiripuvana Dewi of the Great Chola Dynasty".

"Tears roll down from my eyes as this time also I couldn't get a glimpses of my Prince, or I didn't even get to know if my prince was actually present there, I returned to my room; pour some water over the Shiva Lingam that shines in the corner of my house, and began chanting 'Om Nama Shivay".

I whispered to myself "for others, he is the King, for me he is still the Madura", I bow down to the Shiva Lingam again. "If my Lord wants I can still reunite with my child, I can still touch his tender hands, sing some lullaby for him, and make him asleep, that's the only wish I have before I finally face death, if I can see the Prince for one last time, I will feel that my soul have already reached the abode of Shiva".

"For sometimes I went back to the day when the little Madura was born".

## II
### *The Divine Birth*

The whole palace was lightening up with diyas, for the occasion for Mahashivaratri, and everyone was happy and busy preparing for Puja. The Shiva Stotram, which was reciting by our Royal priests, echoed the whole palaces together gave a divine atmosphere. Our Rani Amma was set her foot on the Shiva, when suddenly she cried in labour pain. I grabbed her and ask other maids to immediately inform others, the Rani Amma is about to give birth, suddenly the whole palace come to standstill, the divine Strotram was stopped, and everyone seemed to be worried.

Rani Amma, who was crying in ardent pain, instructs that the celebration and Strotram should not be stopped, because a blessed child would be born to her.

The Little Prince was born after some time, the atmosphere was totally divine, with Strotram heard in background, the diyas lighten up the palaces and a small tender child was born.

"My Shiva was born" proclaimed the Rani Amma, I took the child in hand, and he looks so divine. Everyone in the palace was happy that day.

## III
### *Juvenile Days*

He was affectionate from childhood, and well behaved and I never had felt that I am a mere maid to the royal Prince, he used to treat me with affectionate and care. I accompanied him to the palace of Patteswaram, where I was in charge of him while Choti Amma Kundavai and Badi Amma Madevi was his guardian. He used to treat all people equally with love and affection. He used to hold my hands and called me "Amma", which melts my heart. I used to see my son in him; I used to see my Lord, the Lord Shiva in him. He is a blessing of Lord Shiva for us and from me.

From his childhood only he had dreams to end the sorrows of all the subjects. He used to run towards me, whenever he saw any sorrows of the subjects and said "you will see, one day there will be no sorrows to any people, everyone will be happy and that day we will sit under that big tree with amma, mami, aachi, you, and we will all read Shiva Puran there".

The Royal child I see, had inborn values and virtues and him. An ardent devotee of Lord Shiva, when he used to chant 'Om Nama Shivay' in his voice, I feel like the Shiva himself had come to bestow His divine blessings on us. The sound of his voice directly touches the heart. Not only he was good in Shastras, but he had excelled in all other art form, an excellent archer and sword fighter, and excellent in Marshall Art, and all form of warfare art, excellent horse rider and elephant rider. Oceans, seas and river fascinate him, he loves to swim a lot. Not even the seniors can beat the little child in Shastra Gyan and yuddha niti. No other strong man in this land I have seen in my life had excelled in military art as well as its contradiction dance and music in his life, like I see my little prince. I feel he was born with some divine blessings of Lord Shiva.

The Shiva Lingam the only expensive possession in my small house was built by my Little Madura, with his little hand at young age, although he is a great King today and remain very busy, I feel him in my Shiva Lingam, the little gentle hands, when he used to build small Shiva Lingam for every person he loves in his childhood. For Dasis like me, such a respect from Little prince was no less than blessing of Lord himself. He used to say, "One day there will be big Shiva Temple right there, from where the Shiva stotram would be heard the miles across the seas".

He had dream to conquer across the ocean, the countries which lies across the ocean, I even can't spell their name. Although my little Madura's dream to conquer, but he never wants to kill the innocents. He was just the kind-hearted boy I have ever seen. For him "The cowards are those, who killed the innocent ones, strong man spread their culture and the name of Shiva". The strong yet powerful message echoed the whole palace of Patteswaram.

## IV
## *Last Wish*

Today when his dream of conquering the land across ocean have come true, my tears are not come to a close, his dream has finally come true, I had so many memories with this little boy, whom I have nursed in my lap. Not only me, the other nurses were also cherishing the memory they had with little prince, for his kindness. We Dasis had taste the respect, which we had never expected. Morning time, the sun has yet to come. A knock was heard from the door.

"Who is it?" asked Meena Amma,

Nothing was heard.

'Ah, who was there in this early morning, Sita? Wait, no strength is there in my leg and waist. "Wait, I am coming," said Meena Amma in a trembling voice.

She come and opened the door

"What you need so early in morning Si…", Meena Amma just looked up and to her surprise it's not Sita, The great King Rajendra, her little Madura.

She can't believe in her eyes.

She stood speechless.

"Meena Amma" voice was heard.

"Maharaj?" asked Meena Amma in trembling voice.

"For the world, I may be Maharaj Rajendra, for you I am still your Madura, why are you living in such a small hut. I ask my ministers to find the whereabouts of you and they find you here."

"I had accomplished my service towards you, Maharaj, I need nothing now, my only wish was to see you once in my life before my journey to Shivaloka, I see you as my son, although I know I am not your caste, I am from lower strata for still, still I am grateful for all the love you bestowed on me."

"Amma, I see people as human, for me you are also mother like, come and stay in palace, for all the service you had given me, I need to repay you back in love and care"

"But…."

"Take it as my order"

"No one has right to disobey you Maharaj. I am ready to come but let me take my priced possession my Shiva with me"

Meena Amma took out the Lingam, from the corner of my room. Tears rolled down from the corner of the Great King Rajendra, he remembered the times in his childhood he makes these lingams for all of his caretakers. He was utterly surprised. In these years, everything has changed, he set out to conquer, vast lands of North, South, and beyond the ocean, the Sinhala Rajya, Sriwijaya, Malayur, Pannai, Nakkavaram and so many lands. But a small gratitude from a Dasi of him, makes him think that love and the small Shiva Lingam is her only priced possession, that can never be conquered or captured.

***Ankita Chakraborty***

# Section VII
# The Delhi Sultanate
## *(1206 CE to 1526CE)*

The Islamic conquests began with capture of Delhi by Mamluk raiders from Turkey in 1206. One could say that this was the beginning of integration of Indian and Islamic civilisations. This was not only a period of synthesis but also to some extent modernisation in technology, Indo-Islamic architecture and the beginnings of Hindi-Urdu as a major language. The Mamluk's ruled for the longest period till about 1290 when the Khalji's took over. It was also known for one of the few female Islamic emperors – Razia Sultana (1236-1240). Ghazi Malik took over Delhi in 1320 and started the Tughlaq dynasty. This was the largest dynasty of all, occupying most of the greater India. The powerful dynasty lasted till 1414 when it was taken over by the Sayyid dynasty for a short period. This also saw the decline of the Sultanate power with resistance from the south in the form of Vijayanagara empire – famed for its emperor Krishnadevaraya who extended his empire well into the north India. The Mewars of Rajasthan also grew into a powerful enemy and ate into the sultanate territory depleting their resources to a large extent. Sayyid's were finally displaced by the Lodi rulers in 1451.

Turkish slaves were trained as fighters by the generals of Mohammad Ghori of the eastern caliphate of Ghor and came to be generally called Mamluks. They moved east and attacked Delhi in 13$^{th}$ century. Famed Qutub Minar construction was initiated by the first Mamluk ruler – Qutub al-Din Aibak but did not last long enough to see the completion. The Khalji's expanded the empire further into India and were known for repelling the Mongol hordes from the north – even after repeated attacks by the fierce Mongols who eventually went on to occupy most of the land up to eastern parts of Europe and knocked on the doors of Rome at one stage. Ala ud-Din Khalji was the most prominent of the rulers who extended the empire into the south India under able generals like Malik Khafur. He was ruthless in his rule and taxed the population heavily and loaded his treasury with such treasures as the famed Kohinoor diamond. He was known to be a tyrant with a streak of insecurity. He slaughtered around 30,000 people in and around Delhi with suspicion of insurrection.

Tughlaq dynasty was the longest and most powerful of the four dynasties during this period. They extended their rule to almost the entire Indian subcontinent and had desires of extending beyond the borders. Mohammad Bin Tughlaq was probably the most prominent one of them and ruled the longest. He is portrayed as cruel and often irrational. His order to move the capital from Delhi to Devagiri in Maharashtra – around 800 miles and renaming it Daulatabad is still used as a stark example of irrational behaviour. This move failed miserably due to shortage of water in the area and caused death of thousands of people – some of them killed by his troops for refusing to move. He then decided to move the capital back to Delhi after a few months. His cruelty meant thousands of citizens decided to stay back or move further south causing the spread of Islam into southern India. He was also responsible for the destruction numerous temples. The rulers who came after that were not as effective and towards the end of 14th century was constantly quarrelling between themselves. Timur (Tamerlane) from Turkey used this opportunity and ransacked Delhi in 1398 killing over 100,000 people and carried away the loot on top of thousands of elephants and carriages, including the famed Kohinoor diamond. The massacre took five days and streets of Delhi was littered with rotting corpses for weeks afterwards. He took the loot over to Samarkand and never looked back.

The destruction of Delhi left a vacuum and was filled by a little known Sayyid rulers who did not last very long. It was soon taken over by the Pashtun tribe of Lodi. Sikandar Lodi expanded the infant empire both east and west. He was also responsible for destruction of many temples, including those of Mathura. The last Lodi emperor, Ibrahim Lodi was weak and easily overrun by Babur and the beginning of the Mughal empire. In fact, Daulat Khan Lodi of Punjab invited Babur to attack Delhi and the battle of Panipat in 1526 was the deciding event.

The wealth of the nation reached its peak during the Sultanate period, for reasons that are beyond the scope of this article. It grew by 80% during the period and became a world power.

# Section VIII
# Mughal Empire
## *(1526CE to 1857CE)*

Conventionally, Babur is ascribed with the founding of the Mughal empire. Babur was a minor chieftain from the mountains of Uzbekistan who faced Ibrahim Lodi in the first battle of Panipat in 1526 and spread over the plains of north-east India. However, it was his grandson, the Akbar the Great who expanded the empire and set forward the Mughal empire. Babur has lineage from both Timur (father's side) and Genghis Khan (from mother's side). Babur was a failure in his native Uzbekistan but managed to occupy Kabul with the help of Ottomans and moved further south towards India. His son, Humayun did not fare much better either. He was exiled into Persia for a brief period and died soon after return to India. It was his son, Akbar who consolidated the empire and went on to rule with a benevolent and cosmopolitan rule earning him the title, Akbar the Great.

Akbar modernised the political rule and encouraged all religions and even initiated his own religion – Din-i-ilahi – tolerant to everyone. During his rule the strength and economy of the empire expanded to greater heights. There was links with many of the foreign nations including European. The trading links as well as cultural links he developed is a story in itself. His reign is considered the golden era of the Indian subcontinent by many with prosperity and relative peace in the land.

Akbar's son was an anathema among the Mughal rulers. He was ineffective, addicted to opium and neglected the rule of the state. The country was under a threat of decline when his son, Shah Jehan came into power in 1628. His reign saw the glory days of Mughal art and architecture with Taj Mahal as the pinnacle of beauty even today. Unfortunately, this caused a drain on the treasury from which a recovery seemed impossible. His eldest son, Dar Shikoh took over when Shah Jahan fell ill in 1658. He was an artist and a dreamer, not a warrior. He had visions of his grandfather, Akbar of synthesis of Hindu and Islamic culture. He was weak and was overthrown by his younger brother Aurangzeb and soon executed rather ignominiously. Even though, Shah Jahan recovered from his illness, Aurangzeb declared him incompetent and imprisoned him in Agra Fort where he died looking at the beautiful Taj Mahal from his window.

Aurangzeb was a controversial figure by all accounts. While he introduced strict Sharia law, he encouraged Hindus, built many temples and employed many Hindus into key positions in his government. His son, Bahadur Shah I repealed all of his father's laws and saw the beginning of the decline of the Mughal empire. It was during the rule of Bahadur Shah Zafar that the glorious empire of the Mughals came to an end.

It did not help when Nader Shah of Iran invaded from the northwest, crossing over an impossible Khyber Pass defeating a huge, but inadequate army of Bahadur Shah, despite being overwhelmed six to one. He then ransacked Delhi slaughtering over 30,000 citizens in one day and went back to Iran with the Mughal treasury in 1739, including the fabled Peacock Throne.

The last years of the era saw the break-up of the empire towards Bengal in the northwest and vassal states in the south. Of note is Hyder Ali in the south and the rulers of Awadh in the north. Najeeb SA (Myth, a double edged sword") has given us a poignant story about Hyder Ali's son, Tipu Sultan. Both Hyder Ali and Tipu Sultan were responsible for defending the south against the onslaught of the British and probably were one of the last states the British occupied. Tipu's rule has drawn both praise and criticisms over the years. Mr Najeeb has done a wonderful job in explaining the man and his rule and I must thank him for clarifying many of the mis-conceptions.

Seema Srivastava delves into the shenanigans involving the loss of two of the royal assets of the last Mughal ruler, Bahadur Shah Zafar. Coming from an expert in history, this piece is an embodiment of detail. It is an extensively researched article trying to trace the whereabouts of the Crown and the throne of Bahadur Shah Zafar.

Neeti Parti, ("Takht ya Taboot") an educationist deals with a lesser known son of Shah Jahan – Murad Baksh, who was the governor of Gujarat during Shah Jahan's rule. He sides with Aurangzeb and falls prey to his tactics finally to be imprisoned and executed. The tale of his life and eventual disappearance is not in the mainstream reading and makes it interesting. The story is more of Aurangzeb's cunning than gullibility of Murad Baksh.

The final piece in this section is the harrowing tale of the Nawab of Bengal, Siraj-ud-Daulah. Ranjana Mazumdar gives a detailed portrayal of the trials and tribulations of the man and the ruler who was a thorn in the flesh of the vestiges of Mughal empire and one who thwarted the onslaught of the British only to fail in the blood bath of the Battle of Plassey. He was eventually captured by the traitorous Mir Jafar and executed as part of a deal with the British.

# Myth is a Double-edged Sword

*Najeeb S A*

***Who is Najeeb S A?***

*Najeeb S.A. is a Sydney based freelance writer, whose essays and short stories have appeared in popular publications in India and UAE (where he lived for almost three decades). He has been a regular with Impish Lass since its inception.*

## Myth is a Double-edged Sword

A Muslim ruler who had provided annual grants to no fewer than 156 temples, who had helped restore the tradition of worship in "Sringeri Mutt" (established by the famed Hindu theologian Adi Shankara) after the 'Marathas' had invaded it, who had offered copious financial assistance to the Kanchi temple during its construction, who had retained the temple town of Srirangapatna as his capital throughout his reign, whose army was mostly composed of 'Shudras', who had supported building the first-ever church in Mysore – how could he be projected as a religious bigot?

Tipu Sultan lived and died in an entirely different era when the lexicon held dissimilar insinuations than those of the present, when territorial expansions were the order of the day and engaging rebellions against authority, swiftly and decisively, were accepted norms of statesmanship.

Admittedly, those at the receiving end of Tipu's indignation faced executions, mass migration and forced conversions that were intended to be harbingers for others who might be plotting insurgency. Such deportments, however brutal it would appear now, prevailed in the subcontinent from the medieval times. How fair then will be judging a Gothic ruler's actions that fell within the propriety of kingship that prevailed over centuries against modern statutes of governance?

Apparently, there is a concoction in the interpretation of history here, because facts and derivatives in history books do not add up.

The death of Aurangzeb in 1707 marked the decline of the Mughal Empire. The new geo-politics that emerged soon resulted in the birth of disjointed states like Awadh, Bengal and Hyderabad, yet allowing an underlying power vacuum benefiting foreign traders who had by now started becoming explicit factors in the power equation of the region. Manipulative as it was, East India Company leveraged this situation to their advantage gaining strong footholds wherever there was a hiatus. In the South, 'Company' could not find their way as easily as they did in the North, because in Hyder Ali Khan they also met their match, nearly as motivated and ambitious as themselves. Khan is said to have sought the help of French military experts in organizing his army and formed a corps of European mercenaries as gunners in his artillery. In 1766 with his eye on a port for the transfer of French weapons to fight the British, he invaded the smaller states in the Malabar belt effectively employing the combination of a Mughal model mobile cavalry and infantry armed with fire-locks and bayonets. The British tried to curb his regional expansions by joining hands with the Marathas and the Nizam of Hyderabad, but Khan played his cards close to his chest winning over both the British allies to his camp.

When Tipu was born in 1750, though Khan and his wife Fatima Fakhr Unnisa had named him Fath Ali, they began addressing him after the local saint Tipu Mastan Aulia, as "Tipu", which later gained acceptance as his real name.

At the end of 1782 when Khan died from a terminal back ailment, Tipu succeeded him. But the son also inherited what historians call as the 'Second Anglo-Mysore War' from his father. The period of transition from one ruler to another has always been vulnerable when the new ruler's potency would be tested either by those with grievances or who wanted to disassociate themselves from his authority. Kautilya's (who had engineered the transfer of power from the Nanda dynasty to the Mauryas in 322 BCE) 'Arthashastra' (the Science of Material Gain) categorically states that if such challenges were not met promptly and conclusively, a ruler's control over his kingdom would soon erode. Tipu quelled the revolts of the Christians in Dakshina (South) Kannada who were allies of the colonialists and the Coorgis of Kodagu who were waging a protracted guerrilla war against his authority.

History is vindictive to Tipu. As a matter of fact, he was a radical in more ways than one. He banned the consumption of alcohol in his state, not on religious grounds, but ethical dictum and also in consideration of the well-being of his subjects. He introduced sericulture. He confiscated the property of the upper castes and distributed it among the untouchables. He also sowed the first seeds Capitalism at a time when feudalism was the accepted norm in the social calendar in the whole country. In 1796, he wrote to the Hyderabad Chief Minister, with blatant undertones of what is in the cards, should the 'Company' be allowed to pave inroads unchecked into the subcontinent. Tipu cannot be reduced into a run of the mill entry in the historic journal, because he represented a manifold of traditions and conventions.

Yet, why is he regarded as a tyrant by some and a hero by others? Why is it that while Emperor Asoka, who is also known to have committed the same kind of brutality during his invasion of 'Kalinga', as Tipu is accused of, celebrated as "the great" (the emperor's insignia is the centrepiece adorning the National flag) and Tipu a persecutor? Is it because, among other things, some of his administrative reforms, like renaming of townships with Hindu names to those in Farsi, and re-calibrating existing weights and measures to suit historical Islamic concepts, bore religious preferences? As a matter of fact, the culprits here are, partly Tipu's colonial enemies and partly the mind-set of a predominant section of the population. While all the other native rulers accepted the Company's call for placing a political agent in their courts without much hesitation, both the father and the son refused to give in to such clandestine manoeuvres by the latter. This was perhaps the final strand they were looking for to eliminate Tipu, who had by now become a thorn in their trading path, they could no longer afford to ignore. In 1798 with the arrival of a new spiteful governor-general in

Calcutta, in the form of the Earl of Mornington, the heat was turned on Tipu. With the Marathas and the Nizam already against him, Tipu comes across as a brave-heart who lead the fourth Mysore war from the front and gallantly embraced death in the battlefield. However, some quarters in Britain, who had considered Tipu as a maverick and perhaps even a bohemian, doubted the legitimacy of Mornington's actions. In response, the governor-general and his cohorts justified their attack on Mysore by portraying both the father and the son as belligerents and oppressors of their subjects. That's how the myth of Tipu, as we know it, was created. Over the next two centuries, as the slogans of patriotism and self-rule dug deep into nationalist sentiments, Tipu became the first Muslim martyr. History has witnessed many parallel instances even as far back as 73-71 BC, when most Roman historians were keen to squash the memory of the legendary Spartacus who fought against the mighty Roman empire and very nearly brought it to its knees, and thwart him from earning a larger-than-life stature.

Apparently in Tipu's case, the character of the myth was defined by the need of the hour to suit the interests of those who created it. The irony though is, only a few were gullible then, but more are now, without ever realizing it.

- Najeeb S.A.

# The Journey and Ultimate Location of Two State Regalias

*Seema Srivastava*

***Who is Seema Srivastava?***

*Seema Srivastava, studied at the Universities of Allahabad, Cambridge, and did her doctorate from University of Oxford, UK (2005). She has been the ICCR-Kings College Professor at Kings College, London, UK (2011), and subsequently Fellow, King's College, London (2012). She was Fellow (Reader) at the Centre for Contemporary Studies, Nehru Memorial Museum & Library, Teen Murti, New Delhi (2005-8). Earlier, (1985-1988), she was involved in researching, editing LettersTo Chief Ministers by Jawaharlal Nehru.' (OUP, Delhi). Her book 'The Famine Experience: Power, Politics and Art of Survival,' is being published; and her doctoral thesis /has been digitised by the University of Oxford, UK, therefore, in the public domain. She has considerable teaching experience in higher academia within and outside of India, authored several articles for leading newspapers as Hindustan Times, and for academic journals and contributed chapters to UGC projects .*

*Seema Srivastava, a British Council scholar, has several international awards to her credit including twice awarded the Foreign and CommonWealth Award which enabled her to pursue her doctorate at the University of Oxford, Uk and avail a year's Fellowship at the Centre For South Asian Studies, University of Cambridge, UK. She has presented numerous papers/seminars at international apex international academic institutions and within India.*

*She fills forms, writes complaints, petitions, opens bank accounts for those unable to do so; provides information of welfare schemes. This could easily be an NGO, but the author prefers to help informally, unconditionally. She is deeply attachéd to Gender and environmental issues to gardening; earlier she played the sitar.*

## The Journey and Ultimate Location of Two State Regalias

In recent times books, essays, monographs, print and electronic media discussions, have focused on the continuing controversies relating to the famous diamond 'Kohinoor;' its history, mythology, anecdotes, the circumstances in which this valuable diamond reached England; subsequent attempts made by India to retrieve it, Whether it can be retrieved by India ? In the process other priceless Indian jewels sharing similar fate, have not received the deserved attention.

'Moments in history', as wars, rebellions, natural disasters, wreak tremendous all round destruction. Thus the invasions of Mahmud Ghazni, Mohammad Ghori, Genghis Khan, Timurlang, Ahmad Shah Abdali, outstand in sub-continental history not only for the, human holocaust wreaked, but also for denuding India of its wealth and destroying much of its artistic, legacy. Mahumd Ghazni plundered Somnath temple sixteen times, and carried away camel loads of wealth, jewels to central Asia. In 1739, Nadir Shah drenched Delhi in blood bath, plundered it's wealth, treasures, carrying away the famous Peacock throne of emperor Shahjehan, as a war trophy to Persia, where it is still remains. In more contemporary times the world witnessed the horrific, needless destruction of centuries old world heritage, the *Bamiyan Buddhas,* in the war which still tragically rages in Afghanistan.

Thus destruction of the artistic heritage of the vanquished was/is thus an integral feature of warfare, and was true of the watershed 1857 war. It was the greatest anti-imperial mobilization in Asia, marked not only for the tremendous destruction of demographic, material life, but also witnessed one of worst systematic destruction of the Indian artistic, aesthetic legacy in the war theater. Sources indicate that the popular clamour amongst Britons in India and the metropolitan was for vengefulness, for teaching Indians long, sore, lasting lessons. Even the intellectual fraternity, humanists Charles Dickens, poet Martin Tupper called for 'razing Delhi to the ground,' and some even for 'extermination of the Indian race.' At almost all epicenters of this war, destruction of palaces, *havelis,* edifices, forts, places of worship, followed re-inscription of colonial authority; these were symbols embodying collective history of 1857-8, and likely encourage future nationalist mobilization, therefore to be erased. Even the destruction of the historic Red fort in Delhi was contemplated, but shelved for strategic reasons. Whilst there is empirical evidence, literature, on the destruction of palaces, edifices, forts, not much attention has been accorded to the, the loot, plunder, destruction of the priceless jewels, gems, paintings, libraries, artefacts, much of which embodied history, and also symbolized the grandeur of the fallen mughal dynasty. No chronicle was maintained of such invaluable, exquisite jewels, gems, artistic legacy of the mughals monarchy, its nobility, *rajas, zamindars*. But some evidence, anecdotes, of the loot that transpired in the epicenters of the war give an impression of the huge artistic legacy lost forever.

Thus anecdotally we are aware of the quiet intrigue amongst officers of a particular regiment, who shipped the invaluable 'famous Pink Diamond,' also known as Agra diamond to England. The diamond belonged to the Raja of Agra whom Babur defeated in war. His son Humayun occupied the city, but spared the lives of Royal family. In gratitude the *Raja's* family offered caches of jewels including the famous Pink Agra diamond to Humayun. This diamond then passed on to subsequent mughal emperors, many of whom including Bhadaur Shah 11 were depicted wearing it in their turban. In 1857 the diamond was taken away by British officers from the vanquished Bahadur Shah 11. The officers did not hand over the diamond to the government but decided to smuggle it to England. They made a horse swallow the 'Pink diamond,' and shipped the horse with themselves to England. Inevitably the horse fell sick and had to be killed, the precious diamond extricated from its stomach, and smuggled home. It was sold, resold, and in 1896, the fifth Marquess of Donegall, sold it to the famous London jeweler Edwin Streeter.

Here, I digress to Jhansi, to give readers an indication of the colossal scale of the loot, destruction of the Indian artistic legacy in the war theatre. A Maharashtrian Pandit, Vishnu Bhatt Godse, travelled from Maharashtra to central India, and caught in the 1857 war. He found refuge, employ in Jhansi, as a temple priest, and witnessed the post war the loot, destruction of life and property following the fall of Jhansi. This he chronicled in his travelogue memoirs, entitled *'MajahaPravasa,* in vernacular (Marathi), on condition that his memoirs be published only after his death; such was his fear of government reprisal and concern for his family's safety. Translated into Hindi and English, *'MajhaPravasa'* likened Jhansi, following its fall to colonizers, to a 'vast burning ground,' depicted citizens as filled with fear hiding themselves in 'dark corners,' but hunted down by the 'demons' and indiscriminately slaughtered.

Not only did the English soldiers kill those who came in their way, but they broke into houses and hunted people out hidden in barns, rafters and obscure dark corners. They explored the innermost recesses of the temples and filled them with dead bodies of priests and worshippers. They took the greatest toll in weavers locality where they killed some women also. At the sight of white soldiers people tried to hide in haystacks in their courtyards), but the pitiless demons did not leave them alone. They set the haystack on fire and hundreds were burnt alive.

Most interesting are his detailed description of the systematic looting of valuables for five whole days. According to him the loot was organized, and had an apartheid structure to it. On the first day only the white British soldiers were permitted to loot valuables only. Jewelery, gold, silver, precious gems, works of art, and money; the focus of the soldiers were the prosperous merchants and farmers homes. The *Rani's* palace was completely ransacked, not sparing even the state library' Thousands of books and manuscripts were wrecked, destroyed. Later in the day the *sepoys* of the Madras regiment were given permission to loot utensils of brass, copper, bronze; they looted pots, pans, eating plates and water jugs, including water wheel anything that was made of metal. On the second day, the *sepoys* of the Hyderabad contingent looted textile-silk, cotton, wool- from beds, mattresses, to saris and shirts, *kurtas, dhotis* to curtains, sheets, blankets, carpets,. Godse observes 'that they found their richest haul in the wealthy merchants houses and stores.' The looter bundled all that they could on elephant backs. On the third day *sepoys* of another regiment looted grains, cereals ghee, oil, cardmoms and other eatables; and carried away their loot in the tins and jars. Till three days soldiers were permitted to loot specific items, but the fourth day was for general looting. They took away chairs, charpoys, bedsteads, water wheels, even ropes with which people pulled water from wells were not spared. He noted that people were denunded of almost all worldly possessions '.... There was nothing left to eat, we drank plenty of water and went to sleep.'

Delhi being the capital of mughals, was politically and symbolically very significant. On it's fate depended the fate of the British empire in India; thus Delhi's three month's long siege has been extensively documented, written upon. Almost accounts underline that the outbreak of the 'mutiny,' signaled loot, arson, killings in and around Delhi on a scale that numbed the souls. Post re-inscription of colonial authority in Delhi, there followed extensive street fighting, loot lasting days, which was general and there was no system or organization to it. Whilst the fate of much of looted, stolen treasures is not known,what can be inferred from discussions is the magnitude and pervasiveness of the loot, no doubt much of it was immediately sold, liquidated. But by whom and to whom? Who profited, and who lost?

We may never have answers to these questions. But this essay, delineates the fate of two state regalias that escaped loot and duly auctioned;- the last reigning emperor of Hindustan, Bahadur Shah Zafar's, famous bejeweled skull crown shaped like a cap, and his two gem embedded, ornamental throne chairs, so richly covered with perforated gilt. Several pictures of emperor Bahadur Shah depict him wearing the skull crown cap, and seated on these ornamental chairs. These state regalia's embodied much history, denoted the power of the faded, vanquished mughal monarchy, therefore of political, emotional significance.

The main sources on which this essay relies, besides some empirical evidence, are the several accounts of the three months siege of Delhi, in particular the testimony of Capt. Robert.Tytler of the 38 NI, posted in Delhi, when the '*sepoys* mutinied,' with such intense fury. His wife3, Harriet Tytler, nee Earle (1828-1907), was the 'lone lady,' survivor of the siege of Delhi. She was then eight months pregnant, along with two other children, aged two and four, and French maid Mary; they lived through, hence eye witnesses survivors of the Delhi siege.

Primary reliance therefore is on the first hand eye witness account of this imperially inclined, class conscious, educated lady. Fifty years later, Harriet, retrospectively chronicled 'those thrilling events,' their numerous adventures, tribulations, the human, material holocaust, which 'may interest others,' acknowledged as '..amongst the best sources of life on the Ridge during the Delhi siege, and on the fate of the city after the fall,'

Harriet's '*An Englishwoman in India. The Memoirs Of Harriet Tytler, 1828-1858;* (OUP, 1986),' a fascinating, gripping text, very rich in sociological, historical, gender detail, and distinct for its discussions of the aesthetic aspects of India that goes beyond the national; the extensive loot, the auction of priceless treasures that followed the fall of Delhi to the colonizers. Yet this significant text remains under researched, under publicized, reflected in that it was fully published only in 1986, eighty years after it was written, due to the exertions of its scholarly editor, Antony Sattin, whose comments have also richly contributed to this essay.

Harriet, recounts that in the hot blazing months of May, June and till September, Tytler's, were stationed on the sprawling ridge, far away from the British camp, yet in the protected zone. They lived not in a fort, residency, or even an entrenchment, but literally herded in a strong wooden cart with only a straw roofing; and, subsequently during monsoons in a round shaped stone 'bell of arms,' in which arms, ammunition were stored. This structure became a tourist attraction post 1857, because an officers family had lived in it. Harriet informs us of her rough social life during the siege; that officers often visited them, discussed developments, issues, 'even maters of the heart,' with this 'angel of the British camp,' as Harriet was referred. She was thus privy to much war related information, and such informal information she incorporates in her text, unique for it's imperial, but feminine constitution, and also the rich information it gives; for highlighting India's aesthetic grandeur, the loot, destruction of India's artistic legacy, such discussion going beyond the national.

Europeans including Tytlers, and Gardner's, fled Delhi in late evening of 11 May 1857, for the safety of nearest stations- Meerut, Karnal, Ambala. They witnessed the cantonment aflame, their bunglow's along with all their worldly possessions-buggy's hoses, guns, ornaments, furniture, paintings gutted. But Harriet mourns most for loss of assets having emotional value, 'a dead child's lock of hair, Robert's collections of curios, treasures, his chemical projects, her own paintings, sketches. Harriet's jewellery used to be kept in Quarter Guard for safe custody, and this their trusted servant, Thakur Singh's uncle, possessed himself of, '..and also our last month's pay which came in late,' on Saturday night. Robert asked his servant to keep it till Monday morning. 'Thereby we lost that too.' Tytler's *durzee* (tailor) and *bhistee* (water carrier), left for their home in Kanpur 'in our buggy,' and the table servants became *sowars* and killed 'in fighting us.' 'A just outcome for their treachery and ingratitude.' Such discussion demonstrates the depths of popular, subaltern participation in 1857 war, and that Indians from homogenous servility, split into rebels and sympathizers of the colonizers. Harriet noted the lawlessness, and that the looters did not spare even the dead. On their return journey to Delhi from Alipore, she grieved for 'many of our fine, tall, handsome men lying somewhat swollen by the heat ... and stark naked, for every camp follower robbed them of their gold, silver jewels, and the last comer of the clothes... leaving the poor fellows just as God had made them.' 'such handsome, splendid specimen of high caste Hindus.'

Loot was confined not only to jewels, gems, clothes, but also cash. In the war theatre specially targeted were the government treasuries, 'eleven of the seventeen treasuries being carried away.' by rebels. Robert was in charge of the treasure chest in Delhi, and despite it being heavily guarded, Rs.12, 000, disappeared from the tumbrels under his charge. After much careful investigation the money was thankfully found. Such loot of treasures, cash, was difficult to conceal, and so were often hidden including in pits dug deep, or walled up. In one instance, a *sepoy* was observed lying in a room on his *charpoy,* busily digging a hole on the wall with his bayonet, where he had hidden his looted treasure. He was arrested, brought to Capt. Robert Tytler. In his defense he pleaded that 'we looked upon this money as loot money and are entitled to some of it.' Increase in such incidents compelled a change in guarding strategy- the guards were changed every week to thwart theft, loot. But despite such precautions in Meerut men of the 60 Rifles, were caught playing the same tricks with government treasury there. Harriet suggests that much loot went undetected, and that looter's new found riches reflected in their wives dressing. 'And had you seen their wives come to the Church, dressed up n most gorgeous silks made by the English millner Mrs. Ludlam, at Meerut and with French bonnets that would never have costed less than three pounds, you would have known that they never bought them from their husband's pay. None of their officers wives could approach them in style or magnificence… '

However, Delhi being the capital of mughals, there was some recovery of jewels, gems, which was turned over to the British army officers 'the dreaded prize agents,' duly auctioned, and shipped abroad.– mainly to Britain, Europe, Nepal. The cycle of selling, reselling looted treasures continued, therefore now difficult to trace. But those sold to institutions, and in institutional custody can still be traced, located. Regrettably, government of free India, has done virtually nothing to trace, retrieve, or even make list of such priceless legacy, still existent within and outside of India. This essay makes a small contribution in this direction in tracing the journey, ultimate location of two historically significant crown jewels--emperor Bahadur Shah's skull crown cap and his two ornate, gem embed throne chairs, which escaped loot but were duly auctioned.

Evidence indicates that from early on in the 1857 war, one of the most pressing problems confronting the rebels was the raising of finances. Whilst the colonizers had no dearth of finances, much of it flowing UK, Mauritius, other parts of the empire and from the peaceful parts of India, the rebels had no sources of funding either from within or outside of India. There was little money even for feeding, upkeep of troops, payment of salary, for caps gun, powder, other ammunition, the *sepoys* not even paid their salary, which meant that their domestic lives were negatively impacted. There are anecdotes of *sepoys* confronting the *badhshah,* over non-payment of salary, but the '*Badshah*,' angrily disowned responsibility to pay salary, reminding them that he neither instigated, nor invited them to rebellion, and was but their reluctant leader. In another instance, a frustrated *Badshah* attempted to resolve the problem by offering that his *zenana* part with their jewels, but his tormentors in honor refused this offer. But tired, tormented by persistent recriminations, quarrels, the frail eighty three year old emperor of Hindustan in sheer frustration is said to have angrily thrown his *masnad* (a long, deep pillow), on which he reposed, at his tormentors. This was said to be full of priceless jewels, gems, diamonds, the value of such treasures so great that it was considered enough to resolve the immediate financial needs of the rebel army. What became of the treasures, we may never know.

Financial problems magnified, caused dissensions; and exploiting this problem, the colonizers planted, circulated exaggerated, reports of strife, dissensions, including communal, amongst rebels, no doubt to create suspicions, mistrust and disorientation; hoping that rumours of widening strife amongst rebels would be 'the kill Kenny cats,' that would implode the rebels cause from within.

Following the successful lifting of the Delhi siege, Harriet, children, did not leave for Kolkatta or England as other ladies did. She took up residence in Delhi's *Lalquila* (Red Fort), complex in the *Diwan-i-Am.* Herein she lived in the airy, spacious grand room belonging to queen Kamraum Shah, the emperor's mother, who according to Harriet 'lived and died here.' Harriet, had lived for three months amidst booming guns, falling shells, the cries of humans and animals alike, considered her life in Kamrun Shah's*mahal*, as devoid of excitement, thrill; utilized '..those dull and dreary days' by doing service to her county, watched developments; explored the Red fort complex, unearthing, conserving war related evidence for posterity- valuable jewels, artefacts, including a length of silk on which verses of the Koran were artistically embroidered with gold thread, and belonged to the Emperor. Realizing the importance of visual evidence, she learnt photography from war photographer Felice Beato, and surgeon John Murray; and with her husband toured the war zone, photographed five hundred war sites, sketching, painting heroic deeds, specific battles sites detailing what actually transpired there, therefore important war testimonies.

Certain policies, developments dismayed, anguished her. Harriet was shocked by orders for the systematic destruction of Delhi. She recalls that for one week or more the British artillery was stationed in large mosque, and unrelentingly bombarded the handsome Delhi edifices, mansions, *haveli's* homes of the Indian rajas, nobility, merchants, landlords, even palaces, residences within the Red fort were not spared, taking refuge in colonial community ire, dissatisfaction over continued existence of much of Indian cultural heritage especially of religious, cultural sites as these embodied indigenous beliefs, values, and show cased Indian artistry, craftsmanship, capabilities, some embodied tales from 1857 war, including from the Indian perspective.. In a climate of ultra nationalism that prevailed colonizers leveraged Indian cultural artistic heritage as an issue for erasing tales of heroism, gallantry of the rebels and their fleeting authority over Delhi. Destruction of these therefore became priority. In the process colonizers reasserted their authority and erasing symbols Indian pride, nationalism,. The destruction of Indian artistic heritage was therefore political in nature, and in no small measure encouraged by inflammatory colonial rhetoric.

As individual protest was useless she got the canvas from bazaar, and by a stroke of luck, brushes, paints, from famous British painter Mr. Rood. Harriet set to work, sketching, painting the *mahals,* so that the aesthetic grandeur amidst which the mughal royalty lived, was preserved for future; thus single handedly contributing to cross cultural-creativity, the wider knowledge economy. Thus, such activities enhance our understandings of feminine contribution towards the construction, maintenance of the empire, foregrounding, re-conceptualizing gender in India.

Following the fall of Delhi, Tytler's, along with numerous others, entered Delhi with the victorious British army. Harriet was struck by the 'deathly silence' the 'stillness' of Delhi, which she describes a previously thriving, bustling, densely populated city, but presently deserted, 'a vertible city of the dead.' To unwind, exhausted, Tommy Atkins embarked on a spree of loot arson, breaking of liquor cellars, drunkenness. Mayhem ensued for days, generating safety concerns. It meant that military alertness, was lowered. There were instances of Indian women 'of doubtful reputation,' enticing the soldiery with wine, liquor, and when sufficiently drunk slitting their throat. More than a dozen British soldiers were thus killed. These were dangerous developments, and government ordered that all liquor and wine bottles be destroyed, even though wine was sorely short and required in Hospitals, but saving a few lives at the cost of thousands, was not feasible.

To stem the widespread loot of shops, homes of the prosperous, siphoning off of jewels, other valuables, government, prohibited looting either by men or officers of the British army; but Harriet protested, indicts this prohibition. She was appalled by the discrimination, unfairness in distribution of war spoils as ' a great and unjust mistake;'

given that the proceeds from the auction were distributed in percentage points as per rank,- from Generals to the ordinary soldiers. Thus Gen. Wilson, the British Army Chief during 1857, got the largest and best share of the loot, which she resents. Harriet doubted Gen. Wilson's military capabilities, projects him as weak, indecisive, prone to terrible procrastinations. He 'wavered' at critical times; therefore considered him undeserving of the largess. She informs that it were the junior officers like Col. Baird Smith, (Engineer), Maj. Tombs, Brig. Nicolson, who led from the front, took decisions, decisive actions on behalf of the General. Tommy Atkins toiled, bore the brunt of the hardships, yet got the least share,- hardly enough to buy him 'baccy for a month.' She argued, that the men had fought hard by the side of their officers, therefore entitled to 'and take all they could get,' believed, 'it a wise policy and a just one' to allow soldiers to loot, or everyone apportioned an equal share. .

Despite prohibition, the loot of Delhi 'continued for several days,' much being 'spirited away.' In one instance two Gurkhas carrying two large bags full of riches, jewels, were accosted by an officer who ordered them to 'give it up.' At once their hands clasped their *kookries* (Gurkhas knives), showing what they meant; they respectfully said "Sahib, we do not mean to do any such thing. We have fought hard for it and we mean to keep it.' The officer knew that further protestation was useless, dangerous, for the 'Gurkhas were daring fellows not to be trifled with.' The officer prudently let them go. In another instance two Sikhs in a state of undress were carrying bags with similar loot when an officer intercepted them "You give up that treasure to the prize agent or I will report you to your commanding officer,' which he did, as the men did not obey him. A parade was ordered for the whole regiment to appear in undress which they did. But they looked so like each other that the officer who reported them, could not identify the delinquents. So the *sepoys* got off with their loot, an approving Harriet informs. Further she believed that officers had little moral authority to prohibit sepoys looting, as she knew officer's 'who did loot and made a good thing of their looting in the palaces,' such looting winked at by their superiors. Amongst officers she singles out Capt. William Hodson, infamous for so cruelly slaughtering the emperor's two sons and grandsons, 'as a tremendous looter.'

But the little that was recovered was handed over to the army, duly auctioned by the 'dreaded prize agents.'She interestingly details the officially sanctioned auction whose proceedings she got a good view of, from the *Diawn-i-Am.* She describes the venue, arrangements, method of auctioning, demonstrating her exceptional observational powers for detail. According to her, the auction was held under a large marquee in the *diwan –i- Khas,* converted into the officer's mess since colonizers re-established their authority in Delhi. The auction overflowed with precious jewels, gems, other valuables, much of it belonging to the royal family, mughal nobility, *rajas, nawabs, zaminadars,* landords. Royal treasures included crown jewels, gems, bejeweled swords, draggers, knives, ladies ornaments-neckleces, bangles, bracelets, anklets, broaches,beautiful filigree ornaments, elaborate Kashmiri shawls, golden kincobs, silks, Persian carpets, ornamental tables, chairs, paintings, chandliers, and other items. Auction of these royal jewels infact, signified the sorry end even of the mughal nominal rule.

Harriet, however, does not inform us the composition of the bidders, whether it was an entirely European affair or Indians participated?; and if so, their class, status, region? But she does confirm that though her husband did not loot, he went for the auction. Robert Tytler, born and for most bred in India, was one of the few remaining British officers who could read, write, speak Hindustani fluently. He had a deep knowledge, appreciation of Oriental cultures, arts, craftsmanship, much of such knowledge no doubt inherited from his father, the famous surgeon Tytler, who championed the cause Oriental languages over English medium education, whilst lord Macaulay espoused English language, and ultimately prevailed. Robert Tytler, was equally fascinated by sciences, experimented in chemical projects, including of making gold in collaboration with Mansoor Ali, the *Subedar- major*, who headed the Court martial of the eighty rebel *sepoys* in Meerut on 9 May 1857. This 'gold' making' project had successfully concluded, but for one last remaining test, disrupted by the outbreak of 1857 war.

At the auction, Harriet informs, Robert purchased many 'rare, beautiful objects,' but does not elaborate or list these; but she mentions that Robert purchased the emperor's famous bejeweled skull cap crown 'for a very large sum'. The skull cap crown was of pure twenty four carat gold, 16.4 cm.in height and 7.7 cm in width, and its top was adorned with beautiful feathers, that added to the majesty and height of the crown. The base from where the emperor tied his turban, was embedded with turquoise, emeralds, rubies, diamonds, pearls. Besides, he also purchased the emperor's famed ornate, gem embedded, gilted, two throne chairs.

Tytler's, returned to Britain in late 1860, economically weak, having lost almost all their material possession, apart from their little cottage in Musoorie, in the 1857 war. To overcome the financial crunch Robert decided to raise money by selling the emperor's bejeweled skull crown cap. Aware of its historical value, significance, Robert offered it first to her majesty Queen Empress Victoria, who quoted a mere five hundred pounds for it, but promised a 'fine appointment,' on Robert's return to India. Harriet informs us that London's Bond Street jeweler offered them a much higher price, a thousand pounds for the crown, and Oxford Museum offered a thousand pound just for the cap without a single jewel. But Robert, had struck a deal with no less than the queen empress, remained 'very loyal,' to this bargain. Infact, to the treasure of the skull cap, he also added the two gem embedded, gilt perforated throne chairs, hoping to be remunerated generously.

But when for several months they did not hear from the palace, an anxious Robert, contacted Sir Charles Wood, Secretary of State for India, later Count Halifax. What awaited them stunned, shocked, dismayed Tytler's. Harriet informs that by 'some strange calculation ,'the two invaluable chairs were included in the price of the skull cap crown. Such valuables gone for a mere five hundred pounds!.Robert knew he was swindled, was very bitter, but kept quiet, afraid of making himself 'unpopular,' with the powers that be, and that protest might jeopardize the promised 'fine appointment,' in India. So without protest, he let the matter drop. But his more forthright, dynamic wife vented her ire, felt 'greatly cheated,''swindled,'by the bargain. Harriet, could not comprehend,'how her majesty, for the sake of 'filthy lucre,' deprive 'a poor military man,' who she was aware 'had lost his all in the mutiny.' But after much careful analysis, introspection of the issue, she attributed such cunning, deceit, to Sir Charles Wood, concluding 'I am now satisfied that Sir Charles Wood did it all.' and felt '..sure that he either kept the Chairs himself or presented them to the Queen in his own name.'

What actually transpired we may never know, as no written records exist that detail the transaction between the Queen Empress and Robert Tytler. However, Antony Sattin, who edited Harriet's memoirs, informs us that Sir Charles did write to the Prince Consort on 19 January 1861 'I cannot at all make out what the owner would expect of them(the Chairs), and the skull cap.' Resting all speculation, I would vouch for Harriet's version, that these valuables, worth thousands of pounds went for the throw away price of a mere five hundred pounds! We also know that the bejeweled skull cap crown, and the two throne Chairs, are still in preserve of Windsor Castle collection.

So, what did Robert Tytler receive for his loyalty? The promised 'fine appointment,' was also a huge let down for Tytler's. Robert was made the Superintendent of the Andaman Islands, where a penal colony had been established. It was 'an appointment worth having as a Major, but not Colonel,' but Robert accepted it anyway 'hoping that by doing so it might lead to something better.' In untamed Andamans the Tytler's health suffered as the climate did not suit them. Whilst a dejected, ailing, Robert, was embroiled in controversies, Harriet, overcoming social isolation, health barriers immersed herself in projects including evangelical. She oversaw the construction of a road built by prison labour, and virtually ran the affairs of the Governors's house, founded the first Church 'Christ's Church' there, and attempted to tame, civilize (read as prosleytise, Christianize), 'truly savage;' aborigines; such exertions quietly challenging Clapham conceptualizations of gendered division of work, roles, which typecasted, marginalized, confined, ladies primarily to the domestic sphere. Her labors earned her the deep admiration of many, including Robert, who acknowledged his wife's diverse, rich contributions to competitive state building; honoured her by naming the highest peak in Andamands 'Mount Harriet,' which still remains.

# Takht, Ya Taboot

*Neeti Parti*

***Who is Neeti Parti?***

*Neeti Parti, is an educationist a prize winning poetess and writer, an artist, an editor and a trainer. She is Deputy Director, Academic Practices, of a renowned chain of schools and has more than forty schools in India under her charge. As Founder Principal of a well reputed Senior Secondary School, she received the 'Award for Best Upcoming School in Uttar Pradesh'.*

*She has contributed to more than twenty five anthologies and edited three. She is an RJ and a television artist. She is a keen environmentalist and is associated with many 'green causes.*

*She paints and loves photography. She lives in Gurgaon, India and believes that 'When the Universe smiles, a child is born, nature's greatest tribute to itself!'*


# Takht, Ya Taboot


François Bernier was a French physician and traveller. He was briefly personal physician to Mughal prince Dara Shikoh , the eldest son of the Mughal emperor Shah Jahan, and after Dara Shikoh's demise, was attached to the court of the Mughal emperor Aurangzeb, for around 12 years during his stay in India. Said he, **"Not only was the crown to be gained by victory alone, but in case of defeat life was certain to be forfeited."**

Although each classic period Mughal ruler was the son of his predecessor, the succession was by no means one of primogeniture—the eldest did not necessarily win his father's throne. In the Mughal world, every son had an equal share in his father's patrimony, and all males within a ruling group had a right to succeed to the throne, creating an open-ended system. There were often fierce battles among the princes when a ruler died. The rule of succession could be summed up by the Persian phrase **Takht, ya taboot!**

On 16th September 1657, Shah Jahan fell ill. Physicians tried all remedies but in vain. His legs swelled up, his fever rose, and he was in great pain. His life was despaired for. He could not attend Durbar or make a public appearance, setting off rumors that he had died.

Shah Jahan had four sons. Dara Shikoh, forty-two (his favourite and the one he had formally nominated to be the successor) was with him in Delhi. Shah Shuja, forty-one, was in Bengal. Aurangzeb, thirty-nine was in the Deccan and Murad, thirty-three was in Gujarat.

*This is the lesser known story of his youngest son Murad.....*

Murad, son of Shah Jahan and Mumtaz Mahal had been born in the hill fort of Rohtas during Shah Jahan's rebellion against Jahangir. He was a great soldier but had little wisdom. He could not plan anything beyond his amusements, drinking, singing and dancing.

According to Bernier, Murad was generous and polite and boasted that he had no secrets. He despised cabinet intrigues and wanted to be known for the strength of his sword. He was full of courage and if that courage had been under the guidance of a little more discretion, he could have won the war of succession.

When Shah Shuja, the second son, heard the news of Shah Jahan in Bengal, he claimed that Dara Shikoh, the eldest son had killed his father. He proclaimed himself emperor, had the khutbah read and coins struck in his name. Murad, the youngest son in Gujarat followed suit, first in a secret enthronement, then, two weeks later, in a public ceremony. Murad's astrologers told him that 20th November 1657 was a precious day and too rare to be missed, so Murad declared himself Emperor in the presence of a few amirs. His public accession was on 5th December. The khutba was read out and coins struck in his name. He even sent an ambassador to Persia to announce his accession.

To take over Shah Jahan's empire, Aurangzeb, Shah Shuja and Murad entered into an agreement. They would divide the empire among themselves after eliminating Dara Shikoh. Aurangzeb, unlike Murad and Shah Shuja had not declared himself an emperor. As he moved to Agra, he maintained that he was not a rebel but a dutiful son anxious about his father's welfare and one with the historic obligation to defend the faith. So, at Dipalpur Lake, Aurangzeb was joined by Murad. Together they decided to proceed and deal with Dara Shikoh.

On the other side, Dara Shikoh's plan was to keep in check Murad and Aurangzeb as they advanced. For this, he sent two armies towards Ujjain. He then decided to deal with Shah Shuja in the east (Later Shuja was defeated in the Battle of Khajwa. On the run, he was killed by the King of Arakan). After having done so, he decided that he would wheel his armies to the south to crush Aurangzeb and Murad.

Dara Shikoh had made his plan strategically without considering the emotions of a father. He was unaware that Shah Jahan had given secret orders to the army heading towards Aurangzeb and Murad not to engage in battle with his sons unless compelled. He wanted Dara to win but did not want his other sons to lose, at least not their lives.

The armies of Dara Shikoh met Aurangzeb and Murad in Dharmat and were defeated. When Shah Jahan came to know of this, he suggested that Aurangzeb and Murad be allowed to visit him at the Agra Fort for him to arrange peace. It was an unrealistic plea as Aurangzeb would not withdraw in peace and negotiate away what he had won by the sword.

The battle of succession would only cease with a clear cut winner. There was no way to avoid a war with Dara Shikoh on one side and Aurangzeb and Murad on the other. Dara Shikoh prepared for battle. Shah Jahan bade his favourite son a fond farewell and held him in a long tender embrace before letting him go. Then he prayed for Dara's victory and safety. He would never see Dara again.

The battle ground would be Samogarh, thirteen kilometers east of Agra. The battle was fierce. At a point when Dara was under heavy attack and made an easy target atop an elephant, he was advised to get down and mount a horse (not an uncommon act in a war). This seemed like abandonment to his army which was in panic. A sudden victory flourish was opportunistically sounded by Aurangzeb's band and Dara's army took to its heels. The battle had lasted only three hours and Dara lost some 10,000 men. Dara had to flee (He was hunted down and mercilessly executed later).

Prince Murad had received many arrow wounds on his face and body during the battle at Samogarh. Aurangzeb applied the salve of praise and compliment and wiped away the tears and blood from Murad's face. He credited Murad for the day's victory and declared it the first day of his reign.

Shah Jahan responded to the rout of his son Dara Shikoh and the unfortunate turn of events by sending the celebrated sword Alamgir and many presents to Aurangzeb and invited him to parley in Agra. Fearing a trap, Aurangzeb refused to go. It thus came to be that the issue between father and son had to be settled with cannon and musket. After an initial battle Aurangzeb realized that the Agra Fort was too strong and would take too long to bring down, so he cut off its water supply from the Yamuna. For three days Shah Jahan held out, then with thousands of inmates of the citadel in torment without water in the summer heat, he surrendered. Aurangzeb's son Muhammad was sent in to take the Fort. Aurangzeb ordered the confinement of the emperor Shah Jahan to his apartments, cutting him off totally from the outside world. He never went to meet his father. He did not even attend his funeral eight years later.

Murad was nowhere in the picture. He had been relegated to the background after a brief moment of limelight in Samogarh. Aurangzeb had no further use of him. He could be done away with. Murad resented this. He had been strung along to believe by Aurangzeb that once he, Murad was successfully placed on the throne, Aurangzeb would retire to a religious life. Aurangzeb, it is said, used to address Murad as 'Badshahji'. He had promised him an empire to rule. In reality, Aurangzeb had in his hour of need fawned over Murad, and Murad, impetuous and gullible, had fallen for the fake sweetness of his brother.

As Aurangzeb's power and prestige grew by the hour, Murad's stature shrank by the same measure. Murad felt cheated but he did not have the strength or resolve to challenge Aurangzeb militarily. To show his displeasure, he stopped visiting Aurangzeb. When the two brothers set out towards Delhi in pursuit of Dara, who had fled there with his family, Murad stayed a few kilometers behind his brother. Aurangzeb did not want to close in on his brother Dara without eliminating the threat from Murad. So, he set about in his usual crafty manner to lay a trap by sending beguiling messages to Murad to lull his suspicions.

At Mathura the trap was sprung. One day, when Murad was returning from a hunt and passing by Aurangzeb's camp, he was induced by an attendant bribed by Aurangzeb to stop by. He was received with cordiality and the brothers feasted together. Murad was liberally plied with wine and invited to rest in an adjoining tent with a slave girl to serve him. Soon Murad was fast asleep. Only his personal guard remained. Aurangzeb called him on a false pretext and his men entered Murad's tent and bound his feet in golden fetters – ironically as a tribute to his princely status! Murad woke up and began to curse Aurangzeb for breaking his word of making him emperor pledged on the Koran - to which Aurangzeb replied that he was doing everything for his (Murad's) good and for the good of the state! To insult him further, Murad was dispatched before dawn, on an elephant to Delhi in a covered howdah - the kind used by harem women!

Murad was subsequently shifted and confined in Gwalior Fort. But Murad alive, even if in confinement, was a threat to Aurangzeb. Murad spent nearly three years in prison before Aurangzeb contrived a means to liquidate him under the cover of judicial propriety, which was his preferred means of political murder. A son of Ali Naqi, an amir had been slain in Gujarat by Murad in a rage. He was persuaded to file a complaint against Murad in the courts and to insist on enforcing the Islamic law of blood for blood. Aurangzeb directed the Kazi of Gwalior to carry out the judgement. Sentenced to death, Murad was executed in December 1661 and his corpse buried in the Traitor's Cemetery in Gwalior Fort.

Said Aurangzeb about him, "In regard to Prince Murad Baksh, a man of good qualities and an excellent soldier, I am innocent of his death. It was due to the demands of justice. Nor was he fit to reign, for he was heretic, as I have ascertained since his death. If God made me an emperor, it was from no other cause than that I had been ever a faithful defender of the Koran. Against my design and my will, which was to live as a poor fakir, I was exalted above other men, because that just Lord, who raises the meek and abases the haughty had so determined."

# Siraj ud-Daulah – The Betrayed Nawab

*Ranjana Majumdar*

***Who is Ranjana Majumdar?***

*Ranjana Majumdar, MA, BEd, a resident of Mumbai, India, has been in the teaching profession for the last 27years. She has served as 'Resource Person' for English at state level for teachers of English. She is an ex-Moderator for English of Maharashtra State Board HSC Examinations. She is also the Editor of guide-book of English subject for Std XI of Maharashtra State Board.*

*She has presented 'Academic Papers' at State level as well as at the International Level of English Teachers Association. She is an active member of all India English Teachers Association (AINET) and Mumbai English Educators Team (MEET). She has presided over as a judge in various literary competitions at District and Ward level of Maharashtra.*

*She is a recipient of 'Best Teacher' award, twice.*

*She has contributed in anthologies as a writer and she is also a columnist in newspaper.*

## Siraj ud-Daulah – The Betrayed Nawab

As a lover of history and my ardent desire made me pay a visit to the magnificent Hazarduari palace (1000 doors) in Murshidabad, West Bengal. It was built in the nineteenth century, by the then Nawab but now a museum under the archaeological department. I stepped into the museum with a guide. Here articles used by all the Nawabs and their courtiers are preserved. I had an eerie feeling. The years rolled back, mentally I flipped through the pages of the history book as the guide started his narration, a story of intrigues, hypocrisy and betrayal.

I was transported to the last period of Nawab Alivardi Khan's reign. Bengal province was once upon a time one of the most prosperous provinces in India. Murshidabad was its capital. Nawab Alivardi Khan was the most powerful ruler of Bengal, Bihar and Orissa during 1740-1756. Here I was in the year 1733, Siraj ud-Daulah, his first grandson took birth.

The throne in the museum made me picturize the Nawab sitting on the throne in his Durbar hall, his uncontainable excitement at the news of the birth of his grandson Siraj to his daughter Amina Begum and son-in-law Zainuddin Ahmad Khan. The Nawab had three daughters, without a male heir. Out of his three daughters, only Amina Begum had given birth to a son. So, the Nawab doted upon his grandson, Siraj ud-Daulah. I could visualize the jubilant Nawab's declaration in his court," Siraj should be imparted the best education. Mahamantri, appoint the best teachers for him. Train him also in military arts and administration."

This adoration and indulgence didn't go down well with Ghaseti Begun, the eldest daughter of Nawab Alivardi Khan. She harboured jealousy against Siraj. She fretted and fumed ferociously.

When Siraj was 13 years old he not only rescued his captured grandmother Sharfunnisa from the hands of the Marathas but also together with his grandfather drove the Marathas out of Bengal. The widespread massacre of human lives in this war and the tragic death of his brother and nephew devastated the Nawab physically and mentally. He had a premonition of death. In May 1752 he announced that his grandson Siraj will be the next Nawab of Bengal, Bihar and Orissa after his death.

In the midst of unrest and discontent in the state, Siraj's personal life went for a sea - change. A Hindu girl named Rajkunwari was forcibly bought as a slave and brought to the palace. She wanted to live as a free being and not as a slave. In her accidental encounter with Siraj, she pleaded for the same and Siraj conceded but in-house politics didn't honour Siraj's promise to her. She was kept with Siraj's grandmother, Sharfunnisa Begum. Gradually he became attracted to her beauty, her melodious voice and her sweet nature. One day Siraj expressed his desire to his grandmother Sharfunnisa to give Rajkunwar's hand in marriage to him. His grandmother could not but agree. Rajkunwar became Lutfunnisa through her conversion to Muslim faith. Out of his three wives Lutfunnisa was Siraj's beloved, his principal consort and constant companion in good as well as adverse days. Later she gave birth to their daughter Zohra, an apple of Siraj's eyes.

Life in the palace continued as per the pattern of a Nawab's life. Nawab Alivardi Khan died on 17th April 1756 after 16 years of sensational rule. In his deathbed he had advised Siraj to suppress strongly all rebellions, not to yield to the pressure of the East India Company and to pay whole - hearted attention to the welfare of the subjects of the provinces under his rule.

Siraj ascended the throne at the age of 23. He received immediate hostility from his maternal aunt Ghaseti Begum, Mir Jafar, the paymaster and his cousin Shaukat Jung. They started conspiring against him. People once loyal to Alivardi Khan turned hypocrites. Trade and commerce were gradually declining in once a prosperous state. Siraj was well aware of the conspiracy in the court. His first and swift move was against his aunt, Ghaseti begum. He overpowered Ghaseti begum by seizing her Motijheel palace in Murshidabad and also her huge wealth which was the cause of her power and strength. He also kept her in confinement. Thereafter he made drastic changes in his administration. He transferred the post of the Bakshi (paymaster) from Mir Jafar to his trusted man Mir Madan. Siraj's another trusted man Mohanlal was made Peshkar of his Dewan Khana. Mohanlal exercised great power in the administration. Mohanlal, a Hindu elevated to a high position greatly offended the Muslim nobility, especially Mir Jafar who was originally the head of army, the highest position, second to the Nawab. Mir Jafar took it as an insult to him. On losing the post of paymaster Mir Jafar became a strong rival of Siraj, his arch-rival. Next Siraj sent his army to suppress his cousin, Shaukat Jung, the Governor of Purnia who eventually died in the battlefield due to a mishap.

On the other side the East India Company as a trading company under Lord Clive started exercising their powers in Bengal, the richest state in India. They misused the trade concession obtained for Bengal from the Mughal Emperor. The Nawabs of Bengal were nominally subordinate to the Mughal Empire. The East India Company started free trade without paying taxes to the Government. It was a huge loss of revenue for the Bengal Government. Nawab Siraj ud-Daulah warned them but they did not pay heed and continued their practice. At the same time, they started fortifying their commercial settlements and factories in Cossimbazar. Next, they started interfering in the country's internal affairs for protection of their commercial monopoly in Bengal. This angered Nawab Siraj ud-Daulah. He ordered the company to stop interfering in his Government's affairs, to stop their fortifications and to pay their taxes. The company did not accede to his demand. Siraj ud-Daulah was well aware of the British interest in colonization, their dominance in Bengal to establish their empire. When he heard of their capture of Fort William in Bengal, he rushed there with his soldiers, defeated the English and captured Fort William and Cossimbazaar. The British officials were arrested and kept in a very small hole known at that time as Black hole. Out of 43 officials, only 23 survived, rest died due to suffocation. The British Government criticized the brutality of Indian rulers.

Following this Black Hole tragedy, a huge force under Colonel Robert Clive and Admiral Watson reached Calcutta from Madras Presidency and recaptured the British settlements in Bengal. The British next attacked Chandernagore, a French settlement. This infuriated Nawab Siraj ud-Daulah further. A great discontent arose, and a deep distrust set in between the British and Nawab Siraj ud-Daulah.

In June 1756, Siraj gauged a possible attack from the Afghans in North and the Marathas in the West. Besides these enemies, he was riddled with conspiracy in his court, masterminded by Mir Jafar. Jagat Seth, the richest businessman in India and other traders of Bengal were unhappy with Siraj which was not so during Alivardi Khan's reign. In his court was William Watts appointed by Lord Clive as company representative. He kept Clive abreast of the conspiracy. The main conspirators in his court were Mir Jafar and Rai Durlabh who instigated other merchants, even the officers in the army. The other conspirators were Yar Lutuf khan, Jagat Seth and Ominchund who was Siraj's most trusted servant. Clive took this golden opportunity to manipulate the adverse condition in the state and overthrow Siraj to establish finally the East India Company in Bengal.

Siraj could apprehend the possibility of a conspiracy against him by the Britishers with Mir Jafar and others. As a result, Siraj started secret negotiation with Jean Law, chief of the French factory at Cossimbazar and De Buddy.

The English resorted to vigorous political and secret activities to overthrow Nawab Siraj ud-Daulah and reinstate a puppet in his place. Their first and easy target was the greedy Mir Jafar, the commander-in-chief of the Nawab's army. Clive could lure him with the throne of Murshidabad as Nawab of Bengal if he supported the British in the battlefield. A treaty was drawn up between the British and Mir Jafar to make him the Nawab in exchange of support to the British in the battlefield and compensating them with large sums of money for the attack on Calcutta by Siraj ud-Daulah. Ominchund was also bribed by Lord Clive with a false agreement of handsome payment. After conspiring with Mir Jafar, Jagat Seth, Rai Durlabh, Yar Lutuf khan and other dissatisfied courtiers, Clive finalized his plans and on 14th June, he sent a declaration of war to Siraj ud-Daulah. The irony was that, that the success of the English was decided before the war was fought.

To gain a better understanding of the famous battle and also to feel it in my skin, I reached the battlefield of Plassey by Hazarduari express train. Once a mangrove is now maintained as a memorial. With a bleeding heart I listened to the tragic tale of the famous battle of Plassey. The English forces under Robert Clive and Charles Watson marched towards Murshidabad. At 1.00 p.m. on 23rd June the British force reached the battlefield of Plassey. They were quick enough to occupy the mango grove there called Laksha Bagh. The Nawab's army was already stationed there, a day before. The army lay behind earthen entrenchments. A French detachment under Jean Law reached Plassey to support Siraj.

Siraj with strong determination faced his enemies in the field of Plassey (anglicised version of Palashi) on the island of Cossimbazar, 30 miles south of Murshidabad on the riverbanks of the Bhagirathi, a distributary of the Ganges. Nawab Siraj ud-Dualah had placed a large division of his army under Mir Jafar and Rai Durlabh. Mir Jafar, Rai Durlabh and Yar Lutuf Khan were present with their troops near the battlefield but did not bother to participate actively in the battle. A heavy cannonade ensued from both warring sides. Mohanlal and Mir Madan fought valiantly. When Siraj was sure to win with his huge force, a tragedy occurred. Mir Madan, the faithful commander of Siraj's army was struck by a cannon ball. He died fighting valiantly. This cannon is still there in the palace. It is known as Mir Madan cannon. It was a gift from Dutch Govt to Nawab Alivardi Khan.

Mir Jafar turned a deaf ear to an utterly helpless Siraj's pleas to save the honour of the country though he had vowed on the holy Quran to stand by the Nawab. He remained inactive with a large division of the army under him. Rather he advised the Nawab to stop the fighting as the British troops had retreated for the night. It was a ploy of the British. The Nawab trusting Mir Jafar ordered his army to ceasefire. As his army was retreating, the British attacked. The soldiers were caught unaware. The Nawab, a 23 year old youth fought valiantly. Mohanlal wanted to carry on the war and had advised Siraj not to take the decision of retreat which will be fatal for the Nawab. Siraj could not pay heed to Mohanlal's caution. He became frightened when his army started running away from the battlefield. Deceived by cruel fate he mounted on a swift - moving camel and fled to his palace with his faithful guards. Siraj ud-Daulah's army with 50,000 soldiers,40 cannons and 10 war elephants were defeated by only 3000 soldiers of Colonel Robert Clive due to the non- cooperation of the conspirators. The battle ended in 11 hours. Nawab Siraj ud-Daulah, the last independent Nawab of Bengal, lost the battle of Plassey to the British East India company. On 23rd June 1757 this land was the witness to the last sunset of independent Bengal, the first fight for independence.

A huge monument inscribed with names of Nawab Siraj ud-Daulah, Mir Madan and Mohanlal stands tall in this battle ground. A set of three obelisks of martyrs Mir Madan, Nauwe Singh Hazari and Bahadur Khan were erected here. Siraj's statue erected in the same place made me feel proud not only of his great valour but also of his fight for his motherland.

On 24th July 1757 at midnight, Nawab Siraj ud-Daulah, fled in disguise from his Hirajheel palace in Murshidabad with his beloved wife and four year old daughter, Zohra. He was escorted by his loyal bodyguard Gulam Hussain. Nearby was the Bhagirathi river. Here at Bhagwangola riverbank, he hired a boat and continued his flight. He sought refuge from a Pirzada Dana Shah, a fakir who was once upon a time punished by Siraj. Though he was granted shelter cordially, he was eventually betrayed by this man. His disguise had a flaw. His clothes were simple but the Nawabi shoes which he had forgotten to change gave away his identity. Mir Kasim Ali Khan, son-in-law of Mir Jafar was in pursuit of Siraj. As soon as he received the news of Siraj's whereabout, he captured Siraj and paraded a chained Siraj with his companions in a cow cart down to Zafraganj palace of Mir Jafar in Murshidabad. What a humiliation!

Here Siraj was handed over to Miran, son of Mir Jafar. Miran threw him into the prison at Zafraganj palace, named after Mir Jafar, who ordered to kill Siraj. Miran offered a reward to anyone who would kill him. Only Muhammadi Beg who was brought up from infancy by Alivardi Khan agreed to conduct the deplorable act for the greed of money. At midnight on 2nd July 1757, Siraj was hacked to death and beheaded-a blood-curdling scene indeed! His headless trunk was laid hanging from the back of an elephant and paraded in the streets of Murshidabad. On receiving the tragic news, Siraj's mother Amina Begum ran out in a dishevelled state and fell at the feet of the elephant, wailing. One can imagine what a heart-wrenching, woeful sight it was! The mute spectators to this inhuman act were his devastated mother, his beloved wife and his loyal subjects. Tears welled up in my eyes to imagine such an appalling sight. When I saw the sword with which Siraj was hacked to death, in the museum, it sent shivers down my spine, a chilling experience.

After killing Siraj, Mir Jafar and his son Miran entered Siraj's palace and looted all his jewels and treasure. Lutfunnisa and her daughter were confined in the Jinjira palace in Dhaka for 7 years. Later she was freed and brought back to Murshidabad. Nawab Siraj ud-Daulah's Hirajeel palace in Murshidabad is no more in existence but Jinjira palace is still there. The British East India Company sanctioned a pension for her. Mir Jafar became the Nawab of Bengal, a puppet ruler of the British. Clive, the most efficient and most corrupted British officer made a huge fortune for himself and Britain by looting the rich treasure of the Nawab.

I proceeded to Khushbag, the graveyard of Nawab Siraj-ud-daulah's family. It was originally a rose garden built by Alivardi Khan. Later he was buried here. Siraj's grave beside his grandfather was a smaller one. The reason is that his mutilated body had to be stitched to place it in the grave-an excruciating pain swept over me.

The battle of Plassey is known in history as a bloodbath never seen before. Ghaseti begum though a conspirator was not spared. Miran killed her by drowning her in the Bhagirathi river. In one year, 34 members of Siraj's family were killed and buried here in Khushbag including his mother and grandmother. Lutfunnisa who spent her last days in a hut here, was buried beside her beloved husband. A story runs that people heard a wailing sound and smell of perfume from the graveyard. It is said that she used to sprinkle perfume at Siraj's grave and cried. I bowed in respect to their immortal love.

I didn't forget to visit Jafarganj palace of Mir Jafar where Siraj was brutally killed. The dilapidated gate is the only remain of the palace. It is called Namak Haram deori, a traitor's door.

The conspirators too had a miserable death. Mir Jafar being afflicted with leprosy was deserted in the forest by his family and died there subsequently. His son Miran was killed by the Britishers. Mir Qasim died in penury. Muhammadi Beg, the hacker of Siraj became insane, later drowned himself and died. On not receiving any money from Clive, Omnichund and Yar latif Khan died a madman. Rai Durlabh and Jagat Seth were killed by Mir Qasim. Dana Shahi was killed by the British for betraying Siraj. They believed a betrayer would one day betray them too. In Britain, Lord Clive, on his return was charged with corruption by the British government for looting in Bengal. He was jailed for seven years. Utterly penniless, he committed suicide. William Watts and Charles Watson too had a miserable death. So, all the conspirators were paid back in their own coin.

Today Mir Jafar's ninth generation is suffering due to his treachery. Mir Jafar is called Clive's donkey by locals. People spit on his grave. As per the information from the locals of Murshidabad the present generation doesn't use the word 'Jafar' in their children's name. Everywhere they are targeted and humiliated though they are educated and lead a respectable life. Some of them left Murshidabad due to this extreme humiliation. On the other hand, Siraj's ninth generation leads a respectable life in Dhaka, Bangladesh. Siraj too must be resting in peace in his grave when India became free from colonial rule.

Eventually I bid goodbye to Murshidabad with a heavy heart.

History repeats itself. Isn't history witness to such heinous, ignoble acts?

***Ranjana Majumdar***

# Section IX
# Marathas
## *(1527CE to 1818CE)*

The Maratha supremacy lasted from 1527 till 1818 AD with the defeat of Peshwa Bhaji Rao. The empire did not come into existence till Chhatrapati Shivaji ascended the throne in 17th century. The Great Marathas along with the Vijayanagar kings in the south and the Nawab's of Bengal in the west formed the bane of the last remnants of the Mughal empire and caused the eventual demise of the empire. The Marathas continued to be a thorn in the side of the British empire for a considerable time after that.

Once Shivaji was crowned an emperor – Chhatrapati – he continued his expansion and fought many wars against the sultanates of Bijapur and Golconda as well as the Mughals and the British. He ruled from the fort city of Raigad and instilled the strength of Hinduism and Sanskrit into the culture. He replaced Persian with Marathi as the court language and brought back many of the ancient practices back into fore. His death was followed by controversies regarding ascension.

At the death of Shivaji, ten year old Rajaram was crowned instead of Sambhaji. His rule lasted only three months as Sambhaji came to power by capturing the Raigad fort and dethroning the young Rajaram. The throne eventually passed on to the Peshwas (Minister) in 1720 with the ascent of Peshwa Baji Rao. The Peshwas expanded the empire north and south and at its peak, in the middle of 18th century, they covered most of the India and extended up to Kabul in Afghanistan. There were several wars with the Mughals and lost the third Mughal-Maratha war in 1707. The Maratha rule came to an end in 1818 with the defeat of the last ruler – Peshwa Baji Rao II.

Dr Aparna Bagwe brings out the story of Chhatrapati Sambhaji, the eldest son of Shivaji in a sensitive manner and in some detail going through his childhood and eventual ascent to throne and the rule of Maratha empire as a Chhatrapati.

# Celebrating the Life of Chhatrapati Sambhaji Maharaj

*Dr Aparna Bagwe*

***Who is Dr Aparna Bagwe?***

*Dr. Aparna Bagwe has a Ph.D. in Applied Biology and, till October 2018, was a senior Scientist with the Tata Memorial Centre, Mumbai. She has a flair for writing, excels at editing, is passionate about nature and wildlife photography, and has travelled extensively within and outside the country. She used to be an active blogger on Rediffiland, and, in recent years, her writing has appeared in her Centre's house magazine, in newsletters and websites of professional societies, and on several online literary platforms. She has won several awards for her writing as well as photography in online literary and photography groups respectively. Some of her poems have been included in three anthologies published over the past year. She is presently an Administrator of the Asian Literary Society.*

# Celebrating the Life of Chhatrapati Sambhaji Maharaj

The big celebrations at the birth of the first son of Chhatrapati Shivaji Raje Bhonsle were so different from the deathly pall that accompanied his death at the hands of the mighty Mughal Emperor Aurangzeb, when he – Chhatrapati Sambhaji Maharaj, was less than 32 years old and had ruled over the great Maratha empire for only nine years.

I can see it all in my mind's eye today, as though I was there. I must have been there in a previous life, for I have always felt a bond – an inexplicable closeness to my hero Sambhaji Raje Bhonsle that is beyond explanation. Let me relate to you all that I recall of his tragic life story.

My hero Sambhaji was born on $14^{th}$ May 1657 at Purandar fort. He was the eldest son of Chhatrapati Shivaji Maharaj and Saibai, the first of Shivaji's eight wives. Lest you get judgemental, let me tell you that in those days, alliances of marriage were the norm in a bid to bring various clans close to each other within the empire. Blood and marital relationships forged thus ensured that they would be united against the common enemy, who in those days were the Mughals.

Saibai passed away when little Sambhaji was just two years old, and his grandmother the Queen Mother, Jijabai (mother of Chhatrapati Shivaji Maharaj) took on the task of looking after her grandson. Sambhaji received tutelage under the famed teacher Keshav Bhatta who taught the young prince about politics, and Sanskrit. The young Sambhaji turned out to be a voracious reader and read widely from tomes of those times. He could read, write and speak Marathi, Hindi and Sanskrit. He even wrote poetry and authored three books including one on the science of politics. He also was a keen lover of music and appreciated the nuances of various music gharanas.

After Saibai's untimely death, the mantle of queenship had been taken up by Shivaji's second wife Soyrabai who was a very ambitious and conniving woman. The son born much later to Soyrabai and Chhatrapati Shivaji Maharaj, Rajaram, was much younger than Sambhaji, who looked after his young half-brother with great fondness. However, Soyrabai looked upon Sambhaji as a threat to her own son Rajaram, whom she wanted to make the next ruler of the Maratha empire. The half-sisters of Sambhaji and Rajaram, Ambikabai, Deepabai, Ranubai and Kamlabai were no threat as they had been married off at a young age into reputed Maratha sardar families.

Sambhaji was very open minded and had no hesitation in befriending those who were good to him and had helped him. Thus, in his youth he became a close friend of Akbar - the youngest son of the Mughal Emperor Aurangzeb. Their friendship transcended differences due to religion and their parents' rivalry, but their closeness was misused by the connivers in the Maratha court to malign Sambhaji. Over the years, he became a victim of palace intrigues and a lot of false canards were deliberately spread about him, his supposedly debauched life and his closeness to the Mughals.

The true fact was very different, and this was proved after his father Chhatrapati Shivaji Maharaj's untimely death. Sambhaji, being the eldest son, ascended the throne of the great Maratha empire and was coronated at Panhala on 20th July 1680 immediately after his father's death. His grand, official coronation as Chhatrapati Sambhaji Maharaj took place at the Maratha capital - Raigad fort on 16th January 1681.

It is said that Sambhaji took after his father Shivaji and had great acumen as a king, was a master tactician, and was a well-loved leader of the Mawlas – the brave foot soldiers of the Maratha empire. He had the respect and love of the Mawlas who looked upon him as the natural heir of their revered Chhatrapati Shivaji Maharaj. Like his father, Chhatrapati Sambhaji Maharaj too was very protective of womenfolk, and thus naturally drew deep respect from the soldiers as well as commoners in the Maratha empire.

During the nine years of his rule, Sambhaji came to be known as a great warrior and a just king. He fought 180 battles during his reign and won all of them. He strengthened the Maratha empire, and forged many new alliances with other principalities who opposed Mughal rule. In those days, the Marathas were under threat from all sides, and had to fight against not just the Mughals but the Siddis closer to home, as well as the Portuguese and British who were making inroads into the Maratha empire.

During this period, the battles and skirmishes had led to the killing in battlefield of many brave sardars in the Maratha empire, while several others had defected to the Mughal side. The downslide that had started after the death of Chhatrapati Shivaji Maharaj became much worse when several of the sardars in the Maratha empire in cahoots with the 'never say die' Soyrabai plotted against their own King, which in the long run played a major role in the total weakening of the once great Maratha empire.

The end came rather suddenly and unexpectedly. It is said that the presence of Chhatrapati Sambhaji Maharaj near Sangameshwar was given away to the Mughal emperor by one of his own trusted relatives who had become a vassal of the Mughals. Along with his leading commanders and trusted courtiers like Kavi Kalash, Chhatrapati Sambhaji Maharaj was captured by the Mughal forces at Burhanpur.

Historical records mention that the captured ruler was subjected to inhuman cruelty and torture over the next fortnight to a month. He was taken around in procession to teach a lesson to his people, while the Mughal soldiers heaped insults on him. It is said that he was asked to bow before the Emperor and to convert to Islam. However, Sambhaji refused to do so, and to teach him a lesson the Emperor Aurangzeb ordered his torture till death. His eyes were gouged out, his tongue and nails were pulled out and, after several days of such continued torture, ultimately, he was beheaded at Tulapur, by the banks of the river Bhima, on 11th March 1689.

Thus, a life that had begun with great promise was cut short. For a long time, his character and reputation were subjected to lose talk. However, as the years went by, the true facts behind this and the reasons for his being maligned came to light. His greatness was revealed and came to be appreciated by one and all. Today, historians who have access to documents of the period have celebrated his life as that of a true warrior and hero.

It is sad though that some individuals have to suffer a lot in life and glory is attained only after death. Such is the story of my hero, Chhatrapati Sambhaji Maharaj. Recognizing his greatness and sacrifice, he has earned the title of Swarajyarakshak.

As was the tradition in those days, I would like to present a paean in praise of his life, in the form of a Marathi Powada:

*I bring to you the life of my great King*
*Who was known as Chhatrapati Sambhaji!*
*Greater Kings than him there were few!*

*Wise was he in the science of politics*
*His Mawlas loved and respected him*
*As they knew him well - his heart and soul.*

*A poet was he, as was he a writer too*
*A gentleman was he to his female subjects*
*He protected and revered them as goddesses.*

*Alas, time was unkind to our great King Sambhaji*
*He faced treachery from within and without*
*Captured was he when he was unprepared.*

*The cruel Mughals, the villains, how they tortured him*
*But bend did not, our hero, King Sambhaji*
*He gave his life rather than give in to tyrants.*

*That is why revered is he today*
*Our great Chhatrapati Sambhaji Maharaj*
*O jee, O jee, O jee, O jee.*

***Dr Aparna Bagwe***

# Section X
# The British Raj
## *(1857CE to 1947CE)*

The East India Company sent its emissaries to India in 16th century ostensibly for trade. English East India Company established its first trading post at Masulipatnam (Andhra Pradesh) in 1600 as a factory. Soon they established many more such factories in the south and remained quite inconsequential as the other East India Companies set up by the Dutch, French, Portuguese and Danish expanded elsewhere. The initial desire for trade soon turned into territorial ambition when they saw the Mughal empire decline. By beginning of 18th century they had military presence "to protect" the company assets. An opportunity arose with the puppet Nawab of Bengal, Mir Jafar in 1757. They offered help to Mir Jafar and defeated the erstwhile Nawab of Bengal, Siraj-ud-Daulah at Plassey and gained the rule of Bengal. Soon this extended to include the state of Bihar and they established a capital at Calcutta (Kolkata).

Defeat of Peshwa in 1818 and annexation of the Maratha empire completed the establishment of an English colony. The company bosses made vast fortunes and came under heavy criticism in Britain. The *Sepoy Mutiny* in 1857, saw the end of the East India Company rule and beginning of British rule.

The British controlled the whole of India, Pakistan, Bangladesh and parts of Burma at its peak. We have one entry in this section with Snigdha Agrawal's "Love towards all and malice towards none."

# Love Towards All, Malice Towards None

*Snigdha Agrawal*

***Who is Snigdha Agrawal?***

*Snigdha Agrawal has an MBA in Marketing from IGNOU and Corporate work experience of over two decades. She enjoys writing all genres of poetry, prose, short stories, travel diaries. Educated entirely in Loreto Institutions, and brought up in a cosmopolitan environment, she has learnt the best of the east and west. She is a published author of two books of poems "EVOCATIVE RENDERINGS" and "TALES OF THE TWINS", apart from contributions to several anthologies. She shares her travel experiences in her blog: https://randomramblings52.wordpress.com.*

## Love Towards All, Malice Towards None

They came stealthily, cloaked in the darkness of the night. Wading through rice fields submerged in ankle deep water from the first monsoon showers, they kept slowly inching towards their target. Masked and armed, sticks of country made bombs, swords and sickles, tucked in the waist of their chequered 'lungis', they looked as innocuous as cows grazing in the fields. Fields which belonged to Upendranath Mukhopadhyay, Zamindar of Kashipur in Nadia district, owner of vast acres of lands. Lands they tilled, harvested, and eked a living for generations, like babies refusing to wean from mother's breast milk. Landowner and his field workers, sharing a camaraderie that transcended the statutory norms between employer/employee.

'Malik' he was known to his field workers. When his lands were flooded or hit by drought, his granaries were open to feed the poor peasants and their families. No one returned empty handed from this great benefactor. Possessed of a kind heart with no political affiliations or ambitions, to him the poor were never compartmentalised based on their beliefs, or caste. He celebrated Durga Puja in his mansion where Hindus and Muslims participated with equal fervour, the Hindu priests performing the 'Dhunuchi' Puja to the beat of the Muslim 'dhakis'. On Ashtami day, 'Bhog' was served to all guests present, he personally serving the first spoon of 'Khichri' on all the banana leaves laid out. The only day the rich and the poor sat on the floor and broke bread.

Amongst them sat his farm hands, dressed in their best. On Dashami, dressed in his silk kurta, and gold bordered dhoti, with a Cashmere shawl thrown casually over his right shoulder, he presented the picture of the true 'Malik', hugging each and every visitor, handing over boxes of home-made sweets, as was customary in his household for generations.

"Love towards all, Malice towards none" espoused by Khawaja Moinuddin Chishty was his way of life. Though a 'Kulin Brahmin' he remained undaunted and unperturbed by the criticism levelled at him from his Zamindari friends from Khulna and Chittagong districts. With a mindset different from theirs, he continued his philanthropic activities, visiting families living on his land. When malaria hit in an epidemic form, he got phials of quinine from Calcutta city and went about visiting homes distributing the medicines, out of bounds for the poor farmers. That's how he earned the additional salutation of "Doctor Saab", prefixed to his name.

How then were the same people heading towards his mansion to torch the 'Malik' and raze his mansion to rubble; complying to the sentiments whipped across the new nation that was about to emerge with partition? Misdirected? Misinformed? Or were they simply being nationalistic in getting back at the Hindu landowners evicting them from land, which rightfully belonged to them.

Much before the agitation had gained momentum; they were given the opportunity to exchange their lands with Muslim landowners in

West Bengal. Upendranath's brothers had been more astute in taking up the deal and moving into Calcutta, before the risings accelerated and turning into explosive blood baths. Upendranath had stubbornly hung on!

On that fateful night of 20th December 1946, he stood watching them approaching his home. Marauders out to blaze a trail of destruction. He stood steadfast and refused to budge daring them to torch him and his family members alive and wrest his belongings. His heart and soul would not leave his homeland, never mind the political lines that would be drawn, as a result of the inevitable partition. His home was in Kashipur, where his forefathers had lived and survived for generations.

Decades later Upendranath Mukhopadyay well into his nineties couldn't recall much of his past, except the sequence of events that followed thereafter, on that inky black night when he and his family had to flee to India under the veil of darkness, and to the sounds of owls screeching like sirens, not unusual in war torn countries.

Sitting in his home in Calcutta, he often narrated to whoever cared to hear, the last chapter of his flight from Kashipur to Calcutta. Having heard it so many times, I felt I was living through his experiences, chills running up my spine, once he began, his voice rising and falling like the waves dashing on the Puri sea shore. It was at Puri where he breathed his last on a summer vacation surrounded by his family members.

"I was waiting to hear the swish of swords in the air poised to strike at me. My country guns, well oiled, still hung on the wall staring at me defiantly to pick up and shoot in self-defence. No! My heart disagreed. They were my extended family. I couldn't lay a finger on them. Let them kill me, my family, and burn us here on the soil of my Motherland.

To my utter dismay, the masked, armed, plunderers, all recognisable, prostrated before me and pleaded that I leave the country immediately, as the new regime did not want Hindu Zamindars in their country.

Even before I could react, they sprang into action and helped the ladies to pack up all their jewellery and gold bars into tin trucks, and loaded it on the cow carts, they themselves had brought along with them. All the brass and silver utensils quickly sealed in gunny bags, were loaded on another cart.

The wall mounted taxidermy hunting trophies of heads of a tiger, wild boar, huge eagle with glass eyes, stared accusingly at me, for betraying them; leaving them to their fate. There was just not enough time, nor space to take them along. They seemed to be crying out for help.

Within an hour, we were ready to depart. Blinded with tears, we all turned back to take a last glimpse of the mansion that had been home to our forefathers and us. Abdul, the leader of the group, along with other farm labourers ran along with us, grouped together in the hooded cow carts. Two kerosene lamps carried by Rahim, and Ajmal, provided some light on that dark night. Here and there we passed through burning fields, smoke rising from the burnt standing crops, reduced to ashes. It would take a couple of hours to reach the nearest railway station.

Not a whisper from anyone was heard. Halfway they stopped near a forest cover to take rest; at least that was, what I thought, my heart pounding with fear not ruling out any mal-intentions. They were struggling to open the strings tied to two cloth bags, bulging at the seams. Were they going to gun us down and bury our bodies inside the deep forest, never to be recovered or recorded as missing persons?

I started reciting the Gayatri mantra. Soon my wife and all family members joined in the chorus. If we were to die, let us die with Gods name on our lips. Suddenly I heard Ahmed whispering into my ear....

"Malik here's dinner for you and family, we brought along, knowing you would be missing your meal at home".

Before us placed on banyan leaves were "puris" and dry "aloodom". Pitchers of drinking water stored in mud vessels camouflaged with branches of leaves, stood nearby to wash down the food, and quench thirst and fear choking our throats. Yes...we were hungry and thirsty, but so were they, risking their lives to save ours. We couldn't eat the food alone, without sharing it with our rescuers. They refused, assuring us...'we have already eaten...this is for all of you'. On my insistence, they served themselves small portions, leaving the rest to us. Choking on emotions welling up, each mouthful felt like God had sent us 'prasad' to survive the long arduous journey through the most inhospitable terrain. Far in the horizon, the grey was fading, replaced with the first rays of the rising sun.

A new day, new hope, did little to lift our sagging spirits!

Kashipur station had just one platform, and two parallel tracks, one for the incoming train and the other for the outgoing. One had to cross the tracks to board the outgoing train, not an easy feat with our luggage piled onto three cow carts. Undaunted, they crossed the tracks, urging the malnourished cows pulling the carts, to make it across, looking completely exhausted. The sun hid behind a cloud cover that morning, when the train puffing steam, rolled into the station.

Even before the wheels grinded to a halt, four of my boys jumped into the moving train, seizing an entire coupe. The heavy tin trunks with the precious gems, and gold were pushed deep under the seats over which they dumped gunny sacks, containing the lesser valuable items. "Ginnima" carried in her cloth bag, held close to her chest, the idols she had grabbed from the mandir. Instinctively her mind thought of not leaving the family Gods and Goddesses worshipped in the temple. It would surmount to sacrilege leaving them to be desecrated? Even in the face of death, her thought went to the Gods and Goddesses she worshipped daily, bathing them with Ganges water, (procured in bottles from Calcutta), placing at their feet offerings of fresh flowers from the garden, picked up by none other than Jaweed, fondly nicknamed 'Potol', our cook Amiroon's son. Every morning, before leaving for school, little 'Potol' would leave on the wooden platform outside the mandir doors, a wicker basket filled with the seasonal flowers, apart from blood red Jabas (hibiscus), perennial blooms, which she religiously placed at the feet of Goddess Kali and Durga. In winter the basket would have roses and rajanigandha (tuber roses,) replaced in spring with white jasmine buds, she would string into garlands.

When 'Potol' was stricken with the deadly small-pox and passed away, she was inconsolable and insisted his grave be dug right outside the mansion gates, so she could walk out every morning after her prayers, to place a flower on his gravestone. Quite a departure from her orthodox ways!

Ginnima...Bauro-Ma to all, the doyen of the family, never differentiated between the Hindu and Muslim field workers. They were all treated alike. During the month of Ramzan, she would keep sweet lemon water filled in mud 'kalshis', and big dekchis filled with 'batasha' (jaggery sweet) on a ledge, in the out-house, for the workers to drink and eat, when they returned from the fields at dusk, to collect the day's earnings.

On Id-e-Milad, she personally gifted each and every member of the Muslim families, new clothes and money to celebrate the festival. They looked up to her as their mother and she in return reciprocated with equal measure, as a mother would do for her sons.

It was not surprising that each of them took turns to touch her feet, weeping at the loss of a Mother, they would never see again. Ginnima blessed them, tucking into their hands one gold coin for each of them. Her way of saying "Thank You my sons...may Allah keep you safe".

As they helped us board the early morning train, I saw tears rolling down their eyes, as they folded their hands imploring for forgiveness. The expression on their faces cried out helplessness. They were not misdirected or misguided. They were being driven to do such acts or else face dire consequences. There was no Hindu Muslim divide in their hearts or minds; their loyalty to 'Malik' untethered.

Why else would they personally see me and my family safe on that train going westward into Calcutta. In their perception, our lives were more precious than the land that would inevitably be wrested from us! "

My grandfather often mused over the irksome question of who truly answered to the calling of 'Malik'? Him or those poor peasants? They fit the role of 'Maliks' who saved him and his family before the 1947 partition of Bengal, into East and West. I found this poem written neatly in Bengali, in one of his accounting 'khatas', handed down to me, when my mother was on her death bed.

Translated in English, it reads…

*They took chalk and drew arbitrary lines*
*believing all would be fine.*
*How little did they know?*
*The Tree of life gives shade to both*
*Roots below the surface holds hand tight*
*spread across fenced miles*
*They know not any divide*

*How little did they know?*
*Of the damage they had left behind*
*My home still lies on the other side*
*My 'Tulsi Manch' they never broke*

*Just as I left that child's gravestone*
*Our hearts sing the same songs*
*Of green fields back home*
*Sweet music of bells ringing at dusk*
*Returning cowherds raising dust*

Many years later, after the war was over, grandfather visited Kashipur. No more the one he had left in 1946. This time belonging to another country, another owner. Hints of development were noticeable throughout the journey he took alone, to visit his 'Paitrik Bhita'. Gone were the forests, replaced with road building activities. Gone was the home, gone were the fields, where ripe crops would sway in the spring breeze. Industrialization had taken over! Where once stood his home, was a brick factory; finished red bricks piled up to be taken away for construction activities. 'Potol's gravestone stood out like a sore thumb in its midst. Grandfather introduced himself to the factory-in-charge, who came rushing out to greet him, warned of his arrival.

They exchanged pleasantries, over cups of hot tea and biscuits. His heart broke seeing the 'Tulsi Manch' untouched. But no more evening lamps would ever be lit, the flame carrying messages of amity.

He took leave from them and headed back to Calcutta, filled with remorse. History of his home forever erased.

But a new history was being written!

*Declaration*

*The story is part fiction, part factual, that happened before the 1947 partition towards the close of the British Raj. Upendranath Mukhopadhyay, my grandfather, (mother's father) was the Zamindar of Kashipur, of Nadia District, in erstwhile East Bengal. He had to flee with his immediate family, with just cash and gold, to rebuild their lives in the city of Calcutta. He lives on in my memory!*

*Glossary of Indian words*

*"Aloodam…spicy dry potato curry*

*"Bauro-Ma…Bauro=eldest Ma=Mother. In the joint family structure, the eldest lady was fondly called Bauro Ma.*

*"Batasha"…sweet made of jaggery.*

*"Bhog"…Food cooked for offering to the Gods and then given to guests.*

*"Dhunuchi…A Bengali incense burner used for one of the stages during Aarti, a ritualized dance worship.*

*"Dhakis" …a traditional drummer who plays the dhak or drum, usually suspended from the neck and tied to the waist, played with wooden sticks.*

*"Ginnima" …fondly referred to the eldest female member in the joint family structure.*

*"Kulin Brahmins" …are the Bengali Brahmins belonging to the Hindu religion, who can trace their ancestors to the five families of Kannauj, who migrated to Bengal.*

*"Kalshis" …Mud pots to store drinking water.*

*"Khatas" …Notebook*

*"Lungis" ... a garment similar to a sarong, wrapped around the waist and extending down to the ankles, worn in various countries in SE Asia.*

*"Malik…The Chief of the Village or Community.*

*"Puri" …seaside town on the eastern seaboard of India*

*"puris" ... are small round Indian bread of wheat flour, deep fried*

*"Paitrik Bhita" …Ancestral home*

*"Tulsi Manch" …Cemented raised structure filled with soil to grow the sacred Tulsi (basil) plant.*

***Snigdha Agrawal***

# Section XI
# Mythology

I had to include mythology in this book as no book dealing with Indian history can be complete without a section on Mythology. The Indian history is deeply interwoven with mythology for thousands of years. It is difficult if not impossible to see where mythology ends and where history begins. And at the same time, today's myth could be tomorrow's history. Until end of $19^{th}$ century the story of Trojan war and Troy was considered by everyone to be a myth. Heinrich Schliemann, a German archaeologist started digging in Turkey in 1868 and before long was coming with evidence of the city of Troy. Now the experts agree that Troy was a real place, and, in all probability, the Trojan war took place. We have our own famous archaeologist, Mr B B Lal who found evidence of the city of Hastinapur dating to the Painted Grey Ware period and the great epic of Mahabharat took on a different colour.

We have two excellent articles in this section. One, "The Salvaging womb" is by Barsha Priyadarshini Kar, the youngest author in this book, still studying in class 12. She has done an excellent job at portraying the power of God Shiva at the same time giving some human qualities to the deity as well as his consort, Parvati.

Dominic Arivarasu Mathias comes back again in this book with a story of Khasi tribe from Meghalaya. I had not heard of the "*Nongshohnoh*" before. It is fascinating reading of an old culture and its beliefs and traditions in a contemporary period. It is a sensitive subject as there are rumours of the snake worshippers being persecuted in the region and Dominic Arivarasu Mathias has done an excellent job in handling such a sensitive subject.

# The Salvaging Womb

*Barsha Priyadarshini Kar*

***Who is Barsha Priyadarshini Kar?***

*Barsha Priyadarshini kar is a student of class 12. She is quite fond of English literature and is an amateur writer. Her poems have previously been published in a few other anthologies. She is in the pursuit of winning hearts with her words.*

# The Salvaging Womb

Once Parvati approached Lord Shiva with great enthusiasm. She said," Respected husband, would you mind sharing the "Bramha Gyan" with me?" Lord Shiva was surprised at the request. But Parvati appeared to be very keen to learn and she insisted the Lord to teach. Lord Shiva had no issues in preaching the Bramha Gyan to her beloved. But in a place teeming with people, animals and birds, who were intensely attached to the material world and always strived to be immortal, the knowledge of Bramha Gyan would give them immense power and thus distort the prevailing social and ecological balance. Deeming this to be undesirable, Shiva and Parvati decided to choose an isolated place. It had to be somewhere, far from human civilisation and devoid of any life forms. They searched far and wide and finally found such a remote place (present day Amarnath) and sat down to discuss the sacred knowledge.

In the process of articulating the most sought after knowledge, Shiva was constantly aware of his surroundings. Time and again he was looking around to confirm the absence of any other being. The knowledge of bramha Gyan straight went from Shiva to Parvati and her joy knew no bounds.

Just behind Shiva, there was a large tree with a hole in it. A skeleton of some sort lay abandoned there and it was the third thing besides Shiva and Parvati who got exposed to the supreme knowledge. As the words seeped through the skeleton, life gushed into it and within a few hours, there was a transformation from the bones to a bird. It was a parrot. But to his utter misfortune, shiva's eyes caught it. He became furious and chased the parrot to kill it. The parrot flew helplessly and as fast as it could. Shiva was no less in chasing. From the forest they slipped into civilisation. A young and beautiful lady was doing surya namaskar. With extreme devotion she was looking at the sun with mouth wide open and *namaskara mudra*. The parrot, finding no other way of escape, fluttered into her mouth and in a fidgety manner got into her womb. Shiva had no option, but to kill the lady "killing a woman is a heinous job. The one who kills a woman cannot be forgiven. "Shiva couldn't put down Parvati's request. He gave up the very idea of killing the woman and left the place with a heavy heart.

The lady with the parrot in her womb was dumbfounded. She was the wife of the great Vyasa Deva. The parrot remained in her womb for twelve years. At the end of twelve years, the child was ready to come out. Before the night of delivery Vyasa Dev heard a voice saying "I will not be born naked. Arrange something to wrap me up before I am out." Vyasa Dev approached Shiva and let him know that. Shiva gave "Bajra kachheta" to Vyasa Dev. Finally, the next night, wrapped in the "Bajra kachheta" a little boy was born. Immediately after Being born, he started walking. VyasaDev and his wife (pianla) had great attachment with their son and requested him to stay back but it was in vain. He requested his parents not to stop him and made his way. He grew up to be the most spiritually erudite and informed "SukaDev" who became one of the most brilliant preachers of religion, Veda and Brahma Gyan. In this way Bharat was blessed with a precious jewel to adorn her land.

# Nongshohnoh: A Leaf from the Khasi Lore

*Dominic Arivarasu Mathias*

***Who is Dominic Arivarasu Mathias?***

*Dominic Arivarasu Mathias, MA, BEd, MPhil (Eng), has been in the teaching profession for over 35 years and has taught in schools in Meghalaya, Mizoram and Arunachal Pradesh for 10 years before settling in Mumbai in 1994. Since then he has been teaching students of BCom, BA, BMM, BSc (IT), MBA as well as Junior Colleges in Mumbai. He has been the Chief Editor of his College and School magazines for two decades. He is a Moderator for HSC, BCom and BSc (IT). He has attended innumerable conferences and presented papers in over a dozen national and international conferences. A freelance writer, his letters and articles have appeared in every leading newspaper in Mumbai. Mr Dominic has won several prizes for essay and story writing competitions at different levels. He is a Master Trainer and a Mentor trained by the British Council. He is also a Moderator of CHESS (Continuous Help to teachers of English from Secondary Schools) programme of the Government of Maharashtra. Mr Dominic is a recipient of several awards for his contribution to education. He has also co-authored three guidebooks for Std XI and XII of Maharashtra State board. One of his stories was published by the National Open School (now NIOS) in its Supplementary Reading Materials in 2002. Three of his stories have been anthologized by The Impish Lass Publishing House, Mumbai.*

# Nongshohnoh:
# A Leaf from the Khasi Lore

Just a casual visit to a student's house need not have invited such stern warnings and admonitions: after all it was just a courtesy call.

One evening, after school hours, I happened to stroll into the house of a class IX student, Dahun, not far from the school playground. As is the wont of Khasis, I was welcomed cheerfully, made to sit in the elegant parlour filled with bamboo furniture and double curtains, and offered *kwai*, consisting of a quarter of a raw betelnut, which was plucked from the tree recently, and peeled in front of the eyes of the guest, and folded within a slice of betel leaf smeared with a dash of wet lime.

Dahun's mother was a short and plump woman with a deep dimple on her right cheek and wearing thick golden rings in almost all her fingers. Curious to know how a Khasi house looked like, I took the liberty of having a dekko around, ushered by Dahun. It was a typical Assamese house, an earthquake-proof wooden structure – since earthquakes are common phenomena in Meghalaya – supported by wooden pillars. Often, while travelling between Shillong and Guwahati by road, looking at such houses in the middle of a river at Byrnihat, I would wonder whether the wood wouldn't decompose, risking danger to the house. But the answer I got was always one of reassurance that it would never happen.

Dahun's house had an appearance of affluence. At every door or doorway hung laced curtains with long decorative seashells brought all the way from Kannyakumari in Tamil Nadu, which jingled as one entered or emerged from the room, announcing movement at the door.

Two of the five bedrooms were small, sufficient to accommodate a couple each, (perhaps meant for guests), while the largest one was occupied by Dahun's parents, and Dahun and her kid brother used the other two bed-cum-study rooms. All the beds had thick mattresses stuffed with dried pine spikes, available abundantly everywhere. The pine spikes are warmer than the fancy mattresses we use today.

The kitchen was the most noteworthy part of the house where the family gathered round the fire for every meal. A large squarish hearth was at the centre of the kitchen. Only this section was grounded on the earth, while the rest of the house was a wooden structure, buttressed by wooden pillars. Since firewood, and occasionally coal, was used as fuel, they needed an earth-based fireplace which wouldn't ignite the house while cooking. High above the fireplace was hanging a bunch of unpeeled corncobs, below which, nearer the fire were suspended some unevenly elongated strips of something which I could not identify. Dahun explained that the villagers would buy provisions for the week on market-days which occurred every week, and stock food for a week, and what I saw were strips of meat that was hung to dry over the fire so that they could just chop a slice and cook every day. The cold climate in the hills made daily consumption of non-vegetarian food mandatory.

Above all, what impressed me most was the cleanliness. There was not an iota of dust anywhere, and all the vessels in the kitchen, be it aluminium, copper, stainless steel or china, all were spic and span as if new.

There was a gentle knock on the door and in came Kyntiew, Dahun's classmate and neighbour. She was pleasantly surprised to see the new teacher enjoying the camaraderie of her bosom friend. Having put away the school uniform, she came wrapped in a *tapmohkhlieh*, the local shawl, to keep the cold and leering glances at bay.

Dahun's mother brought on a tray an empty cup and saucer, a glass container with sugar and 'milkmaid', sweetened and condensed milk, and placed it on the tepoy. She poured boiling water from a shiny tiny kettle through a sieve filled with tealeaves into the cup till it almost overflew and added two teaspoonfuls each of sugar and milkmaid. Having stirred till the sugar melted, she handed over the cup and waited for me to take a sip and asked: '*La thing*?'

I looked at Dahun. She asked me whether the tea was sweet enough.

'Yes', said I turning toward the mother.

'I thought the word for sweet is '*thiang*' in Khasi? I queried Dahun.

'*Thing*' is 'sweet' in our dialect. You should start learning our local dialect now', laughed Dahun.

'Let me pick up some proper Khasi before specializing in your dialect.'

Since I was still trying to learn Khasi, the language spoken all over Khasi Hills, with dialectical variations at distant locations, I conversed with Dahun in English, while her mother needed translations into her own dialect. In my heart I was complimenting the teachers of St Paul's

High School, Marbisu, for the yeoman service they were doing in this village, about an hour's drive from Shillong, the capital of Meghalaya. For, every child could speak in English, despite being first generation learners.

I learnt that it was customary to ask every guest this question after tea was served, whether it was sufficiently sweet. And that it was discourteous of a guest not to have a second helping of food, when invited for a meal, as an endorsement to the sumptuousness of the food.

Six-thirty pm and it was pitch dark, and time to get back to my nest. The narrow road in front of the house was uneven and non-motorable despite being classified as a macadam road in official records. The streetlights too being out of order, Dahun offered me a torchlight for finding my way through but, on Kyntiew's suggestion, both accompanied me till my residence to bid goodbye and goodnight.

* * * *

By morning the news of my visit to Dahun's house and her accompanying me to my residence in the night had spread to many people in the vicinity, and most of my teacher-colleagues were casting furtive glances at me, whispering among themselves: I was intrigued.

Babu Donboklang opened the batting:

"Sir, why did you go to that house?" And before I could answer, "Please be careful and avoid that family."

"I'm telling you for your own good. Please, stop going around visiting houses without telling us." This was from Babu Teibor. ('Babu' is a common title give to teachers. So, I was called Babu Dominic.)

"But why? I was just strolling thereabouts, trying to get to know our locality when Dahun called me in. What's wrong with going to that house?"

"We can't tell you that, but did you notice that they are filthy rich and that their house stands alone on that hillock?"

"Of course, they have a beautiful house on a large tract of land." I remembered that they had planted potatoes and pineapples on the slopes of the mountain flattened into several steps of beds, and there were also orange and lemon trees laden with large-sized lemons. Pine trees were scattered on the western slope of the hillock near the house but as one looked farther, they were tall and dense. Behind the house I was happy to notice a thick outgrowth of ferns: ferns always made me happy.

"But why can't I go there? After all, Dahun is studying in our school along with her brother!"

"Sir, we cannot divulge anything more. Only that it is not good for you to visit that damned house again. Period." declared Babu Henry sternly. There was a finality in his voice.

The day went bad. No one would give me an explanation for their consternation. Forbid, they did. But reason? Not one of them was forthcoming with it. The clandestine looks and muted whispers, especially from some otherwise-amiable female mates, made me miserable. As I settled at my desk after school, there were a thousand questions whirling in my head. Did I do anything wrong at Dahun's house? Why didn't I meet any male member there? Why was it a house of 'ill-repute'? Are the girls of questionable character? No. I don't think so. They are but my students. Was anything wrong with Dahun's mother? She seemed to be a decent woman. She had offered me two servings of *kwai* – one as soon as I entered the house and one before I left. The tea was very aromatic and refreshing. What if she had mixed some poison or potion into the tea? Was she a murderer? Or a sorceress? My mind was being assailed by many inexplicable fears, doubts and queries. Worse, no one would come forward with some sort of explanation for their antagonism and animosity towards the family.

Mustering up some courage, I ventured out looking for the house of Kong Ieid, a teacher in our school. She was the first one to speak to and welcome me when I joined the school in April 1984. Taking a student to guide me I went in search of her house in the sprawling village. We meandered through extremely narrow paths to reach her house at an elevated area in the middle of the undulating hamlet, about three quarters of a kilometre from my residence. At times we had to walk balancing our feet on the stones laid to protect them from getting wet in the open drainage water trickling through the lane.

Kong Ieid drew aside a curtain lightly to peer out when she heard footsteps climbing the five steps to the balcony-like landing admeasuring 4 X 10 feet. On seeing us she signalled me to wait for some time and rushed in to tie a '*tapmoh*' over the sweatshirt she was wearing. Having dismissed the boy, she led me straight to the kitchen to sit near the fire to warm myself while we talked. Her elderly mother too was sitting there and knitting what seemed like a purple coloured muffler with broad white stripes.

We had the usual round of *kwai* and pleasantries and tea, while I was itching to broach the topic. Kong Ieid realized that I was edgy but kept ignoring me until I blurted out:

"Why shouldn't I visit Dahun or Kyntiew's house?"

"No Sir, it's a long story and we are forbidden to discuss it."

"But why?"

"You will not understand even if I tell you."

"How can you say that?"

I was flustered.

"But if YOU don't tell me, who else will?" I pleaded. "Let me in to this secret of yours, please."

"First of all, you are a '*dkhar*' (non-Khasi), and, therefore, it is not meant for you."

"Please, please. This doesn't make sense."

"Okay. I shall tell you, but on two conditions…"

"Tell me."

"First, you must keep mum about it. You will neither discuss with anyone nor reveal that you know about it. If you hear people discuss it, just feign ignorance."

"Fine. What is the second?"

"You will never visit this house again nor any such people."

"What do you mean by 'such people'? This condition is unacceptable to me. How can I stop visiting people I want to? I want to understand the people, learn their language and become one among them. For this purpose, house visits and intermingling with people are necessary. Without one-to-one interaction, how can I learn Khasi?" I was desperate.

"Of course, you can meet people. In fact, you should meet children in their home surroundings if you sincerely want to understand the students whom you teach. I only said that you shouldn't meet 'such people', people like Dahun and Kyntiew."

"What is wrong with them? I can't understand. I meet these kids every day in school, since I teach two subjects, English and Value Education, in their class."

"Okay okay. Now listen carefully." Kong Ieid drew a long breath. "THEY ARE 'MENSHOHNOH': THEY KILL PEOPLE FOR THEIR BLOOD."

"What?" I was dumbfounded. My head was reeling. I could hardly believe my ears. "They are what? Kill people? Did you say: kill? You mean, they could have killed me yesterday? Have I just escaped from the jaws of death?" My head seemed to split, and I began to have a severe headache.

"No, Sir." Kong Ieid was laughing. "Not like that. Ha ha. They won't kill you."

"Whom do they kill, then?"

It had been rumoured that they were worshippers of *U Thlen* (a snake) which needs to be fed with human blood every now and then. The '*menshohnoh*' employ people called '*nongshohnoh*' to find human beings and kill them for their blood.

If *U Thlen* is not satiated, he will turn himself on to the *menshohnoh* or *nongshohnoh*' and drink the blood of their own kids. Hence it is imperative that they give a steady supply of human blood. Generally, the *nongshohnoh* chops the extremities of the fingers and draws blood from them before killing the victim. This is the reason why no Khasi person clips his nails in public or discard the clipped nails in public places. Even hair. Nails and hair are used to lure the victim to solitary places for their blood. In return, the snake god made them extremely rich and powerful.

"I don't think Dahun's family are such, what-do-you-call, *men-shoh-noh*! They seemed very decent."

"You see, Dahun is from the XXX clan. And many people from their clan have been accused of being *nongshohnoh* and *menshohnoh*. People feel that the prosperity of her clan is owing to *U Thlen*."

"Do you think that there is a snake at Dahun's house? That they have kept it hidden somewhere?"

"In fact, nobody has ever seen *U thlen*. But these things are not discussed in public. They may be rearing it at home, or it may call on them periodically demanding human blood."

"It must then be an avatar of the devil himself!"

"Possible. It could be *u thlen* or *u ksuid* (the devil)."

Having served me another round of *kwai*, Kong Ieid let me go, reminding me of her two conditions.

Before leaving, though, she slipped two pieces of paper, with instructions to read one before sleeping that night and to open the second one the next day.

With a heavy heart, I left Kong Ieid's house, relieved, however, that I knew the secret and that I was alive, after the encounter with the *menshohnohs*. By the time I reached home, my headache had abated a little, but the internal trepidation occasioned by the discovery that I could have been a corpse just the previous day did not diminish. Somehow, I completed the supper ritual in haste so as to hit the bed early, scared that the *nongshohnoh* might be lurking in darkness, awaiting my approach, ready to waylay me for my blood. Even the night prayers became more of a ritual than heartfelt prayers due to the disquiet caused by the dreadful disclosure earlier.

Suddenly I remembered the note thrust into my hands by Kong Ieid before I left her house. With trembling hands and bedevilled by doubt and uncertainty, I unfolded the first chit.

It read:

**'Don't worry Sir. The *nongshohnoh* will not harm you because *u thlen* does not accept the blood of non-Khasis.'**

What a relief it was! I re-read the note for confirmation: I was speechless for the second time that day. This time out of a sense of emancipation and freedom. Freedom from the clutches of my would-be assassin. I jumped up and punched the air in jubilation.

'Thank you, Kong Ieid, thank you. Thank you for your thoughtfulness. I know that you gave me this last piece of news so that I can have a seamless and peaceful sleep…'

Suddenly my headache too vanished, along with the murderer.

I was too happy to sleep. I kept rolling on the bed, trying to outguess the contents of the second piece of paper, to be opened in the morning. Time was trickling past in slow motion. Midnight… One o'clock... One-thirty… A fresh thought struck my mind. The second paper was to be opened the next day. And now it is already next day. What prevents me from reading it now?

I got out of my bed cautiously, took a gulp of warm water from the flask I had kept on my table and returned to the bed. The slip of paper was in the left pocket of my trousers, appended on a peg at the back of the bedroom door. Carefully I took it out and read aloud. It contained just one simple exclamatory query:

**'What if the *nongshohnoh* does not know that you are a non-Khasi!'**

This thought hadn't occurred to me earlier. *U thlen* may not drink the blood of non-Khasis. However, that does not rule out the possibility of my being killed by an unobservant and illiterate *nongshohnoh*!

I was too troubled to sleep again!

* * * *

Persistent knock at my door shook me awake. The sun peeping through the curtains rapped at my knuckles that it was already time to go to school. Jumping out of bed I rushed to open the door, only to find two girls in school uniform with their school bags hanging on their backs and a parcel each in their hands.

'Breakfast from my mom,' beamed Dahun.

'And from my mom too.' Kyntiew

It sounded like 'poison from my mom'.

For a moment I was at my wits' end. I could already visualize the staffroom scene later in the day.

However, gathering my senses I muttered a 'thank you', accepted the breakfast and shut the door behind me. As I munched the '*pu-maloi*' and '*pu-tharo*', Khasi delicacies, I found myself being gradually weaned out of the fear of the *nongshohnoh* and *menshohnoh.*

* * * *

That it was going to be a tumultuous day in school goes without saying. The previous warnings having gone unheeded, it became an overt enmity and boycotting of my very presence in the staff room.

During the first recess, Babu Donboklang called me outside the college, led me to my room and revealed to me the most shocking revelation of the day. Kong Ieid's husband was the nongshohnoh of Dahun's family and that is the reason why Kong Ieid did not have any living children: all her four children had been 'eaten' by *U Thlen*, the snake, before it consumed her own husband!

I requested Babu Donboklang to inform the Principal that I would not be able to attend school for the rest of the session as I was feeling faint.

***Dominic Arivarasu Mathias***

Printed in Poland
by Amazon Fulfillment
Poland Sp. z o.o., Wrocław

54347362R00120